JAYDEN

HEROES AT HEART

MARYANN JORDAN

USA TODAY BESTSELLING AUTHOR

ISBN ebook: 978-1-947214-33-0

ISBN print: 978-1-947214-34-7

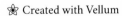 Created with Vellum

AUTHOR INFORMATION

USA TODAY BESTSELLING AND AWARD WINNING AUTHOR

I am an avid reader of romance novels, often joking that I cut my teeth on the historical romances. I have been reading and reviewing for years. In 2013, I finally gave into the characters in my head, screaming for their story to be told. From these musings, my first novel, Emma's Home, The Fairfield Series was born.

I was a high school counselor having worked in education for thirty years. I live in Virginia, having also lived in four states and two foreign countries. I have been married to a wonderfully patient man for thirty-seven years. When writing, my dog or one of my four cats can generally be found in the same room if not on my lap.

Please take the time to leave a review of this book.

Feel free to contact me, especially if you enjoyed my book. I love to hear from readers!

Facebook

Email

Website

As an adolescent counselor for over twenty-five years, I had the opportunity to work with many young people. One young man, upset over a poor choice he had made, came to me. As I listened to his story and his confession, I told him that the true measure of a man was not in the mistakes he made, but in how he handled those mistakes. I remember the look on his face when I told him I was sure he was going to be a good man.

So this book is dedicated to all the students over the years who allowed me to be a part of their lives.

"The wolf, seeing her come in, said to her, hiding himself under the bed clothes. 'Put the cake and the little pot of butter upon the stool, and come get into bed with me.'"

Jayden sat on the bed, his twin, Jaxon, next to him. He glanced over, seeing Jaxon's wide eyes and knew that if he stared into a mirror, his face would look the same and not just because they were identical.

Zander, their oldest foster brother, was reading another bedtime story. Every night, the boys would all gather into one of the bedrooms and listen as Zander read to them, usually from his large abridged version of fairytales. Sometimes he switched it up and read abridged classics. Other nights, they chose smaller picture books to be enjoyed.

But tonight, Zander's expressive voice wove a tale of woods and wolves, dark nights and scary threats, and a little girl who should have stayed on the path.

Jayden felt a shiver but was uncertain if it came from him or Jaxon. He slid his arm around his twin, both to provide and receive comfort. His gaze moved about the room, seeing the others equally entranced. Rafe and Cael sat on the bottom bunk, their eyes pinned to Zander. They were older than Jayden by one year, and he was not surprised to see that they appeared less frightened than he.

Asher, the youngest, had been sitting at the end of the bed but turned suddenly and crawled back closer to Jayden. Asher was small for his age, and he tucked his thin legs up under the covers. Jayden moved to place his free arm around Asher's shoulders.

The room was simply furnished, bunk beds along one wall and a single in the opposite corner. A dresser with three deep drawers stored the underclothing of the three occupants. A closet held their clothes and shoes. A wooden chair and small table with a lamp sat next to the single bed. Simple and comfortable. But tonight, the light from the lamp cast eerie shadows about the room, and Jayden took a deep breath trying to still his racing heart.

The sound of footsteps out in the hall came closer, but instead of fear, the familiar sound sent an ease throughout him. Looking up, he smiled as Miss Ethel walked into the room. Her light blue shirtdress, buttoned in the front, was cinched at her narrow waist with a thin belt. Her legs were encased in stockings, and he liked how her rubber-soled shoes did not create loud clicks on the wooden floors. Her grey hair was pulled back in a bun, and her blue eyes peered about the room from behind her wire-rimmed glasses.

Just having her there made all the difference. The

room seemed a little brighter. A little warmer. Jayden knew that the scaries of the world seemed to stop at her door. He had heard the school social worker tell his teacher that Miss Ethel was the best foster parent in the area. He did not know about that...he only knew she made him happy.

With her presence in the room, Zander halted the story, looking up at her expectantly.

"Please, continue," she said, settling onto the wooden chair next to the bed, crossing her ankles. She leaned over and patted Jayden's leg, a comforting smile on her face as though she knew the story frightened him.

"Grandmother, what big teeth you have got!"

"All the better to eat you up with."

"And, saying these words, the wicked wolf fell upon Little Red Riding Hood, and ate her all up."

Zander finished the story and closed the book with a satisfied expression on his face. Jayden blinked, horrified, hating this version. He much preferred the picture book that ended differently. His mind was firmly stuck on the idea of the little girl now gobbled up, and he swallowed hard, his heart still pounding. He barely heard as the others began to grumble.

"It doesn't make any sense," Cael complained, throwing himself back against the pillows. "Why would she get in bed with the wolf?"

"Because he was dressed like the grandmother," Zander explained, a scowl on his face.

"That's dumb," Rafe agreed with Cael. "She would know what her grandmother looked like, and the wolf couldn't make himself look like a person."

3

Jayden looked over at Miss Ethel and wondered if a wolf would be able to replace her and he not notice. As he stared at her, trying to imagine a long nose and furry face, he startled when he saw her watching him intently.

"Are you wondering if you would be able to tell me from a wolf?" she asked with a wide smile.

Blushing, he ducked his head and nodded. "Yes. If I came home and you had a long, fuzzy snout, I'd definitely notice."

She laughed, her eyes twinkling. "Keep in mind, boys, that the original fairytales were to teach lessons. They were not necessarily stories to entertain, nor were they considered children's stories. But instead, they were used to teach us how we should act or to warn us against dangers."

Jaxon piped up, "But we already know not to talk to wolves. I don't know why they need a story about that, because I can't imagine anyone talking to a wolf."

Miss Ethel looked around at the boys and asked, "If not a warning about wolves, what do you think the author was really warning you about?"

"Bad people," Asher said, his voice barely above a whisper.

Jayden's gaze shot over to Asher and watched as the other boys' did, too. They all had a protective streak when it came to Asher. Jayden thought that it might have been because he was the youngest and the smallest.

Miss Ethel nodded and said, "You're right. The warning is very much about talking to strangers. At the time this story was written by Charles Perrault several hundred years ago, it was a warning for young women to be very wary of strange men. That was a time when a well-bred young woman should never walk alone in the company of a man without a chaperone, and certainly never trust a man they did not know, even if he was charming, sweet, and said all the right things."

"What's a chaper…uh…what was that word?" Rafe asked.

"Chaperone," she replied. "It was usually an adult woman who would accompany a young woman so that she would not be alone with a boy."

Zander barked out a laugh, saying, "Girls are dumb."

She peered over her glasses at him, her voice low. "Zander."

Jayden knew with that one word she meant business, and hearing Zander mumble, "Sorry," he knew that the others did, too.

Peering at Zander over her glasses, she said, "We don't use descriptive words that are not nice. But I am curious as to why you think girls are dumb."

He watched as Zander shrugged, struggling to come up with a reason. He also thought girls could be silly at times but wisely kept his mouth shut.

"I don't know," Zander admitted. "It's just that in all the stories, they end up needing to get rescued. I mean, she talked to a wolf!"

Rafe nodded enthusiastically, throwing his support with Zander, saying, "Yeah, Miss Ethel. That was dumb."

Jayden swung his gaze back over to Miss Ethel to see what her response would be. Her lips curved into a gentle smile, and she sat with her hands clasped in her lap. He felt his body relax at her smile and loved how she spent time with them each night.

"Boys, you have to remember that these were tales made up to teach. They're not a true story of a little girl who actually talked to a wolf. But it illustrates how we can become involved with someone who isn't a good person, and yet we either convince ourselves that they are good, or we simply refuse to believe what is right in front of our eyes. And whether she's a little girl, or a boy like you, we can all learn these lessons."

"I like the one where the woodsman comes in at the end and kills the wolf the best," Jayden admitted, the picture book version held tightly in his hand.

She directed her blue eyes toward him and smiled. "Why do you like that version the best, Jayden?" she asked.

He scrunched his face, pondering her question, and then replied, "Because it ends happy. The woodsman came, cut open the mean old wolf, and saved Little Red Riding Hood and her grandmother."

"That was in the Grimm brothers' story," Zander piped up proudly.

She nodded and confirmed, "Yes, that's true. Some versions have it be a woodsman and others a hunts-man." Looking back at Jayden, she encouraged, "Tell me about the woodsman."

Uncertain what she meant, Jayden tilted his head to the side. "Uh…the book that has the woodsman in it doesn't really tell us anything about him."

She prodded, "Then use your imagination."

"Um, well, he chopped wood." As she nodded

encouragingly, he continued, "I guess that's what he did for a living. He had an ax, and he went around and chopped wood. Since they lived in a forest, that was a pretty easy thing for him to do."

"So," she said, "the woodsman was an ordinary man, just going about his daily work. He wasn't searching for anyone to save. He wasn't a prince, or a knight, or even trying to be a hero. So, what made him special?"

Warming to the task, he let his imagination fly and continued, "He was just working in the woods and heard a scream. Or maybe he just heard the wolf growl. But something must've made him realize that things weren't right, and he could have just left. He could have gone back home, but he didn't. He went to go find out what was happening and saw the wolf at the grand-mother's house."

Jaxon, sitting up straighter, twisted around and nodded. "Yeah, he would've known that a wolf at the grandmother's house couldn't have been right. He must've known something bad was happening."

Cael, not to be left out, jumped in, adding, "He would've known something was wrong because the wolf's belly would've been huge with the grandmother and Little Red Riding Hood in there!"

"Hey," Jayden complained. "This is my story!" Receiving another nod from Miss Ethel, he continued, "He could've been scared and just walked away, but he didn't. He decided to do whatever he could to set them free, even if that meant doing something as icky as cutting open a wolf!"

Miss Ethel clapped her hands and threw her head

back, laughing. "Oh, my, you all are such good story-tellers." She lowered her chin and peered at Jayden once again. "And you are exactly right, my dear. We can learn something from all of the stories. The version with the woodsman definitely teaches us that we can step in and help others that cannot help themselves."

Jayden thought about his brothers. Zander, the oldest, never seemed afraid of anything and always jumped to the defense of the rest of them. Rafe, already big for his age, did not seem to have any problem with the kids at school teasing him. And they both quickly pounced on anyone who made fun of Cael's red hair. And all three of them had chased after some boys that were teasing Asher and calling him a runt.

Before he had time to ponder that further, Miss Ethel clapped her hand and stood, announcing, "Okay, boys. Time for bed."

He, Jaxon, and Asher climbed off the bed and walked across the hall to their room. Exactly like the older boys' room, it had bunk beds and a separate twin bed. Jaxon claimed the top bunk, Asher moved to the single bed, and Jayden crawled into the bottom bunk, loving the feel of being surrounded.

He heard the sounds of Miss Ethel saying goodnight to the older boys in their room before she appeared in their doorway.

She bent over Asher's bed, tucking him in tightly. He could hear her whisper to Asher but did not know what she said. Not that it mattered, because she whispered sweet things to all of them. Turning, she walked over to the bunk bed and smiled up at Jaxon.

"Is my little pirate tucked into his pirate ship for the night?"

Jayden could not keep the grin off his face as he heard his brother giggle. The moment Jaxon had seen the beds, he had turned to Jayden and asked, "Can I have the top bunk? I'd feel like a pirate sailing on a ship!"

Jayden had not minded, so he easily gave the top bunk to his brother. For him, he found the bottom bunk to be plenty of room and comforting...almost like being in a cave in the deep, dark woods.

Once more, he heard Miss Ethel whispering, knowing she had something special to say to Jaxon. After just a moment, she shifted and sat down on the edge of his bed.

"You seem to have something on your mind, Jayden," she said.

"Do you think he was scared? The woodsman, I mean," Jayden asked, wondering if he could ever be that brave.

"All of us are afraid at one time or another," she said. "I think a person is very foolish if they're not afraid in the face of danger. And not everyone reacts the same way. Some are small and weak, like Little Red Riding Hood and her grandmother. That's why it's so important for those of us who are strong to protect others."

He sucked in his lips and thought about his small size. Lifting his gaze, he said, "I'd like to be brave, Miss Ethel, but I'm not very big."

Laughing, she replied, "Oh, my dear boy. You're young, but I have no doubt you will grow to be big and strong and brave. I believe all my boys will discover their strengths and use them to help others."

She tucked him in before leaning over to kiss his forehead. "Don't worry, Jayden. You're my perceptive one. You are wise beyond your years. And just like your brothers, your protective instinct is strong."

Her words moved through him, warm, sliding deep inside. He felt her lips on his forehead and smiled. She walked out, flipping off the light switch, leaving the room illuminated by the small nightlight.

As he drifted off to sleep, he dreamed of woods and wolves, a grandmother that looked like Miss Ethel, and a little girl dressed in red.

Sitting outside the principal's office in an uncomfortable plastic chair, Jayden sat erect, anger and adrenaline still coursing through his veins. At sixteen years old, he was already a big teenager and shifted in the seat of a chair that was meant for someone smaller. The sting of his knuckles drew his eye, causing him to flex them so that he could examine the red, swollen flesh.

Hearing a noise near the office door, he looked up and observed Jaxon, Zander, Rafe, Cael, and Asher rushing through the door as one pack.

"What are you boys doing in here?" the school secretary asked, jumping from her desk.

Almost in unison, the five boys looked over at him, and Zander said, "We're here for Jayden."

"No, no, no," the secretary said, still standing but

staying behind her desk, eyeing them suspiciously. Her hands fluttered in front of her, attempting to shoo them out.

Each of them still had more filling out to do but were already over six feet tall. Zander, their leader and a senior, had already signed with the Army for after graduation. Cael and Rafe were both juniors, Cael already topping them all in height. Asher was a freshman, but Jayden noticed his quiet intensity was burning.

His gaze naturally moved to Jaxon, the understanding of twins passing between them, no words needed.

Before Zander had a chance to speak again, Jaxon said firmly, "We're. Not. Leaving." He walked over and sat down next to Jayden, the others filling in the chairs around them.

None of them spoke, words were not necessary. *If my brother needs me, I'm here. If I need them, they're here.* They sat quietly for several minutes, the only sound in the small office coming from the tick of the clock on the wall and the occasional huff from the secretary.

The principal's door opened, and their eyes turned in that direction. The principal was in the process of calling Jayden when he saw the others and snapped his mouth shut. They all stood at once, and he proclaimed, "Boys, this only concerns Jayden—"

A soft voice could be heard from inside his office, saying, "Now, Mr. Thompson, you know what concerns one of my boys concerns all of them."

Without another word, Jayden walked into the principal's office, followed closely by the other five young men. As soon as he passed through the doorway, his gaze landed on Miss Ethel, composed as ever. He was struck once more with the thought that she had not aged in the years they had been with her.

She was standing, as unflappable as ever, and moved directly to him. She now had to look up to see the faces of her sons, this time her eyes searching his carefully. Jayden noticed she must have been satisfied at what she saw, because she patted his cheek and said, "Come sit down next to me."

Inhaling deeply, the scent of her rosewater perfume calmed him, and he followed her. He and Miss Ethel filled the two chairs in the principal's office, and he stifled a grin as the other boys moved to stand behind them. The principal sat down heavily behind his large wooden desk, an unhappy look on his face. There was a window behind Mr. Thompson, and as Jayden viewed the reflection, he realized the seven of them presented unity. At this thought, his anger abated slightly.

Clearing his throat, Mr. Thompson began, "Jayden, as the evidence has been presented to me, I understand that you were coming to the defense of one of our female students who appeared to be in trouble."

"*Appeared* to be in trouble? *Appeared?* Those two were trying to...*hurt* her," he bit out, his anger ratcheting up again.

"Yes, yes," Mr. Thompson agreed, "but you should have tried to get help and not take it upon yourself to deal with them."

He opened his mouth to defend himself again when Miss Ethel laid her thin hand on his leg. He had not realized his leg had been bouncing, but with her calming touch, he let out a breath, forcing his leg to still.

"I have always raised my boys to look out for those in need. I have also raised my boys to take action to help those in need. If he had done as you suggested, that poor girl might have been violated, more traumatized than I'm sure she already is."

"Yes, but he didn't just get her free, he let his fists continue to do the talking—"

"While I do not normally condone violence," Miss Ethel stated, "I have lived my many years knowing that there are all sorts of people in the world. Thank goodness, most can be reasoned with, and a good, heartfelt conversation can settle differences. But unfortunately, not everyone can be reasoned with, and action is necessary. 'Measure a man's worth by his actions alone. For the devil also promises the moon!' An excellent quote by Avijeet Das concerning actions speaking louder than words. Don't you agree, Principal Thompson?"

The silence in the room stretched for a moment. Jayden did not have to see his brothers behind him to know their mirth at Miss Ethel confounding the principal speechless.

Finally, Mr. Thompson sighed. "Be that as it may, I must enforce consequences for broken rules. I promise the other two boys will be not only suspended from school, but the girl's parents are filing charges against them. For you, Jayden, you will have a two-day suspension out of school. While I commend you for coming to the girl's aid, we do have a policy to uphold."

Jayden did not say anything, instead taking his cue

from Miss Ethel, who nodded quietly. She turned toward him and smiled. "I'm so very proud of you, Jayden." Her eyes swept behind him toward her other boys and added, "I'm so very proud of all of you."

She nodded her head toward the door, and without another word, the boys filed out of the room. As Jayden moved through the door, he heard Mr. Thompson say, "You've done a good job with those boys, Miss Ethel."

She pinned him with her stare and replied, "I was gifted with good boys, Mr. Thompson. All I needed to do was handle my precious gifts with care." With that, she stood and followed the boys out of the office. She nodded toward the secretary, whose mouth was standing open, and Jayden held the door for her.

Once in the hall, they circled around her and headed outside. He had two days suspension, but as he walked next to her toward the old van, he held his head high. Miss Ethel placed her hand on his arm, and he looked down at her.

"I don't know the girl that you saved, but I have no doubt she will sleep easier tonight because you came to her aid." Patting his arm, she unlocked the van.

With the warmth from the sun on his face, his brothers at his side, and Miss Ethel's words ringing in his ears, he felt like a hero.

Every night, even though they were all teenagers, Miss Ethel still spoke to each of them before they went to bed. Zander's nighttime reading had been replaced by each of them reading their own books which they often discussed or shared.

That night, when she came to him, he spoke before

she had a chance to say anything. "Miss Ethel, thank you for coming to the school today and speaking up for me. When I rounded the corner near the back of the school and saw those two jerks trying to go after that girl, I honestly didn't think…I just jumped in to help her and didn't care how much I hurt them in the process."

She patted his cheek and said, "As you continue to mature, you'll learn that your strength will be a service to you and others. You must temper your strength so that you do not cause injury where you shouldn't." She stepped back, and her lips curved into a smile. "Do you remember how much you liked the Grimm's version of Little Red Riding Hood?"

He had not read that story in years, and his brow lowered in confusion. Nodding, he replied, "Yes, ma'am, although it's been a long time since I read it."

She chuckled and said, "You never forget the classics, my boy." She started to walk out of his room but stopped at the door. With her hand on the doorframe, she turned and looked at him. "You, my dear Jayden, are the woodsman." With that, she turned and walked down the stairs.

2

"Jayden!"

He lifted his head from underneath the hood of the minivan he was working on, searching for who called him amidst the sound of engines idling and music blaring. He was trying to diagnose and fix the problem as quickly as he could considering the young mother, with a baby in a carrier and a toddler clinging to her leg, was currently sitting in his small waiting room.

Building his own business, J.C. Tire & Auto, had been his dream ever since he watched Mr. Martin work on Miss Ethel's old van many years before. He had been fascinated as the older man tinkered on the engine in her vehicle. He had watched, with envy, as new minivans pulled up to the school, letting kids out. But she had an old model that she had bought used, saying it held all of her boys.

The mechanic had chatted with Miss Ethel, and it was clear that he knew she needed her vehicle fixed.

Jayden did not know why she did not buy a new one, but when Mr. Martin said, "Don't you worry none, Ms. Wiseman. I know you need this big ol' tank to get all them boys around. It might not be fancy, but me fixing it is a lot less expensive than you trying to buy something new. Don't you worry none. I'll get it up and running."

Hearing the mechanic's words, Jayden had learned at an early age that taking care of six, sometimes more, boys must have been expensive. He had looked up at Miss Ethel's pensive face and declared, "I'm going to learn how to fix cars, and then I can always take care of yours."

Her face had relaxed into a soft smile, and she bent to cup his cheeks with her hands. "Oh, my sweet Jayden, you are such a dear. I want you to grow up and become whatever your heart desires. You don't have to become a mechanic to take care of me. But if that's your dream, then do it with all your heart."

His childish desire had never wavered, and when he left high school and joined the Marines alongside Jaxon, he worked as a mechanic. He spent time in Afghanistan, working on both diesel and gasoline trucks. The cold winters and hot summers had him longing to be back in Virginia, but his plans to open his own shop kept him motivated to learn everything he could.

He saved every dime during his deployment and time of service, and when he was discharged, he took a job with old Mr. Martin who was looking for someone he could sell his business to and retire.

That opportunity came five years ago, and Jayden had turned it into a booming business, offering excellent work at decent prices. Others had told him that he could charge much more, but he cared more about his customers being in safe vehicles than making more money than he needed.

Hearing his name called again, he grabbed a cloth and wiped the grease off his hands. Seeing Jaxon walking over, he turned to his lead mechanic, Cas, and said, "Hey, can you keep working on this for me?" Castiel, another one of Miss Ethel's later charges, had been working for him for a few months after being discharged from the Army. "I wanna get that mom back on the road as soon as possible."

"No problem," Cas replied, looking up. He nodded toward Jaxon, greeting him with a wide smile.

Walking over, Jayden grinned at the face as familiar as his own. Jaxon had his long curls tied back when he was on duty as an EMT, but other than that, they looked identical. He clapped his twin on the shoulder. "Hey, man, what's up?"

Jerking his chin around, Jaxon indicated an ambulance parked outside. "Think the tires need rotating," he said. "It's not quite time for the maintenance, but I felt it pulling a bit this morning. I checked with my captain, and he said since I was on this side of town, I could bring it to you."

"No problem, I can get someone on it right away." Once Jaxon drove it into an empty bay and Jayden assigned one of his mechanics to begin the work, the two brothers walked into the office from the garage. His garage was simple in design, with four bays and a door leading into the office. Customers could wait in the small waiting room near the front, where there was also a door to the office. He settled into the squeaky, metal, rolling chair that had been part of the business when he bought it. Not caring about office furniture, he poured his money into modernizing and updating the shop.

Jaxon poured a cup of coffee from the pot sitting in the corner and sat in the only other chair in the office. "Business good?"

Nodding, he replied, "Yep. Pay my mechanics, pay my bills. I figure I'm doing pretty good."

"Shit, bro," Jaxon laughed. "You can't fool me. I know you still save every dime you make."

Lifting his shoulders in a shrug, he said, "Old habits die hard. Plus, I don't have anyone to spend money on, like most of you." In the last several years, many of his brothers had all fallen under the spell of wonderful women. Zander and Rosalie were married and now had a child. Rafe and Eleanor worked in her burn clinic and had just had a baby. Cael married Regina, now celebrating her continued good health after a battle against cancer. And recently, Jaxon had met Morgan, who also worked in Eleanor's clinic.

Their monthly gatherings with Miss Ethel now had them filling the room when they all got together. He knew Miss Ethel loved her growing family. *"There's always room for more at my table."* Her words resounded in his head and proved to be just as true now as when she was taking in boys years before.

"You're just not looking in the right places," Jaxon quipped. "Other than coming into Grimm's Bar where you just hang out with us, I don't see you getting out much." Jerking his head toward the waiting room, where the grateful mother was now paying since Cas was finished with her minivan, he added, "Not sure I see this place as a good setting to meet girls."

Chuckling, he replied, "You never know. Ms. Perfect might just need her car fixed one day."

Jaxon laughed, saying, "Well, if she does, I hope you recognize it and go for her."

Cas walked into the office and said, "Got 'em back on the road." He looked through the window into the shop and asked, "You want me to help with the ambulance?"

"That'd be great," Jayden agreed. "I don't like having Jaxon's wheels out of commission."

With a chin lift, Cas left the office. Jaxon asked, "How's he doing?"

"He's good. He works hard, does everything I ask, but other than that, keeps to himself."

"He's missed the last couple of gathering at Miss Ethel's," Jaxon stated, not telling Jayden anything he did not also realize.

Turning the conversation to sports, they passed the time, the ease between twins obvious. Within the hour Jaxon was back on the road, and Jayden was close to shutting down the shop for the evening. Having said goodbye to his mechanics, he locked the door and climbed onto his motorcycle. He considered heading to Zander's bar, Grimm's, but turned toward his apartment instead, preferring a quiet evening over the noisy bar. *I can always finish the book I started.*

Later, sitting on his balcony after a re-heated, left-over dinner, he propped his booted feet up onto the railing and sipped his beer. A park behind his apartment building gave him views of the sunset over the trees. Enjoying the peaceful evening, he finished his beer. As the sun moved beyond the horizon, he sighed. *Is there someone out there who'd like my simple life?*

After the sun set, he stayed up late reading in bed. As he tossed the latest mystery to his nightstand, he spied a stack of classics by his bed and smiled at the memory of Zander reading to them as children. That night, for the first time in years, he dreamed of forests, and wolves, and damsels in distress.

The rumble of the motorcycle underneath him propelled him down the familiar street. Each of Miss Ethel's boys returned when they needed to talk, share a good meal, or just to check on her. But it was the monthly gatherings that always called to Jayden.

The neighborhood had only changed slightly from when he was a child, the old houses now being bought by young families interested in both renovating an older home and providing their children with a safe neighborhood. As he neared the house at the end of the street, a smile slid across his face. There were several trucks and SUVs parked in front as well as Jaxon's motorcycle.

He parked along the street and headed up the front porch steps. Forgoing a knock, knowing it was not necessary, he moved to the front door and was immediately assaulted with memories that flooded every time he walked into her house. The light scent of rosewater perfume clung to the air, sparking a sense of contentment. It had changed very little in the last twenty years...hell, probably the twenty years before that.

A new, dark blue sofa sat where the old one used to take a position in front of the window. She had finally given in to allowing them to buy her a few pieces of furniture for her Christmas present last year. But she insisted on never replacing the old, scarred, wooden kitchen table. She claimed it carried too many memories of too many wonderful meals for her to get rid of it.

Some things never changed, besides the kitchen table. The chair with the knitting basket at its feet that sat near the fireplace had been there for as long as he could remember. She had perched in that chair knitting while all the boys would sit around in the evenings and work on their homework. She seemed to be able to help Zander with his reading, Cael with his math, and the twins with whatever they needed while her fingers continued to knit in a continuous motion. It fascinated him then and fascinated him now.

The noise from the back of the house captured his attention, and he walked down the hall leading to the kitchen. There, crowding the space, were his brothers and their women, filling the house with laughter, and in the center of it all was Miss Ethel filling it with love.

He was surprised and pleased to see not only Cas

but also Zeke, making their group complete. Zeke had come to Miss Ethel's when Zander was a senior in high school, but the two had formed a bond, and when Zeke returned from his time in the military, he joined Zander at Grimm's bar. Working first as a bouncer, he had convinced Zander that the bar needed to serve food and took over the restaurant side of the business.

Walking over to Cas, he clapped him on the back, saying, "Glad you came. I know Miss Ethel always likes having everyone together."

He made his way around the room, kissing the women he considered to be his sisters. He tugged on Regina's red hair that was growing after losing it to chemo. She playfully punched his shoulder, smiling widely, and his heart was lighter seeing how healthy she appeared. At six feet, seven inches, Cael was the only brother he had to look up to, and they shook hands before Cael claimed Regina, wrapping her in his arms.

Back-slapping Rafe, he greeted the former model before kissing the cheek of Eleanor. She had finally become less self-conscious of her burn scars and returned his kiss with a wide smile.

Zander walked by, his arms full of his baby girl, Charity. Stopping to say hello to his big brother, he also kissed the blonde, blue-eyed little girl who looked so much like her mother. Seeing Rosalie walk up to them, he hugged her and said, "She's a beauty." Rosalie beamed and offered him a hug.

His soon-to-be sister-in-law, Morgan, bounded from the kitchen to throw her arms around him. "Hey, Jayden," she greeted enthusiastically. He returned her hug and offered a chin lift to Jaxon walking up behind them.

He finally made it to Miss Ethel, enveloping her in his embrace. She leaned way back, staring up into his face, and clucked, "I swear, I think I have to look up further every time I see you. I suppose you're not growing anymore, so it must be me shrinking."

He laughed, bending to kiss her cheek. Her skin was just as soft as ever, although her smile lines were much deeper than he remembered as a child.

"Come look at what Castiel has created," Miss Ethel called out to everyone, walking into the dining room. The others shared questioning glances, and as he looked over at Cas, noted him blushing. They followed Miss Ethel, and for a few seconds, nobody spoke. Jayden looked around the room, but it did not appear different. The table had not been set, and Miss Ethel leaned over, clutched the tablecloth, and pulled it away, exposing the wooden table underneath.

Now, fully visible, it was evident that a new mid-section had been added, extending the table by almost two feet. The wood used was so similar in appearance that someone not used to the room would notice no difference.

As everyone exclaimed over the extension, Jayden bent and examined it carefully. He lifted his gaze to Cas and shook his head. "How on earth did you get it to match so well? It's even got the same dings and scratches!"

His comment caused Miss Ethel to beam and

everyone to lean closer to see how perfectly the new section matched the existing wood.

"I asked the same thing when he brought it in," she exclaimed. Turning to Cas, she demanded, "Tell them!"

He watched as Cas shrugged and said, "I just searched some old wood shops for pieces that would match. Then I added some scratches and hit it a few times with the edge of a hammer, giving it the appearance that it was part of this table to begin with. Once I cut it to fit and got the supports underneath it, I just made sure to keep staining it until it was the right shade."

Miss Ethel placed the tablecloth back onto the surface, and the others called out their thanks to Cas as they moved between the kitchen and dining room, their hands loaded with platters.

Walking over, Jayden clapped Cas on the shoulder. "You did a good thing here, bro. I knew you worked with wood, but I had no idea you were this talented."

"It's just something I like doing."

"Well, maybe you want to think about making a living building furniture. I'd hate to lose you because you're a crack mechanic, but what you do here is art."

Cas' lips curved into a grin, but he shook his head. "I like doing it, but it would never pay the bills. I figure I'll keep on being your mechanic, and I can always do this on the side."

"I'll keep you as long as I can, but if you ever figure out a way to do this full-time, I'll support your decision."

Soon everyone was settled around the now-larger

table, talking, laughing, and enjoying the food. He could not help but look at the four women that had joined their family, and his mind cast back to what Jaxon had said to him about finding someone special. His life had become his garage, and he had only been half-kidding when he said that maybe she would come walking through his door. *Yeah, right. Like that is gonna happen.*

3

With a final hug to everyone as he left, he allowed Miss Ethel to escort him to her front porch. She held on to his arm and they walked slowly down the steps, stopping to look at the flowering shrubs.

"The old neighborhood looks good, Miss Ethel," he said, pride and happy memories filling him as he cast his gaze across the street.

"It's nice to see lots of young families deciding to restore some of the older homes," she agreed. "It reminds me of the days when I first moved here."

Bending to kiss her goodbye, he felt her penetrating stare. Her eyes, now more grey than blue, still held their intensity. "I get the feeling that you're trying to discern how I am," he said. "I'll put your mind to rest...I'm fine."

"Hmph," she huffed. Reaching up, she patted his cheek and said, "I think they're working on the roads around here. I'd hate for you to go over any bumps with your motorcycle."

He held back his laugh, knowing that she worried

about he and Jaxon riding motorcycles, but a few bumps in the road would hardly be an obstacle.

She continued, "Take a left when you leave this street and go through a few of the older neighborhoods to get back out to the main road. That would make me feel better about you riding on that scary, two-wheeled monstrosity."

Giving her a hug, he promised, "Fine, I'll go that way just to appease you."

Making sure she was back on the porch safely, he stalked to his motorcycle. Fastening his helmet onto his head, he swung his leg over the seat and looked toward the house. Expecting her to have gone back inside with everyone else, he was surprised to see her still standing on the porch staring at him. He lifted his hand in a wave, and as always when she waved back, he felt as though it were a physical touch.

Firing up the engine, he pulled out onto her road. When he got to the intersection, he hesitated. He had not seen any construction on his way in and yet found himself turning to the left, following her directions. Chuckling, he realized that even at thirty years old, it was still ingrained to follow Miss Ethel's instructions.

He used to ride his bicycle through some of the old neighborhoods when he was younger, but he never thought much about them. These houses were smaller than Miss Ethel's; some had been kept up, additions built, and others looked in need of repair. Some yards were neat, but others had hedges that needed trimming and the grass needing mowing. As he turned a corner, a flash of red caught his attention. As he rode closer, he saw a young girl struggling with a lawnmower at one of the small but still cared-for houses.

She was petite, her legs encased in blue jeans, her feet in sneakers, and she wore a large, oversized, red, zip-up hoodie, hanging to the tops of her thighs. The sleeves were rolled up several times so that only her hands and wrists were exposed. Her dark brown hair was pulled up in a ponytail. She appeared to be struggling with a cantankerous mower, unable to get it started, and he spied no one else around.

Wondering if she could use some help, he pulled over to the side of the street and switched off his engine. She turned around, and it was then he realized his error. She was not a young girl but a woman. She may have been petite, but now facing him, the curves underneath the large sweatshirt were evident. She was about ten feet away, but it was easy to see that the top of her head would have only come to his shoulders...maybe.

Her flawless complexion gave her a youthful appearance, but it was her eyes that captured his attention. Wide. Sky blue. And as he approached, they flickered with fear.

Halting on his way toward her front fence, he threw his hands up in front of him, palms out, and quickly said, "I'm sorry. I didn't mean to frighten you. I just saw you trying to start the lawnmower and thought perhaps you needed assistance."

She glanced down at the offending piece of equipment, a grimace on her face before turning her head back to him. "Thank you, but no. I don't need any help."

Her voice was soft, and he had to lean forward slightly to hear her. "I know you have no reason to trust me, but I really would like to help. You can even go inside the house if you prefer, and I could get your lawnmower started and finish the job in just a few minutes."

He was not sure if she was going to take him up on his offer, but her response caught him off guard. Her eyes widened as she jerked her head from side to side.

"No! Please, just go."

Before he had a chance to move, the front screen door creaked, and he heard a gasp leave her lips at the same time her head swung toward the house.

A young man pushed the screen door open and stepped through, weaving slightly. His dirty hair was messy, and his wrinkled shirt appeared slept in. His dark eyes narrowed on the girl before shifting to take in Jayden.

Jayden's gaze did not waver, not liking the look of him, nor the way the man was sizing him up, as though weighing his ability to take him down. It only took a few seconds for the man to shift his gaze back to the girl, his mouth settling into a snarl.

"Ruby! What the fuck are you doing?"

"I'm just trying to get the lawn mowed—"

"Then get it done, and get in here. I'm hungry, and there ain't no food around."

A wave of protectiveness washed over Jayden as he continued to stare until the man stepped back in the house, the screen door slamming behind him. Barely holding in his anger, he turned his head to face the woman he now knew was Ruby and said, "Are you safe? Do you need—"

Her face contorted as she hissed, "Just go! Please, you're making things worse."

He hesitated, the notion of leaving her to face the man's wrath going against everything he held dear. He opened his mouth once more, but the look on her face halted his words. He wanted to erase that specter of fear but had no idea how to help in a way that might not make things worse for her.

She whirled around and grabbed the handle of the lawnmower. Instead of trying to start it again, she began dragging it toward the side of the house. He knew that he had been dismissed and could sense the man's gaze still on him from the front window. Hating the feeling of helplessness, he turned and walked back to his motorcycle. Throwing his leg over and securing his helmet, he started the engine. As he drove slowly down the street, he twisted his head to look back and saw her standing to the side of the house, one hand wiping a tear as the other hand lifted in a slight wave.

Continuing down the road toward his own home, his rage burned at his impotence to help her.

Ruby Mantle stood at the side of the house, watching the man on the motorcycle ride away. The very tall, very handsome, very kind man. His thick, curly, dark hair had been pulled back in the front, allowing the length to flow over his shoulders. He had stood well over a foot above her, muscles evident in the way his jeans fit over his thick thighs, and the T-shirt underneath the leather jacket was pulled tight over his chest.

She wondered how a man could be so large and yet not instill fear. Maybe it was his light brown eyes that had been warm when they rested upon her. Maybe it was the way his voice was soft and smooth as he spoke to her. Maybe it was the fact that he offered to help instead of growling more demands.

When he was finally out of sight, she glanced toward the house, her stomach in knots. When she had gone outside to mow the grass, she knew Kevin had already begun drinking. From the look of him when he was standing on the porch, it appeared he was well on his way to drunk.

She dreaded going back inside knowing he was angry. The house was hers, or rather her grandmother's, but when he came over, he tended to take control like he did with everything else these days.

Hearing a crash from inside the house, she jerked out of her thoughts. Dragging the lawnmower around to the back of the small yard, she pushed it into the shed. Locking it with a padlock, she hurried to the back door. Sucking in a fortifying breath, she pulled open the screen door and stepped into the kitchen.

Wondering what the crash was, she was relieved to see that it was not one of her grandmother's possessions but an empty whiskey bottle on the kitchen floor. Stepping carefully over the glass, she opened the closet and grabbed the broom and dustpan. Bending, she began to sweep, but as she heard Kevin's heavy footsteps coming closer, her heart started to pound.

Hoping to cut off the rant she knew was coming, she quickly said, "I'm cleaning up the spill. As soon as I get it clean, I'll fix some supper."

He staggered to the kitchen counter, leaning heavily against it, propping himself up with his palms on the surface. She did not lift her head to look at him but continued to stare at the floor as she swept up all of the glass.

"You think I didn't see you out there flirting," he growled. "Can't turn my back on you for a second."

"Kevin, you know that's not true," she said. "Granny's coming home tomorrow, and I'm just trying to make the place look nice for her."

Sneering, he said, "Granny. Your fuckin' Granny. You're doing all this work for her, but you don't do shit for me."

Standing, she walked over to the kitchen sink and opened the door to the cabinet. Dumping the broken glass into the trashcan nestled under the sink, she stood and considered her words carefully.

"Kevin, you know that's not true. I do a lot for—

"You callin' me a liar?" he snarled.

She whirled around and shook her head. "No, I'm not. Look, are you hungry? I'll fix some supper right now. Why don't you go on back in and finish watching the game?" She swallowed deeply, barely breathing as she waited to see his response. He appeared to waiver, taking one step forward, causing her body to stiffen in dreaded anticipation. She hated when he grabbed her and jerked her around. He never used to be this way...*but when he drinks...* He rocked back, his hip bumping into the counter, before turning and staggering down the hall.

Letting her breath out in a long, slow sigh, she reached behind her, grabbing the edge of the sink for support, afraid her legs would give out from under her. She remained completely still as she listened for sounds coming from the living room. The sound of his body hitting the sofa, an *'umph'* leaving his lips. Then, the thump of his feet landing on the coffee table. The crunch of an empty beer can just before the clatter of it hitting the floor was followed by a sigh of contentment, coming from a man who knew how to wield power.

When she was sure he was not coming back after her, she swallowed deeply, straightened her knees and steeled her spine. Turning, she walked to the refrigerator, knowing if she did not get supper to him soon, she would pay the price.

Jayden had tried working out, went for a run, took a hot shower, watched a ballgame, but nothing could rid him of seeing the face of the girl...Ruby. Her wide, blue eyes and heart-shaped face stayed in his memory. So did the look of fear that had not only seemed to fill every fiber of her body but crackled off her.

Throwing his head back against the sofa cushion, he sighed. He had wanted to bound up the steps and grab the man by the front of his wrinkled shirt and slam him back against the door just for daring to put that expression on her face.

Jesus, I must be losing my mind. I don't even know her. He scrubbed his hand over his face and hefted himself from the sofa. Walking into the kitchen he tossed his beer can into the recycle bin and rinsed off the plate that had contained his sandwich and chips.

Making sure his apartment was secure, he moved into the bedroom. It did not take him long to get ready, and soon he was lying in bed, his hands behind his head, staring up at the ceiling, having abandoned the book he thought about reading. The words from long ago that Miss Ethel had spoken came back to him. *"We can step in and help others that cannot help themselves."*

He had never hesitated to step in before. As he left boyhood behind him, he and Jaxon had grown tall and strong. While he did not condone unnecessary violence, he had never shied away from standing up to bullies, and if that included fists, so be it. But the expression on Ruby's face, when she pleaded for him to leave or he would make things worse, stayed with him. *What if standing up to a bully actually does make it worse for the victim?*

He wondered who the man was…a husband… boyfriend…brother? He shut his eyes tightly, and he tried to remember if he had seen a ring on her finger. He remembered she lifted her left hand to the handle of the lawnmower, and as he replayed the scene in his mind, he was sure she was not wearing a wedding ring. Immediately feeling better that she was not married to the jerk, he still could not rid himself of the guilt of having walked away.

Maybe tomorrow I'll drive by. Not on my motorcycle. My truck will do. It'll be less noticeable. I could just drive by and check on her.

With a plan formulated, albeit a simple one, he breathed a little easier.

Ruby lay in bed that night, curled up into a ball, facing away from Kevin, and looking out the window at the darkness. She had managed to get dinner fixed quickly, and once his belly was full, he fell asleep on the sofa. She had spent the rest of the evening tidying up the house in readiness for her grandmother's return the next day.

He was much larger than her, but she managed to get him up the steps and into bed. Grateful that he had fallen asleep before reaching for her, she listened to him snore. The sound may have kept someone else awake, but the noise did not bother her. It actually brought relief, for if he was snoring, he was sleeping. If he was sleeping, then he would not touch her.

She had known him for years, first meeting in high school. She missed her dad when he died, and her mother's illness gave her little time for friends. Both loners, they gravitated toward each other as friends. He had been so nice then, so easy to talk to. It had been years before he made a romantic move on her, and at first, she was thrilled. She thought going from friends to boyfriend was the natural progression. But then, over time, he changed. He drank more, worked less, and his frustration would slide into anger. The change was so slow, she did not realize how low he had fallen until his words became cruel. He often said she was lucky to have him. *"No other man'll look at you, Ruby. You oughta be grateful for me."*

She thought of how her parents would feel about her life now and winced. *God, they would hate to see me being treated like he does. Maybe it's time I started making my life my own.* Thinking on that, she sucked in a deep breath before letting it out slowly, her decision firmly resolving in her mind. *I'd rather be alone than with someone who treats me like he does.*

She lay staring into the sky until the clouds passed, and she saw the first star twinkling that night. Unable to stop herself, she closed her eyes and made a wish, thinking of the handsome man who had ridden up on his motorcycle and offered to help.

If only wishes came true. Willing herself to go to sleep, she knew that at least the next day would bring her beloved Granny home.

4

"Oh, my, Ruby! You shouldn't have gone to all this trouble," Granny exclaimed, leaning heavily on her granddaughter's arm as they walked into the house.

Ruby beamed proudly although she was exhausted with worry. She had managed to get her grandmother, the suitcase, and the walker into her small car, and thankfully, it started. Her car had been giving her fits lately, but there was no money to get it worked on. Everything she earned from cleaning houses and working a late shift at a diner barely paid for their expenses, which had grown when Granny went into rehab.

Granny had fallen two months earlier, but, thank God, she did not break her hip, although a stay in rehab was required. Ruby was grateful that they found a place for Granny that took Medicare, but there were still bills to be paid. Money was tight, but now that Granny was back home, she felt as though she could breathe a little easier.

Once she had pulled into the driveway with her grandmother, her next concern had been getting her up the four steps into the house. The rehab had worked wonders because Granny was able to make it up the porch steps as long as she had Ruby to cling to.

Now they had shuffled into the living room that she had scrubbed clean and placed a bouquet of flowers on the coffee table. Turning to peer into her grandmother's face, she breathed a sigh of relief. The pieces of her life were now aligned with Granny home.

"It's no trouble, Granny," she said. "I'm just so excited to have you home."

She assisted Granny to the comfortable chair that faced the TV and was also near the fireplace. "You stay here, and I'll get the walker and your suitcase out of the car. I'll fix us a cup of tea just as soon as I get you settled."

"Now, don't you go fussing over me, girl."

Bending to kiss her grandmother's soft cheek, she said, "I'm so glad to have you back." She blinked rapidly, filled with the desire to burst into tears, and hurried back out of the house toward her car. A myriad of emotions slammed into her, and she fought to get a handle on them.

Gratitude that her grandmother was back home warred with financial worries. She had to shift two of her housecleaning jobs to another day in order to pick up Granny which meant she was going to have to work a full day later in the week without a chance to check on her. Hoping that Kevin was not going to come by, she pushed all thoughts of him from her mind, focusing on the tasks at hand.

If only there were more minutes in an hour, more hours in a day, more days in a week. Sighing, she grabbed the small suitcase and the walker from her car and slammed the door. Working to keep her thoughts positive, she quickly headed back into the house.

As she entered, Ruby's eyes landed on the familiar sight of her grandmother sitting in her favorite chair. She had been plump but was now thinner, and her grey hair had lost the slight blue tint that she so adored. *All temporary changes and can easily be fixed with some good meals and a visit from her hairdresser.*

"I'm surprised that Kevin's not here," Granny said as Ruby re-entered the living room, her voice even but her words not warm.

Jerking her eyes upward, she saw her grandmother's sharp gaze piercing her. "I…he…he's at work…uh…"

Granny's face softened, and she shook her head sadly. "Ruby, you don't ever gotta lie to me. I always thought that boy was a real charmer and hoped he'd treat you good. But since you two have been dating, he seems more like a wastrel than a good man. I don't think he's held down a job for a while, has he?"

Shoulders slumping, she busied herself putting the walker close to Granny's chair. Tossing a smile her way, she said, "I'll get some tea and we can sit for a bit."

Hurrying into the kitchen, she put on the kettle and pulled down two mugs from the cabinet. She looked around the small space and wondered how Granny would be able to maneuver with the walker. The house was long and narrow, built to fit the plot of land it was on. The living room took up the entire front of the house, with a kitchen and dining room in the back. A small powder room was nestled under the stairs near the front door, leading to the two bedrooms upstairs. The original house had three small bedrooms, but once Granny's only son, Ruby's father, left home for the Army, Granny and Grandpa remodeled the upstairs. They turned it into two large bedrooms, each with their own bathroom.

But while the upstairs bedrooms and bathrooms were of a good size, Granny was no longer able to traverse the stairs. The one good thing Kevin had assisted with was to help her take the dining room furniture and put it in the storage shed in the yard so that a hospital bed would fit into the dining room.

The whistling of the teakettle startled Ruby, and she quickly poured the boiling water into the two mugs along with the teabags. Throwing in some sugar and a dash of milk, she set them on a tray and walked back into the living room, placing it onto the coffee table.

She handed the mug full of steaming tea to Granny, fussing over her slightly before sitting down on the sofa and taking a grateful sip of her own. The slight tang of orange and cinnamon hit her palate, always providing a sense of comfort. She watched in pleasure as Granny blew air over the top of her tea, sending the steam curling in the air before taking a sip and closing her eyes in an expression of pleasure.

"I can't complain about the food they served in

rehab, but they just could never get a good cup of tea right."

"They seemed to treat you really well there," Ruby said. "They were always nice to me when I came by."

"Oh, they were," Granny easily admitted. "The hardest thing about rehab was the physical therapy. They wanted me up and walking right away and told me that it was okay to hurt, but not hurt too much. I kept thinking how on earth am I supposed to know how much hurt is too much hurt!" She took another sip of tea and shook her head gently. "They knew what they were doing, though. My hip's all better...well, almost all better."

She watched as Granny's eyes shifted toward the stairs, and Ruby said, "Oh, no. Don't even think about it. I rented a hospital bed and had them deliver it to the dining room. I know there's no shower down here, but with the powder room, you can take a sponge bath. I've already made arrangements for Charlene to come in and wash and set your hair once a week."

Granny pursed her lips and grumbled, "That's an awful lot of trouble for you to go to, sweetheart. I can't believe you're having to do all this for me and work as hard as you do."

Blinking at the sudden onset of tears again, she replied, "Granny, don't you know? I'd do anything for you, just like you'd do anything for me."

She watched as Granny blinked rapidly also, and both women looked back down at the tea they were sipping. A movement on the street caught her eye, and she stared out of the front window. A pickup truck rolled down the street, but with the sun glinting off the windshield she had no idea who was inside. It seemed to slow near Granny's house before heading down the road.

Before she had a chance to wonder about the truck, Granny looked up, her forehead scrunched.

"If a hospital bed is in the dining room, where are the table and chairs?"

"I made room for them out in the shed in the yard."

Eyes wide, Granny exclaimed, "You moved all that stuff by yourself? Lordy, girl, you're going to end up in rehab right along with me!"

Laughing, she said, "No. Kevin came over and helped me move the table." As soon as his name left her mouth, she wished she could pull it back, seeing Granny's eyes narrow on her. Sighing, she said, "He does do some good things, Granny."

"Uh huh." The silence stretched for only a few seconds before Granny softly asked, "And did he help you out of the goodness of his heart, or did he want some money for his time and trouble?"

Swallowing deeply, Ruby took another sip of her tea, her shoulders already slumping in defeat. Her voice small, she answered, "He just needed a little bit," she said, "and it didn't seem right to ask him to do some manual labor without paying him."

Sighing heavily, Granny softened her voice. "I knew his daddy and granddaddy. Two meaner men I've never met. Harsh with words and heavy-handed with their wives and children. Kevin Wolfe Senior was mean to the bone, and when he named his son Kevin, I told your granddaddy that I hoped better for him. Then that Kevin grew up to be just as ornery. Lo and behold, he named his son Kevin, and I prayed that the chain would be broken. When you and Kevin first became friends in high school, I thought, 'Praise the Lord, finally a Kevin Wolfe that was good.'"

Her grandmother's words shifted her thoughts back to six years ago when she was a senior in high school. Kevin was not an overly large man, not like his father and grandfather, but considering she was only five feet, two inches, he was still a lot bigger than she was. She saw the vulnerability in his eyes and the bruises on his arms and found herself wanting to reach out and make it better.

Her father had died when she was thirteen, and then her mom was diagnosed with cancer just before she turned sixteen. When her mother died two years later, she sold their small house to help pay for her mother's medical costs and funeral and moved in with Granny.

The kindness that she had shown Kevin was returned when he helped her with homework on the days that she had to miss school to take her mom to the hospital and then again when he helped her through the sale of her house and the move. He was such a dreamer. He always had a plan, a way to make money and have a good life.

"One of these days, I'll be rich and can take care of you." "I'm onto a new deal, and as soon as this pans out, I'll have money." "I hate seeing you work so hard, Ruby. I've got a line on a sure thing, and the money will be rolling in soon."

They had only been officially dating for the past

year, but as his get-rich-quick schemes never came to fruition, he became angrier over time. Then the drinking would start, and he would fall into a depression. She felt sorry for him, but begging him not to drink did little good.

"I'm going to ask you a question, Ruby, and I want an honest answer," Granny said, once more startling her from her musings.

Before she had a chance to steel herself for whatever Granny was going to ask, the question came.

"Has he ever taken his hand to you?"

A quick denial was on her lips, but seeing her grandmother's eyes peering deeply into hers, she knew she could not lie. Swallowing deeply, she replied, "Only a couple of times, Granny, and it wasn't bad. Mostly, he just grabs me and jerks me around." She watched as Granny shook her head slowly. Lifting her thin shoulders slightly, she added, "I know I shouldn't let him, but I guess I just keep hoping that he'll go back to the nice boy I once knew."

"Is he drinking? Both his daddy and his granddaddy drank to excess."

Unable to answer directly, she nodded.

Granny sighed audibly and said, "Yeah, I figured as much. Probably gets meaner the drunker he gets. Throw in money problems, because that boy never could hold onto a job since he was always trying to find an easy way to get rich, that makes it worse."

Not knowing what to say, she drained her teacup before setting it on the coffee table.

"Ruby, sweetheart, I've never filled your head with

the idea of a prince coming along and taking all your cares away. But I believe that life is hard enough without surrounding ourselves by those who just want to gobble up our souls. There are men out there…good men who would take care of you, and you can take care of them, and you'd make each other happy. That's the kinda happily ever after I want for you. I had a man like that. Your daddy was a man like that. I don't know when you'll meet a man like that, but I know he's out there. And you know in your heart that Kevin Wolfe is not that man."

She knew her grandmother was right about Kevin. She had known for a while that she needed to break things off with him and distance herself, even if that meant being alone.

Her grandmother's words had her mind slide back to the handsome man on the motorcycle from yesterday. The stranger who stopped. Who offered to help. She remembered the look on his face when Kevin had staggered to the door calling out his threats. She could tell he wanted to step in, but she forced him away out of fear.

She had only spent a couple of minutes in his presence yet felt instinctively that he was the type of man her grandmother was describing. *He could have been a prince.*

5

ONE MONTH LATER

Jayden loved the freedom, the roar of the engine under-neath him, the rush of fresh air blasting against his body. Leaving the crowded city streets behind, he rode on back country roads not slowed by traffic. Having worked in the garage late last night, he was taking a rare morning off. Deciding to go for a ride, he headed out to the country, inhaling deeply as woods, farms, and pastures slid by him.

It was a pleasure that he used to share with Jaxon and still did, though not as often now that Jaxon was engaged. Asher also enjoyed a motorcycle ride out in the country, but he had been busy lately, rarely getting away from the homeless shelter where he worked.

The rest of his brothers were at work or with their women, so today was a lone sojourn. It had been a month since he had met Ruby, but she had never left his mind. He told no one about the encounter but had driven by the house weekly hoping to catch a glimpse of her again. At first, he tried to convince himself that it was only to check to make sure she was all right. But in the dark of night, lying in his bed, he knew that was only part of the reason. The other was that he wanted to see her face again. He wanted those wide, blue eyes to stare up at him. He wanted to be the one to take the fear away. He wondered if she was still there because he had never seen her outside on any of his drive-bys.

Bringing his thoughts back to the ride, he left the country road and moved onto a slightly busier road heading back into town. The traffic was not heavy, but he was forced to go a little slower. Up ahead, he could see cars slowing as they moved around a vehicle that had pulled to the side of the road, their lights flashing, indicating a problem.

Not one fucker is stopping to help, he grumbled to himself, flipping on his blinker and moving to the shoulder. The sight of an oversized, red hoodie grabbed his attention. His breath caught in his throat as the driver who had been standing to the side of the immobile car turned and faced him. *Ruby!* Her wide, blue eyes stared at him, and this time he saw a flash of confusion as she tilted her head to the side, her mouth open slightly.

Swinging his leg over his bike, he pulled his helmet off, his hair curling about his shoulders. Walking over, he could not deny the sense of pleasure he felt at seeing her again.

"What's the trouble?" he asked, observing her cross her arms in front of her tightly. Recognizing the defensive posture, he stopped several feet away from her.

"I don't know," she replied, her voice as soft as he

remembered. She glanced back toward her car and said, "It's been running a little funny for a long time, but I was hoping that it would keep going a bit longer."

"May I take a look?"

She sucked in her lips, then nodded her reply.

He walked around her, making sure to not pass too closely, opened the hood and peered inside. It only took a few minutes to determine that the repair would not be something quick he could fix on the side of the road. She had edged closer to him and was now standing at his side, looking at the engine as well. He glanced down, observing her hand resting on the metal of the frame. Her wrists were thin and her fingers delicate. She was just as tiny as he remembered.

"I'm embarrassed to say I don't know anything about cars," she said, her eyes moving from the engine up to his. "I just always stick the key in the ignition and pray that it starts and gets me where I need to go."

He smiled as light pink dusted her cheeks. "Don't be embarrassed. That's a lot more common than you think. But you're in luck because I'm a mechanic."

Her eyes widened, and the shy smile she offered warmed his heart. "Seriously?"

Pleasure shot through him at her beautiful smile directed at him, and he nodded. "Yeah." He reached for his wallet and pulled out a business card, handing it to her. "That's me, Jayden. Jayden Chapman."

She stared at the card in her hand, studying it before looking back up. "I'm Ruby. Ruby Mantle."

"I'm pleased to meet you, Ruby. And even though I own a mechanic shop, I don't actually advise that people ignore their cars. I'd rather see people take care of their automobiles and know what they need to do so that they don't end up stranded on the side of the road."

She glanced around at the traffic passing by, her brow lowered as her lips thinned into a grimace. He had not meant to lose her smile but did want her to realize she had put herself in a precarious situation. "Hey, but don't worry. I'll call for one of my men to bring out a tow truck, and we'll you get you back to the shop."

"Oh…um…okay." Worry lines appeared on her brow, and her mouth tightened even more.

He felt concern rolling off her and rushed to say, "Don't worry about the cost. You didn't call for our service. I came across you and volunteered. So that means we'll tow you for free." He hoped his offer would work, but her eyes pinned him to the spot.

"I know that can't possibly be true," she said, shaking her head. She bit her lip and glanced back down to the car engine. Finally, heaving a sigh, she nodded. "I don't want to be towed for free, but I know I'm in a pickle. I've got to get back to town to check on my grandmother, and I've got to get my car fixed. If I can't get to work, I can't get paid."

Relief flooded him that she was going to allow him to help. Pulling out his phone, he placed a quick call to his shop, giving their location to one of his mechanics. Sliding his phone back into his pocket, he said, "They should be here in about thirty minutes." He glanced up the street and saw a few shops, including the familiar yellow arches of a McDonald's. "While we wait, how about we go grab a cup of coffee?"

She swung her head around, squinting into the distance. "Oh, I didn't even see that down there."

He peered at her carefully and asked, "Should you be wearing glasses?" He watched as another pink blush rose from her neck to her forehead and wondered about the cause.

"I broke my glasses a couple of months ago and haven't taken the time to get them fixed." She looked quickly up at him, and rushed, "I can drive fine. It's just things that are very far away are a little fuzzy for me."

It was becoming evident to him that money was tight for her, and his protective urge came out even more. Hoping to put her at ease, he said, "Well, since I'm the one who wants a cup of coffee, it'll be my treat if you accompany me."

"What about your motorcycle?"

"Oh, I won't be leaving that here. You can ride on the back with me, and since the McDonald's is just down the road, we can be there super-fast."

"I've never ridden on a motorcycle before," she confessed, concern causing a new crinkle between her brows.

"There's a first time for everything," he said, holding his breath, hoping that she would agree to go. He watched her expressive face, seeing the inner battle that she was struggling with. "Look, I know it's asking a lot. You don't know me, and you're right to be wary. It was just a thought, but we can stay here and wait for the tow truck."

Her front teeth bit her bottom lip for a few seconds before she lifted her face up toward his and smiled. "No,

I want to go. I've been thinking that I need to try new things lately, and with you, this doesn't feel like a risk."

Without giving it a second thought, he reached down and took her hand, guiding her over to his bike. As soon his fingers touched hers, he jolted, both at the shock that he had been so forward and that she had allowed him to do so. He grabbed his helmet and put it over her head, concentrating on tightening the chin-strap, not his reaction to her touch.

"I know this is too big for you, but we'll make it work."

"Since this is my first time," she said, "you'll have to tell me what to do."

He blinked, his thoughts first going to the double meaning of her words. *Jesus, get a grip.* Forcing his cock to calm down, he shook his head. Checking the helmet, he grinned and said, "Throw your leg over the seat behind me, and wrap your arms around me. Hold on tight. I'll do the rest." Wincing at the double meaning of his own words, he was glad that she did not seem to notice.

Her shy smile slipped out again, and she nodded awkwardly with the helmet on her head. "I can do that."

"Well, all right." He settled himself on his bike and waited while she maneuvered herself behind him. He twisted his head and said, "Put your arms around my waist so that your hands are tightly holding on. If we were going for a longer ride, I'd give you more instruc-tions, but we're just going right up the road. You'll be fine as long as you hold on."

She did as he asked, and as her hands pressed against

his abdomen, he closed his eyes for just a second, memorizing the feel of her touch. Before he let his imagination run away with the idea that this woman could be more than just someone he was helping, he started the engine and roared the short distance to the McDonald's.

It had been months since Ruby had eaten at a restaurant and that included fast food. Expecting only a cup of coffee, she sat at a table when Jayden insisted that she wait while he ordered. She continued to stare at his broad back, pinching herself that she was here with him. Lost in her daydreams, she was stunned when he returned to the table with a tray laden with food.

"Wow, you eat a lot," she blurted, unable to keep the incredulity from her voice as she stared at several wrapped burgers, two large orders of French fries, a coffee, and two large sodas.

"Once I got up there," he explained, "I decided I was hungry and figured you might be, also. So, I got a coffee for you, but also figured we could split the food."

She was ready to deny that she was hungry when her stomach let out a loud rumble. Ducking her head, she tightened her arms about her middle, squeezing in hopes to quell the noise. She admitted, "Well, I suppose I could eat something since you've already paid for it."

His smile widened, and her heart skipped a beat. She decided that sight was something she would not mind seeing more of. It was not just that he was handsome and friendly, but that he seemed genuinely happy that she was going to eat with him.

She unwrapped what looked like the smallest burger but was still surprised to see that it was much bigger than what she normally ate. Two pieces of meat. Lots of lettuce and tomato. The scent of the greasy burger rose up to meet her, and she wondered how she would get her mouth around it.

"Go on. Dig in," he commanded before taking a huge bite of his own.

He chewed and swallowed, washing it down with a large sip from his Coke, and she watched, mesmerized. His eyes twinkled, and he moaned as though it was the best bite of food he had ever tasted. She had seen Kevin eat many times, but he always shoveled food in, giving no evidence that he was enjoying it. But Jayden...*how can a man look so sexy just eating a hamburger?*

Catching the quizzical tilt of his head, she took a bite, unwilling for him to discern the trail of her thoughts.

She ate over half the burger, along with half of one of the containers of French fries, and half of her soda. As she glanced at the tray, she realized that he had finished all of his food and was watching her carefully.

She immediately brought her napkin up to her mouth and mumbled, "Do I have food on my face?"

He shook his head and smiled. "No. I just really liked watching you eat."

An unbidden snort erupted and she said, "You like watching me eat? That seems like a rather boring experience." Unlike him, she was sure there was nothing special about her eating.

He shook his head and said, "Not at all. You ate like you really enjoyed it. I like that."

They were quiet for a moment, and she felt the awkward silence hover over them, wishing that she knew witty things to talk about. She glanced around and saw the stares a few women were casting toward Jayden. *Who could blame them?* After all, he was the most handsome man she had ever seen.

"What are you thinking?" he asked, reaching across the table to place his hand on top of hers.

"I'm thinking that all the women in this McDonald's are staring at you like they wished you were on the menu, and they're wondering what you're doing with me." She was only half joking but was surprised when his eyes flashed in response.

"They're thinking that I'm the lucky one, being here with you," he stated emphatically.

She opened her mouth to retort, then snapped it shut, uncertain what to say. She had no idea how to respond to that statement, but her insides began turning cartwheels. Pulling in her lips, she could feel the heat of blush moving across her cheeks again and grabbed her drink, sucking loudly on the straw to give her something to do. With a grin on his face, he squeezed her hand again before letting go, reaching for the last of her fries to eat. Grateful he must have understood, she breathed a sigh of relief.

"So, why were you out here?" he asked.

"I have a house that I clean just south of town. It was

the last one on my rotation today, and I was praying that my car would be able to make it back home."

"Is that what you do for a living?"

She nodded and replied, "Part of what I do. I work the late shift at a diner and make decent tips, but you can never count on that. My mama always said that I was such a good helper around the house, so I figured I could make some money doing that for others. I've got houses that I clean on a rotating basis during the days to bring in more money." She held his gaze, pleased to see no judgment in his eyes. Shrugging, she admitted, "It's not very exciting, but it's honest work."

He threw his hands up and smiled. "I can't say being a mechanic is very exciting either, but I like doing it."

His phone vibrated and he grabbed it from the table. Looking at the screen, he sent a text, and then said, "We need to head back to your car. My guy is almost here with the tow truck."

As she helped to clean the refuse from the table, a wistful feeling slid through her. She knew it was only a simple meal between acquaintances. He was a good guy, and he was doing her a favor. *That's all.* But deep inside, part of her wished it was a date with someone who really wanted to get to know her. Squaring her shoulders, she pushed those thoughts away. Turning, she smiled up at him as he led her back to his motorcycle. *One day at a time, and right now, I need to get my car fixed so I can get back to Granny.*

6

An hour and a half later, Jayden stood in the office of his shop, his hands on his hips, scowling down at Ruby. "I don't know why you're being so stubborn." She stood in front of him, her hands clenching and unclenching as she held them tightly. Blowing out a breath, he took a step back, not wanting her to feel crowded, when all he really wanted was to step closer and pull her into his arms. Running his hand over his face, he said, "Look, I'm not trying to be forceful, but I want you to be reasonable. It's going to take at least a day to get the parts for your car and another day to get them installed. You don't have any other mode of transportation, and I know you need to get to work."

"I can take a bus to the diner," she protested, crossing her arms tightly about her waist as she twisted her head to stare out the window between the office and the garage. Seeing her old car up on the lift made her head hurt as much as the imagined the cost of repairs, and she rubbed her forehead.

"Yeah, and you'd have to pay for the bus, plus it's not safe late at night. And what about the houses you clean?"

She pinched her lips and lowered her chin. "I don't know," she all but moaned. "I'll figure something out."

"Ruby, look at me, please," he begged, softening his voice. He waited until she lifted her gaze to his, and he stared into the depths of her blue eyes. "The loaner car is just sitting out in the shop's parking lot. It's old, but it's in good condition. I haven't sold it because I'd get absolutely no money for it, but it serves a purpose here. I'm not like one of these big fancy shops, but if I can offer a customer a loaner car while their car is being worked on, then it helps them out, and I might get their repeat business."

She did not reply immediately, but he could see the wheels turning in her mind, her expressive face not hiding anything. Pushing his advantage, he continued, "I just want to help."

"Why?"

Blinking at her question, he replied, "I don't know, Ruby. I just do."

"I don't need your pity," she said, her voice quivering. As soon as the words left her mouth, she closed her eyes and lowered her chin again, as though too embarrassed to look at him.

He dropped his hands from his hips and sighed. "Everyone needs help sometimes. That's how the world works…we need help, we accept it, then we pay it back when we can."

She raised her chin and stared at him, her chin no

longer wobbling, but her eyes searching his deeply. Suddenly, she blurted, "I remember you. I remember you tried to help me once before."

He stepped closer and fought the desire to reach out to her. "I know. I remember you, too."

Stunned, she whispered, "You do?"

"Yeah, I do. And while I'm so sorry you had car trouble today, you have no idea how thrilled I am that I'm the one who stopped." Deciding to confess, he said, "I felt badly that day that I couldn't help you. I left you to...to..."

Her shoulders slumped, and she looked back down at her feet and said, "It was better that you left when you did."

His gut clenched as he asked, "Did he...was he...?"

"No" she answered, her face flame-red. "He was too drunk to care by the time I got inside." Before he had a chance to speak again, she said, "He's gone. I finally broke up with him."

The air left Jayden's lungs in a rush at her response. He had no idea why it was important that the asshole she had been with was gone, but her words filled him with joy.

She swallowed audibly and said, "I guess I must seem pretty pathetic to you."

The urge too strong to deny, he lifted her chin with his knuckles. "No way. Not at all. Like I said, we all need help now and again. Please, take the loaner car. It would mean a lot to me."

She nodded, her chin pressing against his knuckles that rested there. "Granny always told me that I should be grateful for the good things in life that happen. I suppose I've seemed ungrateful today, but it's just kind of embarrassing that I'm in a place of such need." She filled her lungs with air and straightened to her full height—which was still a foot below him—and held his gaze. "But you're right. I need to work to be able to pay my bills and certainly to be able to pay for my car. And I would be a fool to turn down your offer of a loaner car for the next couple of days. So, I'll take it with gratitude."

Feeling lighter, he smiled. "You don't owe me gratitude. Just knowing that you'll be safe is good enough for me."

Driving home like a little old lady, her hands gripping the steering wheel so tightly her knuckles ached, Ruby carefully stopped at every light and every stop sign. She made sure to drive five miles under the speed limit and heaved a sigh of relief when she turned onto her street. Pulling the loaner car into her driveway, she turned off the engine and very slowly loosened her grip on the steering wheel, flexing her fingers. She had been terrified of doing something to the car Jayden had loaned to her, even though it was probably as old as her own car.

She sat for a minute, glancing about the unfamiliar interior of the car, noting it was clean and detailed, and her lips curved in a smile as she allowed herself to inhale deeply and catch a scent that reminded her of Jayden.

Kevin had always worn cologne, and when she was a teenager, she thought it was so mature and manly. The longer she was around him, the more he wore, and she eventually realized it was to cover up the smell of alcohol and tobacco.

But the scent that filled her nostrils now was not of cheap cologne, but a mixture of vinyl cleaner, oil, and the faint odor from inside Jayden's garage. She closed her eyes and inhaled again, knowing that it might make her seem crazy, but the combination was truly the scent of a man. Just like Jayden.

She had never been inside a mechanic's shop before, but he had taken her through the bays once her towed car ended up in the garage. The deafening sound of equipment whirring mixed with country music playing from speakers was energizing. The area was neat, tools lined up for the mechanics to use, and the ones not necessary were hanging on the wall or in chests. The men that worked for him, dressed in blue coveralls with his logo on the front, were respectful, and if their expressions were curious, it only lasted for a few seconds before they went back to work.

He had escorted her into his office, and that was also a surprise. A desk holding his computer. A filing cabinet and two chairs. A counter with a coffee pot. It was a basic office, but stacks of papers scattered about gave evidence that he cared more about his shop than his office. She had not seen a receptionist or secretary but had no idea if mechanic's shops normally had one of those.

Before she had time to consider the fate of her car in

Jayden's hands or his shop, she jerked when the front door opened. Granny was standing there, clutching her walker, staring out at her.

Grabbing her purse, she jumped out of the car and carefully locked the door, calling over her shoulder, "Granny, it's me!"

Rushing up the steps toward the front door, she chastised her fanciful notions, hating that she had worried her grandmother. "I'm fine, I'm fine."

She made it to the front door and gently assisted her grandmother to turn around and move back into the living room. "I'm so sorry you were worried about me."

Granny sat heavily in her seat and smiled up at her. "I just wasn't sure who was in the driveway," Granny said, staring intently at Ruby. "Where'd you get that new car?"

"Oh, Granny, you wouldn't believe the day I've had." She bent and kissed her grandmother on the cheek and said, "Let me get dinner going, and I'll tell you all about it." She hurried into the kitchen and threw open the refrigerator door. After staring for a moment, she knew she needed to squeeze in a visit to the grocery store soon. Deciding it was going to be hotdogs, mashed potatoes, and baked beans, she pulled out what she needed. *Not fancy, but it'll fill an empty spot.* Her lips curved slightly, remembering the saying her mother used to say about a simple dinner. Chasing the memory away, she pulled out the pans and got busy.

It did not take long for her to reappear in the living room to assist Granny into the kitchen. With the dining room being used as Granny's bedroom now, a small table and two chairs had been placed in the corner of the kitchen. Once seated, she fixed their plates at the stove and brought them over. Putting ice into glasses, she filled them with water from the sink.

Sitting in the chair, placed at a right angle to Granny's, she lifted her hotdog and took a large bite. As she was chewing, she glanced over and saw Granny staring at her, one eyebrow lifted in question.

Trying not to choke, she finished chewing and swallowing before she said, "Sorry. I guess you're curious."

"You might say that," Granny replied, cutting her hotdog into smaller bites.

Wiping her mouth, she said, "In a nutshell, my car died on the side of the road after I left the Smithfield's house. Thank God I got their house clean before it died because she would not have been very understanding if I had been late or had to reschedule."

Granny's eyes widened, and she exclaimed, "Oh, my goodness! Were you stranded on the side of the road?"

Nodding, Ruby said, "Yeah. I wasn't sure what to do because I dreaded having to call for a tow truck. But I didn't have to wait long, because good fortune shone down on me and a man stopped who happened to be a mechanic."

Her eyes still wide, Granny said, "Well, bless me. That was good fortune!"

"He was really nice, took a look at my car, and told me that it would need some work. He called somebody at his shop—"

"His shop?"

Chewing and swallowing again, she nodded. "Jayden is not only a mechanic, but he's the owner of the shop."

"Jayden?"

Hearing the difference in Granny's voice, she looked over and saw her grandmother staring at her. Wiping her mouth with a paper towel, she said, "His name is Jayden. Jayden Chapman."

"Well, tell me more about this Jayden Chapman."

Shrugging, she said, "He was really nice."

Granny grinned and said, "You've already mentioned that."

"Oh…uh…well, he called for his tow truck and then took me to McDonald's for lunch while we waited."

"McDonald's!" Granny cried out in surprise, her smile wrinkles deepening. "What a treat!"

Grinning, Ruby agreed. "It's been a long time since I've eaten out, so I have to admit it was kind of fun." The two continued their meal for a moment, before she continued, "We went back to his shop as my car was towed, and he took a look at it." Sighing, she said, "It's going to take two days to get it fixed because they have to order some parts."

She watched as Granny's face fell, and she said, "Yeah. Looks like I'm going to have to add a few more hours at the diner to cover everything."

"Oh, Ruby, dear. I hate that you work so hard."

She lifted her shoulders in a little shrug and said, "Granny, lots of people work hard just to make ends meet. I'm no different from them."

Granny was quiet for a moment, then asked, "And the car in the driveway?"

"That's a loaner car that Jayden said he kept at the shop in case someone needed it while their car was being worked on. I tried not to take it, but he insisted." She held Granny's gaze and said, "I really didn't have a choice, you know. It's embarrassing to have to take it, but if I don't have a way to get to work, I won't get paid. And if I don't get paid, I surely can't afford to get my car fixed."

Granny sighed, shaking her head. "Work hard just to be able to have a car so that you can turn around and work hard."

Ruby laughed and said, "That's about the size of it."

Granny reached across the table, taking Ruby's hand in her gnarled one, giving a little squeeze. "If I could do anything to lift the burden, I would."

Tears stung Ruby's eyes as she stared at her grand-mother. Her hair was tinted blue-grey once again, and her face was slightly fuller from eating well. Granny's complexion was soft and smooth, although her smile lines were deep. Ruby's heart warmed every time she thought of how lucky she was to have Granny in her life. "You're not a burden at all. You're my gift, Granny. The greatest gift I've ever been given, besides my parents."

The two women held each other's gazes, both blinking back tears, before Granny sucked in a deep breath and said, "So, tell me more about this Jayden."

Ruby bit her lip and hesitated. She hated the instant look of concern on Granny's face, so she decided to blurt out the whole truth. "I'd actually met him once before. Well, not really met him. Just…um…encountered him."

"Child, now you've got my curiosity up," Granny exclaimed, leaning forward, her gaze intent.

"It was a while back…right before you came out of rehab. He drove by once on his motorcycle and offered to help me because I was out struggling with that stupid lawnmower. You might think that I'd be scared…a big guy driving up on a motorcycle. But he took his helmet off, and he was so handsome. But mostly, his eyes were just so kind."

"What happened?" Granny asked, breathlessly.

Her face twisted in a grimace, as she explained, "Kevin was over here. He'd been drinking and was belligerent."

Granny leaned back in her chair and pinned Ruby with a hard stare. "Are you telling me that you were outside struggling with that cantankerous lawnmower, and Kevin was lying about the house, drinking and eating our food?"

Ruby did not answer but simply sighed in response.

They were quiet for a moment, and then Granny encouraged, "Tell me more about Jayden."

Smiling shyly, she said, "I thanked him for his offer but insisted that he leave. Kevin was at the door and was just itching for a fight. I knew he'd never go after Jayden because it was obvious Jayden was such a big man…"

Granny's voice softened, and she choked as she said, "Oh, baby girl. You were afraid Kevin would take it out on you." When Ruby did not reply, Granny continued, "I'm so proud of you for breaking up with him. So proud of you for finally standing up to him and standing up for yourself. You deserve nothing but someone special. A real prince of a man."

"Oh, Granny, you always told me that there might not be a prince out there and raised me to be a woman who doesn't need one, but I'd take a good man. A good man who'd take care of me and treat me right."

The meal over, she jumped up to assist Granny to stand before taking their empty plates to the sink. Washing them, she heard the walker come right up beside her and twisted her head to stare at her grandmother.

Granny lifted her hand and sifted her fingers through Ruby's hair and said, "Don't ever forget, sweet Ruby, that the right man, a good man, can be your prince."

Granny turned and moved slowly out of the kitchen toward the living room, leaving Ruby standing at the sink, her hands buried in suds, staring after her. The image of Jayden's face filled her mind, and she closed her eyes. It was not hard to imagine him as a prince, but if there was one thing life had taught her, it was not to put all your faith in dreams. There was no way a man like him was going to be hers forever, but that did not keep her from being grateful for the help he had already given her. *And it can't hurt to dream a little, can it?*

7

"Here you go. Best nachos in town," Zeke called out, setting a huge platter, piled high, in the middle of the table. Jayden's eyes grew wide staring at the loaded nachos, and a quick glance around the table at his brothers, whose eyes were just as big as his, let him know he needed to jump in.

Reaching over, he began loading nachos onto his plate, barely managing to throw out a thanks to Lynn, one of the servers, as she brought his beer.

Jayden scooted over so that Zeke could sit next to him. Zander, Rafe, Cael, Asher, and Jaxon rounded out the group. He was glad that none of their women seemed to mind the brothers getting together at Grimm's bar for a chance to catch up with each other. For several minutes, there was very little talking as each man shoveled in Zeke's nachos.

Looking up, he watched as Cas walked into the bar, his eyes immediately going to the table. Waving him over, he shoulder-bumped Jaxon and said, "Scoot. Make room for Cas."

They all shifted around so that another chair could be added, and he was glad that Cas had decided to join them. "All good?"

"That Toyota you've got me working on?" Cas began. "I've found quite a bit that it needs to get it running really well."

Nodding while shoving a plate of nachos in front of Cas, he said, "Whatever. Fix it."

"You want me to call her with an estimate, or did you want to do that?"

Shaking his head, he swallowed before replying, "Don't call her. Whatever it is, just fix it, and the shop will cover it."

If Cas was surprised, his expression did not change, but Jayden's words caught the attention of the others.

"You givin' free work at the shop now?" Cael asked.

Rafe jumped in, "Must be some *her* for you to fix a car for free."

Before Jayden had a chance to respond, Jaxon asked, "What gives, bro?"

Not holding anyone's gaze, he took a pull from his beer and answered, "Just a woman I met who's down on her luck. Thought I'd do her a good turn."

"Good turn?" Cas commented. "He found her stranded on the side of the road, rescued her, brought her back to the station after calling for a tow, and is now going to completely overhaul her car for nothing. On top of that, he gave her a loaner car to use."

"You want to shut the fuck up?" Jayden asked, scowling at Cas.

Cas, a grin playing about his mouth, mumbled, "Sorry, man."

His brothers at the table had grown quiet, and he looked around at their questioning faces. Raising his hands, he said, "Honest to God, guys, there's no story to tell. I'd seen her about a month ago in a neighborhood not too far away from Miss Ethel's, and it seemed like she needed help. I was unable to do anything for her at that time and always felt bad about it. I came upon her yesterday on the side of the road, and it looked like she was in a bad way. Her car's a piece of crap. She works several jobs to pay her bills. That's all I know. Like I said, just seemed like she could use some assistance."

The others must have accepted his explanation, because their conversations resumed. Jayden's mind wandered to Ruby, although he knew that, quite frankly, his mind had never been far from her. She had mentioned that she had broken up with the man that was at her house, and Jayden was thrilled he was no longer in her life, hoping he was gone for good.

Lost in his musings, he did not realize time had passed until Jaxon nudged his knee and quipped, "You still here?"

Ducking his chin, he said, "Yeah. Just thinking over shit." Eyeing the others at the table, he realized that Zeke had left and was heading back to the kitchen, and Rosalie had appeared, stealing Zander's attention. Rafe and Cael were also getting ready to leave, both wanting to get back to their wives.

"You do know that I know you better than anyone, right?" Jaxon asked, his gaze penetrating.

Chuckling while shaking his head, Jayden replied, "Yeah, I got that figured out a long time ago." Appreciating that Jaxon remained quiet, he gathered his thoughts before saying, "I don't know what it is about this girl. There's just something about her that calls to me…something so vulnerable, and yet, I swear, this isn't about some hero complex. I don't know what her story is. I just know that I'm drawn to her."

"Then keep helping her," Jaxon said. "It doesn't have to be forever. Hell, it might not be next week. But if you think she needs help and you can provide it, then go for it."

He nodded, having already come to that decision. But what he did not tell his brother was that he wondered if there was the possibility she could be more.

Leaving Grimm's, he climbed onto his bike, deciding on a detour on his way home. He had checked her address when she left it at his office and knew that she was living in the same place where he had first seen her. As he headed down the road, he wondered about his sanity. *Now I feel like a stalker.*

She had told him she worked late at a diner so she probably was not home, but he was drawn by a magnetic force to just to check on her. *Yeah right.* He wanted to do a lot more than check on her. *See her, talk to her, laugh with her, just watch her smile.*

Figuring that most neighbors would not appreciate the roar of a motorcycle late at night, he slowed down, vowing to just pass by. Nearing, he did not see a car in the driveway, although the front porch light was on. It was almost midnight, and he hesitated.

Suddenly, headlights appeared at the corner and came down the street. He watched as a car turned into her driveway and recognized the loaner from his shop. Ruby alighted from the car, bending over to grab something from the passenger seat. She was wearing a short skirt, and his eyes dropped to her ass that was barely covered by the material.

Unable to quell the desire to speak to her, he rolled into the driveway, stopping behind the car. She whirled around, her eyes wide with fright, a squeak leaving her lips.

He jerked off his helmet so she could see who was there. "I'm sorry, it's me," he rushed, swinging his leg over the seat and stepping closer.

He was glad to see her stance relax even as her hand stayed at her throat. "Oh, my goodness, Jayden. You gave me such a fright."

His gaze moved over her clothing, now able to see a pink, tight blouse with the logo of Carter's Truck Stop Cafe embroidered over her breast, and the tight, too-short black skirt. In her arms, she clutched the large, red hoodie, a Styrofoam food container, and her purse. She had dark circles underneath her eyes, attesting to fatigue, and her face was pale.

"You work at Carter's?" he asked, unable to keep the incredulity from his voice.

Her smile fell, and she nodded. "Yeah," she said, crossing her arms in front of her.

He heard her defensiveness in that one word, but continued, "That's a rough place. Why the hell are you working there?"

Now her smile dropped completely, and she stared up at him, her narrowed eyes pinning him to the spot.

"I have to work, and Carter pays decently," she said, her voice still soft but her words clipped.

Jayden scowled, and she huffed, amending, "Okay, he doesn't pay decently, but I make good tips." She lowered her chin and heaved another sigh. "Why are you here anyway?"

Stepping closer, Jayden reached out and lifted her chin with his knuckle. He was so close that she had to lean her head back to maintain eye contact. "I just wanted to check on you."

Confusion passed through her eyes as her brows drew together. "At this time of night?"

"I know it makes me sound like a stalker, but honest, I was just heading home and decided to come by. I assumed I'd see the loaner car in the driveway, and I'd be assured you were in, safe and sound. I had no idea that you would be getting home at this time or where you were working."

"Oh, yeah," she mumbled, her hand tugging on her skirt. "Look, I know it isn't a great place to work, but I do get good tips, and for the most part, the customers leave me be."

"As beautiful as you are, I can't believe they don't give you any trouble."

Her eyes narrowed as her face scrunched. She stepped back and said, "Fine. You've checked to see that your car is here and still in one piece. It's late, and I need to get to bed."

He watched, stunned, as she whirled and stomped away. "Wait...Ruby...wait!" He caught up to her and reached out to place his hand on her shoulder. "Please, wait."

She stiffened at his touch, and he jerked his hand away. She turned around, and he saw her flinch.

"What did I say that upset you? Please, let me know," he begged.

"I don't know what your game is, Mr. Chapman. I might have to take your charity, but I don't have to take your lies."

"Lies? What lies? I've never been anything but honest with you," he protested. He thought back to what he had said to her. "I only said that you were so beautiful, I had a hard time believing that the men at the diner would leave you alone."

"That! That right there. You don't have to tell me I'm beautiful." She took a step backwards and added, "I know I'm not. I'm just plain ol' Ruby."

Understanding mixed with disbelief slowly dawned on Jayden. Her skittishness had him battling the desire to step closer. "What did he do to you?" he asked, his voice low and soft.

She jerked her eyes to the side, biting her lip. If he had had any question in his mind that the man she had been with was the cause of her insecurity, her confusion pointed it out plain as day. "Ruby," he called, gaining her attention. "I don't know what he said or what he did, but if nothing else, always believe that I'll tell you the truth. And the truth is, I think you're beautiful."

Ruby stood, her heart in her throat, as she stared up at Jayden. Everything about him was so handsome it almost hurt to have him so close and not be able to reach out for him.

His eyes held her captive, and the more she stared, the more she saw truth. *He really thinks I'm beautiful.* She sucked in a ragged breath, the memories of Kevin flooding her, threatening to push out the simple honesty from Jayden. She clutched the red hoodie in her hands tighter to her, trying to still the quivering she felt deep inside her stomach.

Swallowing, she whispered, "Then I thank you for the compliment."

"It wasn't just empty words," he said, continuing to hold her gaze.

Nodding slightly, she repeated, "Thank you." She glanced to the side again, her eyes landing on the loaner car and latched onto a change in the conversation. "I didn't get a call about an estimate for fixing my car. You probably don't know how much it is yet, but if you can have someone give me a detailed estimate along with what are the absolutely necessary items to fix, then I can take a look and figure out what we can do."

He hesitated, and her eyes moved back to him. He seemed to be struggling with what to say but finally nodded. "Yeah, sure."

An awkward silence passed between them, and she said, "It really is late. It was…um…nice of you to check on me."

He stepped forward, his large body moving slowly as though he understood she preferred having a bubble around her. He reached down and placed his hand on hers over the red hoodie and gave a little squeeze. "It was nice seeing you again, Ruby. I'll give you a call about your car tomorrow or the next day. Are you working?"

"I've got two houses to clean in the morning, and then I have an earlier shift in the afternoon at Carter's. I can have my phone with me when I'm cleaning but not at the diner."

With a final squeeze, he nodded, and she watched, mesmerized, as he turned and walked back toward his motorcycle. He threw his leg over the seat, but before he put his helmet on, he called out, "Go on in. I want to make sure you're tucked inside."

She jolted out of her perusal—and appreciation—of his muscular body and turned, jogging up the steps to the front door. Letting herself in, she locked the door behind her and walked over to the living room window overlooking the front yard. She lifted her hand in a wave and watched as he secured his helmet, started his motorcycle, and threw his hand up in a return wave before heading down the street.

Staring out of the window toward the dark street, her feet stayed rooted to the floor for several minutes after he had left. Her mind a whirl of emotions, thoughts flying at her faster than she could process.

Why did he stop by? What does he want? Why did he seem upset that I'm working at the truck stop diner? Why was he worried?

Of all the thoughts that flew at her, the one that cried out loudest of all... *He thinks I'm beautiful.* With that firmly settled in her mind, she fairly danced to the back and checked on Granny, finding her snoring slightly, sound asleep. Going upstairs, she pulled off her diner uniform and stepped into the shower, glad to wash off the smell of greasy fries and burgers. Shortly, she was tucked into bed, staring out the window, searching for a star to wish upon. When the clouds parted and a star finally appeared, she smiled. *Maybe wishes do come true.*

8

Jayden had no idea if Ruby was home from work the next afternoon but drove to her house anyway in his pickup truck. She told him she cleaned houses during the day, but he was uncertain of the times. And, of course, there was her evening job, which he hated. He had been to Carter's Truck Stop Diner a couple of times when he got called out for a job on that side of town.

It was a clean diner and the food was not too bad, but he had seen evidence of a clientele that could get rough. Some truckers just wanted a place for a meal, and others thought it was a place to pick up prostitutes. Bikers came through, and like the others, some came for a meal and some looking for trouble. The idea that Ruby worked the night shift there worried him.

As he neared her driveway, he saw that the loaner car was not there. He parked in the front, wondering if he should call her or leave a note. As he sat for a moment in indecision, he looked up and saw the front door open slowly.

A grey-haired woman leaning on a walker was looking out at him through the screen door. He jumped down from the driver's seat and walked quickly to the bottom of the steps.

"Hello, ma'am," he said, making sure to stay far enough away that he was not threatening. "I was hoping to speak to Ruby, but don't see her car here."

The woman's light blue eyes seemed to peruse him carefully as she looked him up and down. "What do you want with Ruby?"

Her voice was not unfriendly, but neither was it full of warmth. He maintained his distance while he called out, "I wanted to come by and let her know that her car is ready." Before he had a chance to finish, he watched her expression change from suspicious to something different…excitement crackled from her as her eyes gleamed.

She smiled widely and said, "Oh, you must be that nice young man Ruby was telling me about. The one who rescued her from the side of the road. I'm her grandmother."

"Yes, ma'am," he said, smiling, pleased that Ruby had spoken of him. "I'm Jayden Chapman. I own a mechanic shop, and—"

"Come on in," the woman called, her hand waving. "As you can see, I can't stand for very long."

"Ma'am, I don't want to be a bother. I can just come back when she's—" The woman was already backing slowly away from the door, and he was uncertain if he should move toward her to assist or stay where he was.

Before he could ponder what he should do, she called out from inside the house.

"Ruby'll be home soon, and you can keep me company until then."

She had already left his sight, so he jogged up the steps, opening the screen door. Stepping just inside the house, he could see that she was making her way into the living room. She stopped at a chair and maneuvered her walker around. He hastened forward to support her arm as she lowered herself into the chair.

She beamed up at him, thanking him profusely. "It seems like you're destined to help me and my grand-daughter at just the right time." She shifted back against the cushions and waved toward the sofa. "Please, make yourself at home. Ruby will be here shortly, and I know she'll want to see you."

He stepped around the coffee table and settled his tall frame onto the sofa. The room was smaller than Miss Ethel's but felt so familiar. Spotless, it was filled with comfortable, lived-in furniture. A small end table sat next to her chair, and he observed the TV remote, a couple of magazines, and a glass half full of water.

She suddenly looked concerned and shifted forward as though to stand again. Interpreting her movement, he hastened to offer, "Ma'am, can I get something for you?"

"I just realized I hadn't offered you anything to drink. Would you like some iced tea?"

Shaking his head, he replied, "Oh, no, ma'am. I'm fine."

She leaned back against the cushions again and

smiled benevolently. "My goodness, you must think I'm rude. I never introduced myself properly. I'm Jewel. Jewel Mantle."

Before he had a chance to respond, she laughed, her face wrinkling into laugh lines. "Yes, it's quite true. My name is Jewel. My mother's name was Pearl, and I can only assume my parents had a sense of humor by naming me Jewel. I only had a son, but then when he had a daughter, he continued the line by naming her Ruby."

He tried to keep the smile from his face, but it slipped out anyway.

"That's all right, son. You can laugh. Lord knows I've laughed at our names most of my life." As her mirth ended, she said, "But you can call me what most of the neighborhood children call me, and that's Granny."

"Granny," he said, as though trying out the name on his tongue. "I'd be honored to use your favorite name."

Her smile slowly left her face, but she remained quiet. She cocked her head to the side and peered at him for so long he battled the urge to squirm. This house, this room, and her expression brought to mind growing up with Miss Ethel, and he almost expected his foster mother to walk through the door.

"My Ruby is a good girl," she said, her voice soft.

"I'm sure," he agreed hastily as she continued to hold his gaze. He was uncertain what more she wanted to say, so remained silent to give her the opportunity to collect her thoughts.

Not waiting long, she explained, "My son died about the time she was thirteen. We were always so close, so

Ruby's mother, and she, and I clung together in our grief. He had a small insurance policy that covered the funeral costs, but then Ruby's mother was diagnosed with cancer when Ruby was sixteen. I'm afraid the rest of the small nest egg was taken up with her medical needs."

Jayden leaned forward, his forearms resting on his knees as he devoured every word she was saying. The need to know more about Ruby filled his entire being.

"Ruby worked while still in high school to help offset the costs. When her mama finally died, Ruby was eighteen. She sold the family house to finish paying off the medical bills that her mama had left and moved in with me. I was so thankful to have the help around here, but more than that was just having Ruby with me."

"I'm very sorry for your loss, ma'am—Granny."

She glanced upward to a framed photograph on the mantle and said, "That's us in better times, when my husband was still alive. Oh, how he used to dote on Ruby. Said she was the light of his life."

He followed her gaze and looked at the picture, seeing a young Ruby, her smile wide as she was surrounded by her family. She was a beautiful child, but he recognized the happiness in her innocent eyes had now been replaced with a weariness.

Eyes locked on the frames, he focused on the family togetherness captured by the photographer. Whenever he looked at family pictures of others, he always wondered what could have been in his own life had his mother not been an addict. He had long stopped wishing that he would have family photos like other people, satisfied that the pictures he had of his brothers and Miss Ethel were the ones that truly mattered.

Granny broke into his musings when she said, "I need to ask you why you're helping Ruby."

His head swung back around to see her now pinning him with a hard stare. Before he could answer, she continued. "Ruby works hard, and I won't see her taken advantage of. Not again. And while I won't deny that we can use some help, I need to know at what cost."

Shaking his head slowly, he replied, "I have no ulterior motive for helping Ruby other than I'd like to get to know her better. I'm not looking to have her be indebted to me. I know what it's like to be in a position of need, and now that I'm in a position to help, I'd like to do so."

His palms began to sweat as he watched her continue to stare as though taking the measure of him, and he fought the urge to wipe them on his jeans. She slowly relaxed her shoulders, and her lips curled into a smile once more.

"That's a very good answer, Jayden. I hope you don't take offense at my asking."

"No. Not at all. It makes me feel good to know that she has you looking out for her."

She was silent for a moment, her gaze on her hands in her lap. "It's a strange thing, need," she said. "Ruby and I were doing quite well, but as you may know, most of us are only one crisis away from financial difficulty. I fell a few months ago, and even though my insurance paid some, the medical costs from the hospital and then the two months in rehab depleted our resources. Ruby took on nights at the diner because the tips were bigger, and then she took on a few more houses to clean. All this just to make sure my bills were covered, there's food on the table, and a house with heat."

"I know she works hard. I told her the truth when I pushed the loaner car on her. It was sitting in our lot, not being used, and I wanted her to have something safe to drive."

She leaned forward, wincing slightly from the movement and said, "You have no idea how glad I am that you were the one that stopped when she was on the side of the road. That could have ended in such disaster. Knowing that she's had something to drive while her car is being worked on has made a world of difference in her being able to get to her housecleaning jobs and not have to take a bus to the diner. You're a good man, Jayden."

He offered a small smile, but shifted in his seat again, this time uncomfortable with her praise. "Honestly, it was no big thing."

"And her car? She said that you were going to provide her with a list of what needed to be done in order of their importance."

"Yes...well...yes," he stammered, heat infusing his face. "Um...that was one of the reasons I wanted to come by today, was to talk to her about her car."

Her eyes widened, and a tiny gasp flew from her lips. "Oh, my, please tell me that it can be fixed."

Nodding quickly, he assured, "Actually, it's already has been fixed. It'll be ready for her to pick up tomorrow."

Her assessing gaze hit him again, and he could hear a tremor in her voice as she spoke. "Already fixed?"

Before he had a chance to explain, the sound of a car door slamming outside caused him to swing his head around toward the front door.

Ruby came barreling through the door, her eyes wildly searching until they landed on her grandmother. Chest heaving, she blurted, "Granny! Are you okay?"

He stood, and Ruby's eyes darted over to him, widening.

"You? What are you doing here?" As she spoke, she rushed to Granny's chair, squatting so that they were face to face.

Patting her shoulder, Granny said, "Now, child. I'm fine. Jayden came by to talk about your car, and we've just been having a nice little chat, getting to know each other."

He watched Ruby's shoulders relax, and she twisted her head around to look at him. "I didn't recognize the truck in the driveway, so I got scared."

"I didn't know when you were working today, so I just took a chance on coming by. Your grandmother was nice enough to let me know that you'd be home soon and invited me in."

She swung her head back around toward her grandmother and said, "Granny, you're supposed to be resting, not entertaining."

Waving her hand dismissively, Granny said, "Oh, fiddlesticks. All I did was walk to the door and invite him in. Since then, I've been sitting right here in my chair."

"It's true, Ruby," Jayden assured. "I promise she hasn't been doing anything strenuous. No jogging, no dancing, no jumping. We've just been chatting."

Ruby looked back at him, a chuckle slipping out. She lifted an eyebrow and asked, "Chatting?"

"Ruby girl, why don't you have a seat on the sofa so you won't have to keep swinging your head around. You're going to make yourself dizzy."

She looked back at her grandmother and blushed. Standing, she bent to kiss her grandmother's cheek before turning and walking toward the sofa, sitting on the opposite end from Jayden.

Her hair was pulled up in a ponytail, but several tendrils had fallen about her face. She tucked a strand behind her ear and peered up at him. "So, um…why did you come by? Is it about my car?"

Deciding to just get the words out, he rushed, "I wanted to let you know that it's ready. You can pick it up whenever you want."

Her eyes widened, and she croaked, "Ready? As in, already been fixed?"

He shifted his body to face her, struck once more by the expressiveness of the sky-blue eyes staring at him. She wore no makeup, and she was dressed in a green T-shirt and blue jeans with sneakers on her feet. And she was beautiful. There was something about her that pulled him in. It was more than her outward beauty. It was more than wanting to help someone in need. She was a tiny powerhouse, was not afraid of hard work and caring for those she loved.

"Jayden?"

He jerked, realizing he had not answered her as his thoughts about her had taken flight. "Yeah, it's fixed."

The air left her lungs in a whoosh, and she said, "You were supposed to call. You were supposed to tell me what items were needed and how much each was going to cost. You didn't call!"

Her pitch rose with each word, her hands fluttering in the air, and he explained, "I didn't call because we fixed everything." He saw her body jerk, and panic flew through her eyes. Rushing to calm her, he said, "It's my gift to you, Ruby. To you and Granny. You don't owe anything."

Her chest heaved, and her gaze did not leave his, every emotion she was feeling passing across her face. He watched incredulity morph into an instant of relief before becoming suspicious.

"Ruby, darling," Granny said, shifting forward in her seat to stand, pulling her walker in front of her to use for leverage. "I'm going to go have a bit of a lie down, and you and Jayden can keep talking."

Ruby jumped up to assist and cast her gaze over her shoulder toward Jayden. "Stay here," she hissed. "I'll be back."

He leaned against the cushions on the sofa, watching as Granny walked down the hall, Ruby next to her in case she needed assistance. He blew out his breath and wondered how Ruby was going to take his offer. *She sure as hell didn't look like she was very pleased.*

9

As she settled Granny into bed, she was about to turn away when her grandmother reached out and grabbed her hand. Looking down, her eyes full of concern, she asked, "What is it?"

"I've been around a long time, girl. I've met a lot of people that I thought the world of, and I've met a few that weren't worth anything. But I've had a chance to talk to that young man sitting out there, and he's a good man. My instincts are usually right."

Ruby bit her lip and whispered, "That may be, Granny, but I just don't know why he's doing this for me. I've got nothing to pay him back with."

"I don't think he wants payback, girl."

Her brow knit with confusion, and she asked, "Then why?"

Her grandmother's grasp on her hand relaxed, and she closed her eyes. "That's for you to find out, Ruby girl. You go on now. I'm gonna have a little nap."

She stepped back, her thoughts tangled. Sighing

heavily, she walked down the short hall, glancing into the mirror in the tiny half bathroom. One look at herself, and she shook her head, wishing she had time to get fixed up. *Even running a brush through my hair and changing out of my cleaning clothes would be better.* But there was no time—*or reason*—so she hurried back to the living room, seeing Jayden stand once more as she entered.

In all the time that she had been with Kevin, she could not remember one single instance of him standing when she, or Granny, left or entered a room. While it would not have been necessary, she could not deny that Jayden's manners were refreshing.

He waved his hand toward the sofa and asked, "Will you sit with me? Will you give me a chance to explain about your car?"

She nodded and walked over, sitting down. Toeing off her sneakers, she twisted her body so that she was facing him and tucked her feet up under her. Sighing, she began, "I don't want to sound ungrateful, Jayden. I just can't imagine how much money it took to fix my car."

She watched as he hesitated, appearing to consider his words carefully. Leaning forward, she placed her hand on his arm and added, "I won't be angry. I just need to understand what's happening."

His warm eyes focused on her, and she felt that warmth move between them, slowly caressing her. His hair was down today, pulled away from his face but hanging about his shoulders. The thick waves appeared soft, and she itched to reach over and touch the tresses.

Kevin's hair used to always be trimmed, but he had let it grow longer in the last few years. But it was never luxurious...instead, it became unkempt and certainly not sexy.

The muscles underneath her fingertips felt strong, and it was not the first time she wondered what it would feel like to have him embrace her.

"Ruby," he began, drawing her attention back to his face and away from his hair and muscles.

"The simplest answer I can give you is this. We did not have to order many parts for your car, and the ones we did order were not expensive. They were some that we should have had in our shop anyway, so I simply ordered for you and a few extra to have for the next Toyota that comes in. I pay my mechanics a good salary, and they get paid whether we're having a busy day or a light one. The last couple of days, I had at least one mechanic with some time on his hands, so it was no big deal to have him work on your car."

She cocked her head to the side and said, "If all that's true, Jayden, then why me?" His jaw ticked, and she wondered about the tension.

"When I first saw you here that day, I was furious that you were struggling in your yard with a perfectly capable man, half drunk, inside. But I didn't know you, and I didn't know him, and you begged me to walk away. I figured he was the kind of man that would've made things worse if I had insisted on staying. So, I left, but you have no idea how that gutted me inside."

She tilted her head to the side and asked, "Gutted? But I was a stranger. "

"Ruby, you don't gotta know somebody to know that they need help. I didn't know you, but I could tell you needed help, and I still walked away."

She bit her lip, pondering his words. Before she had a chance to question further, he continued.

"You stayed on my mind. Not just because you needed help and I walked away, but because there was something about you that made me wish I knew you better. When I saw you on the side of the road, I couldn't believe that I had a second opportunity to do something for you. And you better believe, that time, I decided I was not going to walk away."

She quietly considered his words. "That day, when you walked over to me, you already seemed to recognize me," she said, voicing what she had wondered about.

He grinned and nodded toward the red hoodie that she had dropped near the front door in her rush to get to her grandmother. "You were wearing that the first time I saw you. It's kind of big on you, and when I saw you in it, standing next to the car, I just knew it was you."

Her gaze followed his, and she stood, walking over to the door. Bending to pick up the hoodie, she held it tightly to her, her hands fingering the thick but worn material. Settling back on the sofa, she explained, "It was my father's."

Jayden hesitated, and she saw a flash of unease move across his face. Anticipating the reason, she asked, "I suppose Granny told you my whole life's story before I got here, didn't she?"

"No, not really. I mean, she told me some. She mentioned that your parents were gone." He appeared flustered, but added, "I'm sorry. I admit I was curious about you, but I should've waited and let you tell me yourself in your own time."

Shaking her head, she smiled. "Believe me, I know how Granny loves to talk." She lifted her shoulders in a little shrug. "It's okay, really. There's not very much exciting about me, so I don't really have any secrets." Looking back down at the red hoodie in her lap, she said, "There was a park near where we used to live, and Mama didn't ever care much for walking. But I loved it. Taking walks with my dad was our special time together. He had this red hoodie jacket that Granny had bought for him years before, and I told him that I liked it because I could always find him in a crowd. One day, he gave it to me and said he wanted me to have it so that he would always be able to see me as well. I think perhaps he knew then that he was dying. Anyway, I kept it and wear it all the time. Kevin hated it and used to ask why on earth I wore this old jacket. He never understood how much it meant to me."

"That was the man? Kevin?"

She nodded and replied softly, "Yeah."

"I don't suppose you need to hear me say I thought that guy was a jerk."

Shaking her head, a giggle slipped out. "No, you'd be right—he was a jerk." A moment of silence passed, and she said, "What are we going to do about my car? It doesn't feel right for me to take all of your generosity. Can I please do something to help?"

He reached his hand over and placed it on top of hers, his calloused thumb smoothing over her soft skin. "Your grandmother admitted that you could use some help."

She winced, but he continued before a denial could cross her lips.

"I know about your mother's medical bills. I know you've been working hard since you were eighteen years old. Hell, even before that, since your grandmother said you were working in high school to help defray the costs. I don't know how old you are now, but I know you're still working hard."

"Lots of people work hard, Jayden. Lots of people are down on their luck."

"I know that, too, Ruby. And I help when I can, just like you do."

She stared at him and understanding dawned. "I'm not the first person you've helped with their automobile, am I?"

He shrugged, but she knew the answer. *Who is this guy that's such a good man?* Before she could stop herself, she asked the question that had just passed through her mind. "Who are you, Jayden Chapman?"

Her question caught him off guard, and Jayden pondered what to say. Unable to think of a pithy response, honesty was the only thing he could come up with.

"Ruby, I know what it's like to be in need. I know

what it's like to have absolutely nothing and be dependent on a system to take care of me." She had flipped her hand over and he linked fingers with her, desiring that small physical connection and hoping she did as well.

"My mother was a drug addict and died when I was very young. My grandmother took me and my brother in, but she was old and died soon thereafter, also. Then we were shuffled over to our aunt, who was a nice woman, but too young to be raising two small boys. She decided she couldn't take care of us anymore and turned us over to the system."

Ruby gasped, her eyes wide as she stared at him. "Oh, Jayden, I'm so sorry."

He shook his head and squeezed her hand again. "It's okay. My brother and I landed in a safe place. We ended up in a foster home run by a wonderful woman that I consider to be my mother to this day. She took in other boys, so I was raised in a loving family."

Shaking her head sadly, she said, "I'm so glad you had that, but it breaks my heart for the reason."

He smiled, shifting his body slightly closer to hers on the sofa. His left hand stayed linked with hers, and his right arm stretched along the back of the sofa, his hand close to her face. "The day I drove through your neighborhood, that big, red hoodie caught my eye. At first, I thought you were a much younger girl struggling with the lawnmower. That's why I stopped initially."

He watched a blush cover her face, and she grimaced.

"I've always been small," she sighed. "I look at tall,

long-legged models and am so envious. At five feet, two inches, I'm often mistaken for someone much younger than I am. I'm actually twenty-four years old."

He heaved a sigh of relief and said, "Good, then I don't feel like I'm robbing the cradle!"

At that, a giggle slipped from her lips, and he wished he could pull the words back. "I don't mean...I'm not trying to say...Well, all I meant was...Oh, hell!"

She burst out laughing, her fingers flexing against his. "I don't think I've seen you flustered before."

He pretend-glared but was glad she had not taken offense. "Anyway, when I saw you struggling, I felt a sense of protectiveness that I can't explain. When that guy came out on the porch, though, I didn't know how to help and sure as hell didn't want to make things worse. So, when I saw you again on the side of the road, I knew I wanted to help you in any way that I could."

They settled into a comfortable silence for a moment, and then she gave a little jerk as though a thought had just popped into her mind. "The loaner car! I need to be able to get my car from you as soon as possible, so I can give you back loaner car. I know there must be someone else who needs it."

"There's no rush, honest," he replied. "I know you've been working all day. Do you have to work a shift at the diner tonight?"

Shaking her head, her smile showed her relief. "No, thank goodness."

"What did you have planned for this evening?" he asked.

She glanced about the room and said, "Nothing very

exciting. On nights that I don't have to work at the diner, I make sure the house is clean and the laundry is done. I also try to cook a good meal for Granny." She looked back at him and said quickly, "But I've got time to go by your shop and pick up my car."

He decided to press his luck and asked, "How about this? I've got nothing else to do today, so I can drive the loaner back to the shop and then bring your car back here. Since you've got work you want to do here, how about I pick up some dinner for you and Granny?"

She blinked slowly, before asking, "Dinner?"

He shrugged his wide shoulders slightly and said, "You've got to eat, I've got to eat, why not eat together? You've got work here that you need to do, and my day is finished. I'm not much of a cook, and it would be a treat for me to not have to eat alone. I'd love to share a meal with you and your grandmother."

He watched the denial perch on her lips but not be uttered aloud as the wheels turned behind her eyes. She was the hardest woman to convince to let him do something for her, but every fiber of his being cried out to get to know her better. Much to his surprise and relief, she finally offered a little smile.

"I'll agree, Jayden, but only if you let me do the cooking. "

He opened his mouth to protest, not wanting her to work more, but she rushed, "I really do like to cook, and it would make me feel less indebted to you if you allow me to do this one small thing for you."

It was not what he had intended, but the desire to share a meal with her was so strong, he agreed. Grinning widely, he stood and said, "You've got a deal." Holding his hand out, he waited as she hesitated before placing her hand in his, and he gently pulled her from the sofa. "Give me the keys, and I'll go switch the cars."

Standing at the front door a few minutes later, he said, "I don't want you to go to any trouble tonight. When would you like me back here?"

"Can you give me two hours?"

It was on the tip of his tongue to tell her that he would give her anything, but he wisely chose to simply say, "Absolutely. I'll be here in two hours."

Taking her hand, he squeezed her fingers once more, fighting the urge to pull her in for a hug. Taking a quick look at the time, he made a detour to the store, deciding that if she was going to cook, he could bring dessert.

10

Ruby sat on the sofa for a few seconds before hopping up and pacing the room, glancing out the window. In the two hours since Jayden had left her house, she had washed a load of clothes, taken a quick shower, fixed her hair, applied a coat of mascara and lip gloss, vacuumed and dusted the living room, and fretted the entire time as she fixed a simple dinner. Now, it was almost time for him to come back, and she could not sit still.

"Ruby, please sit down," Granny ordered, her voice firm but smile wide. "You are going to wear a hole in the rug." Granny sat in the chair she had occupied earlier, her walker nearby, and patted her hair, which had also been recently brushed to fluff up the side that had flattened when she took a nap.

She whirled around, plopped onto the sofa, and dropped her head into her hands. "This is such a disaster."

Granny's eyes settled on Ruby, and her smile slipped

into an expression of concern. "What? What is such a disaster?"

She did not lift her head but spoke to her knees and said, "All of this. I don't know why I agreed to let him give me a loaner car in the first place."

Her voice gentle, Granny said, "Honey, look at me." She waited until Ruby lifted her head obediently and continued, "Talk to me."

Swallowing deeply, she said, "He's so good looking. He looks like some kind of model that stepped right off the pages of a magazine. He's the kind of man that women would turn their heads and stare at, but he's not stuck up. It's like he doesn't know he's all that. He's going out of his way to help me for no other reason than he knows I need it. He owns his own business, and I know he makes a lot of money if he's able to help other people. On top of that, he's really nice just to be around."

Granny leaned back in her seat and placed her hands on her lap. "Okay," she began slowly, as though speaking to a skittish animal. "So far, what you've described is a wonderful example of manhood. I guess I'm not seeing the reason for concern."

Sighing softly, she said, "Granny, I just don't get it… his interest in me. At first, I thought he was just being nice. But this…inviting himself to dinner. Well…it seems like more." She looked up and watched as Granny nodded in agreement, and continued, "I'm just not sure about any of this." Her hands, also in her lap, clasped together tightly. "The only man I've been around was Kevin, and I obviously didn't read him correctly. I think he really just wanted me so he wouldn't be lonely but not for really wanting me."

Granny sucked in a deep breath through her nose before letting it out slowly. "My dear, I call bullshit."

Ruby startled at her grandmother's use of the word 'bullshit', and a snort of laughter erupted. "Granny!"

"No, really. That's the only word I can think of that is appropriate at the moment. Kevin may have been your friend and then boyfriend for a time, but he was certainly not the only man you could learn from. Your father was a good and loving man, and you would do well to think back on him."

"Of course, I think back on him," Ruby protested. "But I was talking about a—"

"I know exactly what you were talking about. And I'm telling you that when you finally broke up with Kevin, you did it because you realized he was not good for you, nor to you. And one of the reasons you know that is because of your father. Your father treated your mother with kindness. He loved her and was not afraid to compliment her, do things for her, want to make her life easier. You grew up seeing that example. And right now, you've got a good man in front of you, wanting to be with you. And darling, you are worthy of him."

The sound of a car door slamming outside ended their conversation, and Ruby jumped up from the sofa again. "He's here!"

Granny grinned and nodded. "Normally I would tell you to wait until he arrived at the door, but I know you're anxious to see your car."

With a flash of a smile toward her grandmother, she

darted to the door. Taking a big breath, she opened it and stepped onto the porch, seeing Jayden unfolding his tall frame out of her small car. A wide smile split her face, unable to hide her delight in seeing him again.

Jayden glanced up to the porch, and his heart leapt at the sight of Ruby standing there beaming down at him. Her dark brown hair was not pulled up, but instead was falling in gleaming waves around her shoulders. Her eyes appeared even wider, and her lips had a shine of pink. She was wearing dark jeans and a light blue, short-sleeved sweater, the color making her eyes even more blue. The outfit was simple, but it showcased her delicate curves.

Not wanting to waste a moment to get to her, he stalked forward as she rushed down the steps.

"You washed it?" she asked, her eyes darting behind him toward her car, clapping her hands in glee.

"There's a carwash down the street from my shop, and I just ran it through on my way over here," he explained. Pleased she noticed, he shrugged and said, "It was no big deal."

She moved closer and reached out to grab his hand. "It might not be a big deal to you, but Jayden, it's huge to me." She gave his hand a little squeeze, and he felt his heart beat harder in response. He did not know what it was about this young woman that made him feel this way, but he was determined to break down her barriers and get to know her.

She turned her flawless face toward his and smiled once more. "Come on in. Dinner's almost ready, and I know Granny would like to see you again."

"Yeah, let me get something out of the backseat first." He walked to her car and opened the back door. Leaning in, he carefully lifted out the flowers and turned back toward her. Holding them out, he said, "These are for you and Granny."

Her eyes widened impossibly as she sucked in a huge breath. She exclaimed, "Oh, my God! They're beautiful!" She rushed forward and took them from him, burying her nose as she inhaled deeply. Looking up, she said, "Granny is going to be thrilled. She used to love raising flowers but hasn't been able to do so in several years."

Relieved that his first gift was received so well, he leaned back into the car and lifted out two pies. Hearing her squeal behind him, he turned and shrugged. "I wanted to bring dessert but didn't know what you liked. One is apple and the other is chocolate."

He watched as she gave a small hop as though his gift were gold, and her smile was evidence that she liked both of them. Closing the car door with a bump of his hip, he nodded toward the house. "Let's go in and see Granny."

She nodded enthusiastically and fell into step next to him as they walked to the house. He wished their hands were not so full, the desire to reach out and link fingers with her was strong. She threw open the storm door and backed against it, holding it open for him to pass through first.

As tiny as she was, his large body brushed against

her arm as he stepped into the house, and he felt a tingle of electricity pass through him. He glanced down, observing her blink up at him, and knew she felt the same. Shooting her a grin, he moved further into the room and looked to the left, seeing Granny sitting in her chair, her face turned expectantly toward him.

Ruby skirted around him and announced, "Granny, look who's here! And he brought flowers for us!"

"I'm not deaf, child," Granny laughed. "You don't have to shout, but my, my…aren't those flowers beautiful." She clapped her hands in glee, and Ruby rushed forward, laying the bouquets in her lap.

"I'll run and find a vase," Ruby said, and she darted out of the room.

Granny looked after her and shook her head in amusement before lifting her gaze to Jayden. "My Ruby's been running since the day she could barely walk." She sniffed the flowers, inhaling deeply, and then said, "Welcome back, Jayden. The flowers are not necessary but are very appreciated."

He grinned in reply, the two pies still in his hand. Before he had a chance to ask where he should put them, Ruby rushed back into the room.

"Granny! I found the vase that Grandpa gave you one year for Christmas. The one you used to put your flowers from the garden in."

Jayden watched as she placed the bouquet into the vase, already filled with some water. She placed it on the coffee table right in front of her grandmother, both women still beaming.

Granny exclaimed, "Oh, how lovely they are."

Looking up at Jayden, she directed, "Ruby, show him where to put the pies in the kitchen. He can keep you company while you're finishing dinner, and I'll just sit here and enjoy the pretty flowers."

Ruby glanced up at Jayden, her cheeks rosy with blush and said, "Come on back."

She turned and headed toward the kitchen, and he followed eagerly. He had noticed the scent of spicy tomato sauce when he had entered the house. As he stood next to her, he also caught a whiff of her floral shampoo.

"That smells good," he said, sniffing the air appreciatively, meaning both the dinner and her scent.

"We're going to have homemade, baked spaghetti with garlic bread." She looked up quickly and added, "I hope that's okay? I didn't even ask what you liked to eat."

He observed the adorable furrow in her brow and without thinking reached out to smooth it with his forefinger. "I eat just about anything, especially if it's home-cooked by someone other than me," he said. "But anything that you would take the time and trouble to make for me, I'll love."

Her lips curved in a shy smile, and she ducked her head. "It's really nothing," she demurred before opening the oven door to check on the food. Grabbing the potholders, she lifted the bubbling dish from the oven and set it on top of a trivet on the counter. Reaching for the baking sheet of heavily buttered garlic bread, she slid it into the oven and closed the door. Turning back to Jayden, she smiled and announced, "It'll be ready in just a few minutes."

"Have you always liked to cook?" he asked, leaning his hip against the counter.

Nodding she said, "Granny was a wonderful cook, and my mom learned a lot from her. Mom always admitted that when she married my dad, she didn't know anything about cooking. She figured her mother-in-law would really hate that, but Granny just took her under her wing, and taught her everything she knew." She tilted her head to the side and peered closely at him. "If you don't cook, what do you eat?"

He laughed and said, "I didn't say I didn't cook, but I don't cook well."

She smiled at his response, and he loved seeing the easy, relaxed smile on her face. "One of my brothers owns Grimm's Bar and Grill, and another one of my brothers runs the restaurant side of it. I usually grab a meal there twice a week. I'm also lucky to get invited to eat with one of my other brothers and their wives or girlfriends—"

"Wait," she said, her brow lowered as her nose scrunched. "How many brothers do you have?"

"Oh, I didn't really mean brothers. Well, I did, but—"

Just then the ding of the oven timer went off, and she fussed, "Oh, phooey. I need to get these out so they don't burn, but I really do want to learn more about your family."

"Don't worry, Ruby," he assured. "We got lots of time to learn about each other."

At his words, she twisted around and looked up at

him, pulling the bread from the oven. Her expression was one he was not certain about, but he could have sworn he saw a flare of hope in her eyes. Before either had a chance to say more, they heard the sound of the walker tapping down the hall.

"I'll help your grandmother," he said with a wink and watched the blush move across her cheeks once more.

An hour later, the dinner had been enjoyed, the pies delighted in, the food put away, and the dishes washed. Jayden had moved back to the living room to give her and Granny privacy as she assisted her grandmother to get ready for bed. She had assumed he would want to leave after dinner, but he appeared to be in no hurry, for which he was glad.

Once her nightgown was settled over her body, Granny moved to her bed and allowed Ruby to tuck her in. Smiling, Granny said, "You know, I think I'm getting stronger every day."

Nodding, she smiled and agreed. "I think so, too."

Kissing her grandmother goodnight, she flipped off the lights in the kitchen and the makeshift bedroom and walked back to the front of the house. She stopped at the doorway and watched as Jayden sat on the sofa, his large body looking strangely comfortable in the small space. She thought of how at ease she was with him, unafraid that he might suddenly turn angry and raise his voice or take his hand to her. She bit her lip and reminded herself that she had once thought the same thing about Kevin.

She sighed softly, and as his head turned at the sound, his eyes found hers, and his smile widened.

"Hey," he said.

"Hey, back."

"She settled okay?"

Nodding, she replied, "Yeah. When she goes to sleep, she'll sleep all night." Giving a small laugh, she said, "My grandfather always said that his Jewel could fall asleep quicker than anybody he'd ever seen."

She watched as a shadow of uncertainty crossed his face, and he stood. "I should go. Dinner was really good."

She hated for him to leave but had to admit she was exhausted. Walking him to the door, she leaned her head way back to peer up at him. "I know you don't want to hear this," she said, placing her hand on his arm, "but I have to say it. I appreciate what you've done for me and Granny more than I can say. You're right…it's hard when you find yourself in a position of need, and if it was just me, it would be easier to turn down offers of assistance. But you fixing my car for me has meant a lot… Actually, it's meant the difference between being able to work and eat, or not. I still hope that I can find a way to at least partially pay you back, but until then, just know that you have my gratitude."

He simply nodded, staring at her small hand on his much larger arm. "Piglet noticed that even though he had a very small heart, it could hold a rather large amount of gratitude."

She was not sure she heard him correctly and whispered, "What?"

Deep red spotted his cheeks through the dark stubble. "Shit, Ruby. I'm sorry. I didn't mean to say that out loud. That was just a quote I thought of. It was from—"

"Piglet? It was from Winnie the Pooh?"

Mumbling, he admitted, "Yeah. I used to read a lot as a kid."

A giggle slipped out, and she said, "Don't be embarrassed. I like it. No one's ever quoted anything to me before."

He nodded, turning his body so that he faced her fully. Lifting his hand, he cupped her cheek as his fingers slid through her hair to the back of her head. "I'll accept your gratitude, Ruby. But I'd so much rather accept your friendship." He leaned down and placed a barely-there kiss on her forehead.

Her breath caught in her throat as he leaned back, and his eyes were warm upon her. She replied, "That, you have."

With a wide smile on his face, the sight filling her with joy, she watched as he jogged down the front steps to his truck. She stayed at the front window, watching until he was no longer in sight, the flicker of hope sparking brighter.

Quoting Winnie the Pooh? Jesus, she probably thinks I'm crazy. No wonder I haven't been dating recently. Riding back to his apartment, Jayden could not stop thinking about Ruby. When she had thanked him, all he could think about was how small and perfect she was.

Miss Ethel had taught him that to accept gratitude was a gift to the one giving it, and the A.A. Milne quote about Piglet had just popped into his mind as he stared at the small woman.

Forcing the embarrassment from his mind, he focused on the way she had smiled at him and the sight of her in her window as he drove away. And could not wait until he saw her again.

11

Jayden pushed the kickstand down on his bike and swung his long leg over the seat. Hanging his helmet on the handlebars, he bounded up the familiar steps to Miss Ethel's front door. He found it unlocked, but considering he called her earlier to see if he could come by, he was not overly concerned at her lack of security. He did not see her in the living room, so he continued down the hall to the large dining room and kitchen, finding them empty as well.

"Miss Ethel?" he called out but heard no reply.

He saw movement through the glass of the back door leading from the kitchen to the patio. Stepping closer, he peered through, seeing her in the flower garden. The flowering season was over, but he knew she always pruned certain plants in the fall. Her head was covered with a large floppy hat, protecting her face from the sun. Her long-sleeved dress was adorned with an apron, and at her feet lay a basket with plant cuttings.

He hesitated a moment before calling out, memories flying through his mind. The backyard filled with shouts from the boys as they played ball. Birthday parties held at the picnic table underneath one of the trees. A tall privacy fence built along the back led to an alley that wove between the houses. The poor fence had served as a backdrop as they practiced baseball and tennis, sometimes being a supporting wall of a fort, and certainly being scaled when they were chasing each other.

Every inch of the yard was familiar and filled with memories. Good memories. His mind rolled to Ruby, and he was glad that her childhood had also been filled with good memories.

"Are you just going to stand there staring into space, or did you come over to talk to me?"

Jumping, he grinned sheepishly at Miss Ethel and walked toward her. Towering over her small frame, he bent and kissed her cheek. "Sorry, I was completely lost in thought."

She reached up and patted his shoulder fondly and shook her head. "I was just teasing. There's no reason to apologize. Sometimes we all need to just let our thoughts wander wherever they choose to go." She bent over, picking up the small basket, then tucked her pruning shears and garden gloves inside. "I'm all through out here for now, so let me put these into the shed, and we can go in."

"I'll get them for you," he said, gently taking the basket from her.

Her eyes crinkled as she smiled and said, "Then I'll go start us a cup of tea."

Placing the gardening implements into her small shed in the back corner of the yard, he could not help but grin. Miss Ethel may have raised all boys, but she believed in the recuperative powers of a cup of tea. Something to this day they still enjoyed with her.

Once inside the kitchen, he sat at the counter while she readied the tea. They made small talk, and when the tea tray was finished, he carried it into the living room, setting it on the coffee table. She lowered herself into her chair, sighing slightly once she was seated. "I enjoy staying active, but it's good to just sit sometimes," she laughed.

Peering at him through her wire-rimmed glasses, her grey eyes staying on his face, she sipped her tea. "Is there something new with you, Jayden, or did you just want to visit?"

"I met someone," he blurted. It was not hard to catch the flare of interest in her eyes. "Do you remember the day that you told me to take a ride through another neighborhood?"

A slight smile curved her lips, but after she nodded, he continued. "A woman caught my attention because she was wrestling with a lawnmower, and I stopped to see if I could help. It turned out that there was a man with her...well, inside the house. He was inebriated and angry, so I left when she begged me to go. I was furious...I felt forced to leave, and yet, if I had stayed, he might have made things more difficult for her later on."

Nodding slowly, she said, "Sometimes it's hard to

walk away when you know someone needs us. But we can only handle each situation as it comes."

Buoyed by her understanding, he said, "Exactly. It bothered me, but I didn't know anything else to do that day. But a few days ago, I ran into her again. Her situation is different now...it appears that guy is gone. But she and her grandmother are down on their luck, and I was able to help out by fixing her car."

She leaned forward to place her teacup back on the coffee table. Sitting back, she asked, "Do you remember that I used to tell you boys that the true measure of a man was not in the mistakes he made but in how he handled those mistakes?"

Nodding slowly, a crease marred his brow as he silently waited to see what she wanted to say.

"Well, it was not a mistake for you to leave...like I said, we have to take each situation as it comes. But, my dear, the fact that it has bothered you, and you are now able to make her life easier, then you understand the true measure of a man."

Heaving a sigh, he released the burden he had carried for a month. Breathing easier, he leaned back in his seat, his heart warm.

Taking another sip, Miss Ethel expressed her curiosity, prodding, "Her grandmother? You mentioned a grandmother."

"Yes, sorry," he said, bringing his thoughts back to why he came to see Miss Ethel in the first place. "Jewel Mantle is her grandmother. Her name is Ruby."

A slow smile spread over Miss Ethel's face. "Ah, yes. I know Jewel. It's been a while since our paths have crossed, but I remember her well." Her smile fell slightly as she appeared to be pondering. "I know she lost her son about ten years or so ago, and I believe her daughter-in-law not too long after that."

Stunned Miss Ethel knew her, he nodded enthusiastically and said, "Yes, that's true. Since then, her granddaughter, Ruby, has lived with her and helps to take care of her."

"She's unwell?"

"I understand that she fell a few months ago and was in the hospital and then rehab for a while. Anyway, they've fallen on hard times since Ruby's mother had a long battle with cancer before she finally passed away. Most of their money is gone, and Ruby works days cleaning houses and nights at a dump of a diner."

"Then I must certainly go and visit Jewel," Miss Ethel pronounced. "I've been very negligent in keeping up with some of my old acquaintances." She leaned forward and set her teacup on the table, her gaze warm on him. "So, is Ruby the woman who has caught your eye?"

His brow scrunched in frustration, but he nodded, saying, "Yes...and...um...no." Seeing her wrinkles deepen as confusion crossed her face, he said, "I feel a real pull toward her. I want to help, but she's very stubborn and has a lot of pride. But it's more than that. I really want to get to know her better, but also feel like she's been scarred in the past and doesn't understand how amazing she is."

"You said there was a man before?"

"Yes, but I don't know the whole story. I know that

Mrs. Mantle was not taken with him, and I get the feeling that he was abusive in one way or the other toward Ruby. I also know that he's no longer in her life, but whatever he said or did to her, she's kind of skittish."

"Skittish?"

"She's very petite, and I know I'm rather large." Seeing Miss Ethel's knowing smile, he continued, "She seems rather nervous around me, and I want to make sure that I never use my size to intimidate."

"Oh, posh, Jayden. You've always wanted to protect and never shied away from jumping in to help somebody. I know a few times when you were young you defended your brothers, but I was never afraid that you were going to use your size for anything other than good."

"I would never want to intimidate her, but I just think she has to get used to me. I also get the feeling that maybe this other guy really put her down because she doesn't seem to realize how very special and beautiful she is."

"I see," Miss Ethel said, setting the now empty cup back on the table. "Well, it certainly seems as though you have your work cut out for you."

He drained the last of the tea from his cup and set it next to hers. Leaning back against the comfortable cushions on the sofa, he sighed again. "Any advice, Miss Ethel? I know I could go to my brothers or any of their women, but I trust your wisdom most of all."

Her smile brightened, and she replied, "I do believe that's one of the nicest compliments I've ever received."

"Well, it's true, and you know it."

She chuckled and said, "When each of my boys came to me, no matter what different backgrounds you had, there was one thing that you all had in common...and that was a fear of abandonment. Zander had been on his own for a while, and it took him a long time to trust that I was going to stick around. Cael had not only lost his parents, but when his grandmother was unable to keep him, he felt that loss again. Rafe lost his parents in a car crash, and he feared that anyone he cared about could quickly be taken away. And then, of course, you and Jaxon lost your mother, your grandmother, and then your aunt. I essentially had a house full of skittish boys."

Shaking his head slowly, he replied, "I never really thought about us like that. You really had your work cut out for you, Miss Ethel."

Waving her hand, she said, "Oh, my, I didn't say that for you to feel sorry for me. I loved having all my boys, but I did have to learn how to deal with someone who had been hurt before and who was scared about caring again."

"How did you do it?"

"You can never convince someone that they should trust you or trust that you'll be around. What you have to do is show them. And you show them by being consistent. I consistently talked to each of you at night. I consistently helped you with your schoolwork. I consistently made sure that you had everything that you needed. And each of my boys—in time—realized that they could trust me because my actions showed that I would be here."

"So, that's what I need to do? Show her what kind of man I am."

She nodded and said, "It sounds like you're already doing that by helping her. You can't buy her trust. You just need to keep showing her that you like her, you care about her, and you'll be there for her."

"I can do that," he said, nodding emphatically. With a firm plan in mind, he relaxed and enjoyed the rest of his visit. As he was getting ready to leave, he gave Miss Ethel the address of Jewel and Ruby Mantle. "I know Mrs. Mantle is home most of the time, so I'm sure she'd love a visit."

Climbing back onto his motorcycle, he glanced at the time. Knowing that Ruby was working at the diner, he decided that a greasy burger might be just the thing. Roaring down the road, he made his way toward Carter's Truck Stop and Diner.

Ruby stepped through the kitchen door, her hands filled with platters of hamburger sliders and wings. The tables were placed closely together, because the owner, Carter, determined it was good for packing in as many customers as he could into the space. She had to weave amongst the tables while dodging the patrons that were crowding the area.

The sound of loud talking and laughter filled the air, making it difficult to take people's orders. It was a booming night at Carter's, not only bringing in long-haul truckers but locals who had been to the nearby racetrack. She could always tell when it had been a race night because the diner was packed. It was hard for her to complain about the rowdiness because the tips were higher. Ruefully, she admitted that it was not because each customer was an exceptional tipper, but the sheer numbers of them resulted in more money.

Many of the truckers were just looking for a good meal and a friendly smile, but some were more handsy, hoping for a tumble in the bed of their sleeper cabs. She had turned down her share of drunken propositions, usually after they had already been turned away by one of the bustier waitresses.

There were times she thought of leaving Carter's, but when she checked out other restaurants, she found that their pay was not much better than his, and the tips would probably not add up to as much. Plus, Carter did not mind having her work nights. Another restaurant would want her to work days sometimes, and that would interfere with her housecleaning clients.

One of the cooks in the kitchen also helped her out. If he was having to throw out some of the food at the end of the night but it was still good, he would send some her way. She often took bread and vegetables home with her. Occasionally, if he made too much chili or cooked meat for nachos, or wings, he would send those home with her as well.

But the reality was that Carter wanted his customers to eat and drink and expected his servers to do whatever it took to make sure that happened. They had to wear short skirts, and he preferred for them to toddle about in high heels. She had tried heels for the first year she worked there, but now her feet screamed if they even thought of being squished into the tight shoes, so she only wore sneakers. Carter hated them, but so far, he had not made her change.

She wondered if her tips would go down when she gave up her high heels but found that most of the men thought she looked cute in her sneakers. As long as her feet were comfortable and her tips were good, she did not care what they thought.

She set the platters down onto one of the tables and checked to see if their drinks needed to be refilled. Glancing at the clock on the wall, she sighed. Even though she was not working to closing, she was not nearly finished. *Two more hours to go on my shift.* She walked to the counter to fill their drink glasses again, and as she sat them down, found herself daydreaming of Jayden.

Having him meet Granny, and the two of them get along so well, was such a bonus. Kevin had grown to resent the relationship she had with her grandmother and grumbled when they spent time with her. Jayden not only tolerated Granny but seemed to really like her. A smile slid across her face as she thought back to how he wanted to be her friend.

"Hey, Ruby, darlin'," the man closest to her said.

She did not recognize him, but with her name tag pinned directly over her breast, where Carter demanded they wear them, she knew it was easy for him to see her name. She noticed the man's eyes never left her breasts as she asked, "Do you need a refill?"

"No, but I'd like to fill you up," he said, grabbing her arm and jerking her into his lap.

She pushed against him, but he was much stronger, and she looked around for help. Carter always promised his girls that they would be safe, but she noticed he was never around when one of the servers needed him. "Let me go, now," she demanded.

The man laughed, his breath foul, and his arms

tightened. "Now, that's no way to be, Ruby darlin'. You and me are just getting to know each other."

Before she could scream, her arm was taken in a gentle but firm grip, and she was pulled away as the man flew backwards, his chair tipping over. She watched in stunned silence as the man hit the floor with a thud, his arms and legs waving in the air like a beetle in its death throes.

Whirling around, she felt the grip loosen on her arm, and she was even more stunned to see Jayden towering over the man. His long hair was loose, its thick waves flying about his shoulders. Fire shot from his eyes as he bent over and grabbed the man on the floor by the front of the shirt hauling him to his feet. She could feel the rage pouring off Jayden but stood immobile, entranced by the scene playing out in front of her.

"How do you like someone else grabbing you, asshole?"

To her disbelief, the man swung, but Jayden reared back and punched him in the face. The man dropped like a stone to the floor, his friends scrambling to pick him up.

As Carter rushed over, a grease-stained apron tied around his ponderous stomach, his face red with anger, Jayden continued to stare at the man and said, "That's how you treat a woman? By grabbing her and mauling her?" He sent his glare to the men sitting at the nearby tables, and she observed their wide-eyed nervousness.

"J...Jayden?" she managed to choke out. He whirled around, his hands still in fists at his side, and she stepped back instinctively. She had seen that look on

Kevin, and it sent fear throughout her whole body. Strangely though, as soon Jayden's eyes landed on her, the anger fled from his face, and his fingers relaxed.

"Ruby, are you all right?" he asked softly. He must have noticed her backward step because his eyes filled with concern.

She was nodding her head when suddenly Carter pushed between them. He stared up at Jayden, and yelled, "Who the fuck are you? How dare you come in here and start a fight in my place! I ought to call the police!"

Ruby was mesmerized as she watched Jayden turned toward Carter, his jaw tight, and he peered down at the man. Snarling, "You're Carter? What kind of place do you run that you allow your employees to be manhandled? No man should ever allow a woman to be treated that way and sure as hell not an employer. You want to call the police? Go ahead. We'll see whose word they take and who just might get shut down."

At that, Carter paled but turned toward Ruby. "Get your shit and get outta here. You're fired." With a last glare at Jayden, he stomped away.

She gasped and turned her attention back to Jayden, hissing, "What are you doing? I need this job!"

He placed his hands gently on her shoulders and assured, "No, Ruby. You don't need this job. There are lots of jobs out there, and ones that can pay better. You do not need to work yourself to the bone every night at this dump, putting up with men like this. And you sure as hell don't need to work for an ass like that!"

Heart pounding, she felt her control slipping as

reality crashed around her. "You come waltzing in here, causing a ruckus that I was trying to handle, and now I'm fired!"

He scrubbed his hand over his face and said, "Don't worry. I'll take care of you and Granny until you find something else."

Rearing back as though he slapped her, she said, "This is ridiculous. You barely know me, and yet you're swooping in to take care of me. I don't want to be taken care of. I just don't want life to always be quite so hard." Her voice choked out the last words and her chin began to wobble. Blinking furiously to keep the tears at bay, she turned and walked toward the back.

She grabbed her purse from the workroom, and passing Carter's office, she saw him sitting inside at his desk. Forcing her feet to propel her forward, she moved toward his desk. Steeling her resolve, she demanded, "I want my full paycheck and the tips that I earned for tonight."

He looked up, his face hard and his mouth pulled back in a sneer. "You'll get nothing—"

She watched as he stopped in mid-sentence, his eyes moving from her to over her shoulder and up. And up. She felt Jayden's presence behind her but refused to take her eyes off of her former boss.

"You'll pay her final paycheck and the tips she earned tonight. You'll pay them right now in cash."

Jayden's words came from directly behind her, but she dared not turn around. Heat was pouring off him, but instead of searing her back, she felt comfortably warm instead, hoping Carter gave in. *If I walk out now,*

Carter won't ever pay me what he owes. Forcing herself to continue to stare at Carter, anger filling her, she wondered if he would acquiesce to Jayden's demands.

Opening his cashbox, Carter counted out the money that she would have been paid for the past two weeks, including a fairly accurate amount for the tips she had earned that evening. Shoving the money to the other side of his desk, he growled, "Take this and your boyfriend and get the hell out. You'll never get a recommendation from me, and don't come back, begging to me when you and your grandmother are starving."

Drawing herself up, she straightened her spine. "Don't worry, I won't be back." Whirling around with the idea of stomping out, she practically ran straight into Jayden's chest. Not giving him a chance to react, she ducked around him and hurried to the back door, glad for the cool night air to hit her burning cheeks.

She stumbled to her car, placing her hands against the cold metal, leaning forward until her forehead touched the window. Dragging in the night air, she shivered but did not know if it was from cold, fear, or adrenaline.

A hand touched her shoulder, and she yelped, whirling around with her purse in her hand, whacking the person who dared to come near her. Hearing his *'umph'* before she looked up to recognize Jayden, she groaned, "Oh, it's you." Sucking in a breath, she cried, "Jayden, you got me fired."

He scrubbed his hand over his face and then dragged his fingers through his long hair, pulling it away from his face—his handsome face—that she wanted to punch right now.

Sighing heavily, he stepped closer. "I know you're upset, but honestly, you'll feel different when this sinks in. Getting fired was the best thing that could've happened to you."

She had dropped her chin, but at his words, her head snapped back up. With sparks shooting from her eyes, she threw up her hand and said, "Are you kidding me? The best thing that could've happened to me? Let's see, Jayden, what do my salary and tips pay for? Groceries, electricity, gasoline for my car, the most basic cable package so Granny has something to watch during the days, homeowner's insurance, car insurance, Granny's doctor bills that aren't covered by insurance, and that's praying that I don't get sick because I don't have health insurance." As she ticked off each of these items, she poked his chest with her finger every time. Throwing her hands to the side, she added, "Now, do you want to tell me how this was the best thing that could happen to me?"

After Ruby went through the litany of her bills, Jayden watched as her shoulders slumped, and her body leaned against her car as though all her energy had drained from her. *Shit, this was not how I expected this evening to go.* His plan had been to show up at the diner, make sure to sit in her section and simply surprise her. True, he knew the clientele could be rough at times, but he hoped that his presence would let it be known that he was staking a claim. Well, that was his plan until he walked in and saw her being mauled.

"I'm sorry, Ruby," he said, his heart aching at the sad expression in her eyes. "I'm sorry about surprising you, but I'm not sorry about you not working there anymore. You said yourself that he didn't pay well, and I'm sure there are other jobs that will pay more."

A heavy sigh left her lips, and she lifted her chin to stare up at his face again. "I'm sure you're probably right, Jayden. But now that means that I have to pound the pavement looking for a new job, all the while knowing that each day that passes, what little money I have is disappearing."

At that moment, she appeared so tiny, almost waiflike, the weight of the world bearing down on her thin shoulders. Without hesitation, he stepped forward and wrapped his arms around her, pulling her into his warmth. He held her tightly, her cheek resting against his heartbeat, and he willed her worries away.

She remained stiff for a moment, then he breathed easier as he felt her body relax and her arms lift to slide around his waist. They stood in the parking lot, silent, holding each other.

Finally daring to speak, he said, "Let's go home, Ruby. I'll follow you." If she had any questions, she kept them to herself and simply nodded against his chest.

As he followed her home, an idea that had already been forming in the recesses of his mind came slamming back. He did not want to say anything to her yet. *Probably any suggestion from me right now isn't going to be well received.* Plus, he needed to put something into motion before saying anything to her.

As he pulled behind her in her driveway, he felt better about her situation but was afraid that she had spent the time driving home building up her anger against him even more. Climbing from his bike, he stalked toward her, shooting up a grateful prayer as he saw her alight from her car, steam no longer rising from her.

"Hey," he greeted, not wasting any time wrapping his arms around her for a hug, feeling her body stiffen and then slump into his.

"Hey, back," she replied, her voice barely a whisper.

They stood in her driveway for just a moment before he kissed the top of her head. "I know you're exhausted, so I want you to go on in and go to bed. I want you to fall asleep, safe in the knowledge that you no longer work at a place that allows you to be abused. But also that I'm going to do everything I can to make sure you have what you need."

She tilted her head back so that she could stare into his eyes. "Right now, Jayden, I'm so tired I can't even think of anything. I glanced at the money that Carter gave me, and it looks like he may have been extra generous just to get rid of me or because he was afraid of you. So, at least for a week, I don't have to worry about money. That'll give me a chance to find another waitressing job that hopefully won't need a reference from him."

"It'll all be fine, Ruby," he promised, bending to kiss her forehead.

He watched as she nodded slowly, and with a last small smile that did not reach her eyes, she moved to the front door. She suddenly stopped and turned around, her head tilted to one side.

"Jayden? How'd you learn to fight like that? You took that man down, and he never landed a punch."

"I was in the Marines," he answered without hesitation.

Her eyes widened, and she sucked in her lips, not saying anything else. With a slight nod, she turned and hurried up the steps and into her house.

Climbing back on his bike, he roared down the street knowing what he needed to do the next day.

13

"You do know what fuckin' time it is, right?"

Jayden winced at Zander's early morning greeting. "Not all of us can sleep in, bro. My shop opens up at eight in the morning."

"And my bar doesn't close down till after midnight," Zander grumbled.

"Okay, okay. Normally wouldn't call this early, but I've got something I need to talk to you about. My day around here is kind of crazy, so is there any way you can stop by on your way to the bar later?"

"No problem," Zander replied easily. "How about I drop by around lunchtime?"

"That'd be great. I really appreciate it. See you then." Disconnecting, Jayden leaned back in his chair, his thoughts a tangled mess.

Cas knocked on the doorframe to the shop's office. Looking up, Jayden greeted him then waited to see what he needed. Cas' gaze drifted around the office at the piles of papers before he said, "How the hell do you keep anything straight in here, boss?"

Jayden's brows lowered, and he asked, "You come in here this early in the morning just to bust my balls about my office?"

Chuckling, Cas shook his head. "Sorry, no. I wanted to see if you had the work orders up yet for today."

Startled, Jayden looked down at his desk and begin shuffling papers. "Jesus, I must be preoccupied. Can't believe I didn't already have it posted." Finding the paper he was looking for, he handed it to Cas, who nodded as he took it and walked back out.

Knowing he needed to get his head straight before he started working on cars, he grabbed a cup of coffee and headed out to the garage.

Just as he was getting ready to take his lunch break hours later, he grinned as Zander walked up. The two men greeted with hugs and back slaps before moving into the office. Having given no thought to lunch, he was thrilled when Zander handed him a bag.

"Zeke sent one of his subs," Zander said, causing a groan of appreciation from Jayden.

"Let's dig in, and then I'll get straight to the point." A few minutes later, the sandwiches decimated, he leaned back in his squeaky chair and stared at the man he considered his oldest brother. From the moment he and Jaxon had landed at Miss Ethel's, Zander had taken that role seriously. Quick-witted and equally quick with his fists when needed, Zander had made sure that all of Miss Ethel's boys knew that he was in their corner...a trait he never outgrew.

"I've met someone."

Zander's eyebrows lifted, but other than a twitch of his lips, he remained perfectly still.

Rubbing his chin, Jayden floundered, suddenly uncertain of the idea he had come up with last night. "Right now, we're just friends, but I'd like it to be more. From the moment I met her, all I wanted to do is take care of her. She's a tiny sprite of a woman but has a huge heart. She's worked hard since she was a teenager, making money to help pay for her mom's medical treatments. When her mom died, she moved in to take care of her grandmother, who recently fell and had to have several months of expensive rehab. Ruby cleans houses during the day and has been working at Carter's Truck Stop Diner during the night shift—"

Silent no longer, Zander growled, "Carter's? That shithole?"

"Yeah, well. She said it was because the tips at night were bigger, but…uh…after last night, she doesn't work there any longer."

Quirking an eyebrow, Zander asked, "And does that have anything to do with you?"

"I might have gone there last night and caused a bit of a ruckus when some asshole was manhandling her."

Nodding his head, Zander said, "Good for you."

"Yeah, well, tell that to her. She was pretty pissed last night because now she's worried about a job."

"There're better places for her to work than that diner. Safer places, too."

"You and I know that, but right now, she's afraid of the bills piling up. "

Zander's lips twitched again, but he lost the battle to hide a small smile. "You wantin' to see me have anything to do with me needing a new server at Grimm's?"

Nodding his head, he met Zander's smile with one of his own. "Yeah. I don't know if you've already hired someone, but I can vouch for Ruby. She's a hard worker, and I know you treat your employees right. She'll have trouble getting a recommendation since Carter is pretty pissed right now."

"Fuck him," Zander said. "I wouldn't take a recommendation from that asshole anyway. Your word means everything to me so if you vouch for her, that's good enough for me."

Blowing out a breath he had not realized he been holding, the tightness in his chest eased. Zander eyed him for a moment, then asked, "I just want you to be sure, though. You said right now that you two are friends, but you'd like it to be more. If this doesn't turn out to be more, or your friendship goes sour, she'll still be working at my place, at least until my other server comes back. Is that gonna be a problem for you?"

Shaking his head emphatically, he replied, "Absolutely not. I want her in a safe place, and if something doesn't work out between the two of us, at least I know she'll be taken care of." Grinning, he said, "But don't worry. I plan on doing everything I can to make her fall for me."

He eyed Zander for a moment, then added, "She's real independent, and we've got to make the idea of working at Grimm's sound like it didn't come from me."

Zander barked out a laugh and said, "Gotcha. Now, how do you want to play this?"

Rubbing his chin for a moment, Jayden thought. Then he and Zander put their heads together and came up with a plan. As Zander walked out of his office a little later, he just hoped their plan worked.

"I can't believe I let you talk me into going out this evening," Ruby said, worry still gnawing at her.

"Look, I know yesterday things looked bleak, but I've been wanting to ask you out anyway, and this is as good a time as any. Your neighbor wanted to come over and visit with your grandmother, so you can relax knowing she's got somebody with her."

She huffed but leaned back in the seat of his truck, inwardly thrilled that he had asked her out. Sneaking a glance to the side, she noticed his worn-but-clean jeans. His T-shirt stretched across the muscles of his chest and biceps. Glancing down, she even thought his motorcycle boots were sexy. She wiped her sweaty palms on the thighs of her jeans, glad that he was dressed casually considering she was wearing a simple pink sweater with her jeans.

She had lain awake the previous night, fretting about her loss of employment, yet strangely relieved that she was not going to be putting on her short, tight Carter's uniform anymore. Instead of being upset, Granny had been thrilled when she told her what Jayden had done and her subsequent firing.

"Thank God, hallelujah, praise the Lord!" Granny had shouted, much to Ruby's surprise. She knew her grandmother was not a fan of Carter's but did not realize how much Granny really hated her working there.

The parking lot at Grimm's was three-quarters full when Jayden pulled in, and she was surprised, considering it was only five o'clock. Carter's usually had not kicked into high gear until about seven or eight which is why she often had the late shift. She glanced at the automobiles in the lot, seeing pickup trucks, SUVs, sports cars, even expensive sedans.

Per his instructions, she waited until he opened her door and assisted her down. The outside of the building was unassuming, and once they entered, she realized the inside was the same. Not fancy but exuding a welcoming vibe.

The bar ran along the left side of the room, mismatched bar stools lining the old, wooden bar counter. Round wooden tables filled most of the floor space, wooden chairs circling each. Two bartenders worked the bar, laughing with the patrons that were seated on the stools. Several servers bustled among the tables, chatting with the customers while serving the food and drinks.

She immediately noticed that the servers were wearing blue jeans and simple T-shirts with Grimm's logo on the front. Not too tight and certainly not revealing. Music was playing from a jukebox toward the back, and she saw several tables had been pushed to the side, allowing a few couples to dance if they wanted.

The clientele was as diverse as the cars in the parking lot. Singles, couples, and what appeared to be gatherings from workplaces all filled the space. Interestingly, she noted two large men, one near the bar and one near the back, standing with their legs apart and their arms crossed over their chests, eyeing the crowd. Recognizing bouncers, she was at first surprised since the crowd was orderly, but also relieved knowing that help would be quickly on its way if there was ever a problem.

She jumped as Jayden startled her out of her musings when he placed his hand on her lower back and guided her to a table filled with people. Jerking her head around and up toward him, her eyes widened with uncertainty. Leaning down, he whispered, "It's okay. It's just some of my brothers."

They were at the table before she had a chance to come up with an easy excuse for why she needed to dart out of the room. The men at the table stood, and she blinked at the smorgasbord of masculinity before her.

"Everyone, I'd like you to meet Ruby Mantle. Ruby, this is Cael and his wife, Regina." She greeted the huge man and beautiful woman, both with red hair and wide smiles. Cael was one of the tallest men she had been close to, and Regina was his perfect physical match. Tall with serious curves, she wore a cute top with little cap sleeves, dark jeans that fit her like a second skin, and stiletto heels that screamed class.

Feeling tiny, she shook their hands and forced a smile just in time for Jayden to move to the next couple.

"This is Rafe and his wife, Eleanor."

She dragged her eyes from Regina and turned to the next couple. Offering her hand again, she noted the dark-haired man had the looks of a model she had seen in a magazine spread. His beautiful wife's shy smile greeted her. Eleanor tucked her hair behind her ears, and Ruby noticed what appeared to be burn scars on her neck, but the diamond studs in her ears drew her eye. Eleanor was slender but was also decked out in stylish comfort. Before she had time to process more, Jayden turned her to another couple.

"And this guy here is the oldest of us, Zander, and his wife, Rosalie. He owns Grimm's, so if there's anything you don't like tonight, you can complain to him." Zander smiled, his cool, blue eyes assessing. Swallowing, Ruby felt her lips tremble as she continued to hold on to her smile. Rosalie was closer to her own height but with a curvy body and long blonde hair glistening in the bar lights.

Ruby felt the heat of blush creep over her face as she greeted them and murmured, "I'm delighted to meet you, and I'm sure I'll have no complaints." She shot Jayden a glare, but he just grinned in return.

"I'd like you to meet Asher, another brother, and Zeke, who runs the restaurant here."

Zeke met her with a wide smile and said, "I can guarantee you won't have any complaints about the food."

She appreciated his easy-going manner before greeting Asher, a much quieter man who offered a gentle handshake.

There was one other woman at the table, and just as

Jayden was getting ready to introduce her, his carbon copy jogged over. She blinked, staring in surprise between the two men.

"As you can see, this is my twin brother, Jaxon, and his fiancée, Morgan."

As she got over her shock at seeing Jayden's twin, she greeted his fiancée, recognizing the woman who had been in the news as a former Olympic hopeful swimmer, injured in a car accident. Morgan, with her long, dark russet hair and fabulous, athletic body, greeted her warmly. But it was Jaxon who caught her off guard when he shoved past Jayden and gave her a huge hug.

Working in a full shift in the diner had not been half as exhausting as she felt the past five minutes had been. *At work, I just serve and don't have to impress anyone. But this?* She continued to force her smile as Jayden held a chair for her. Sitting down, she tried to steady her heartbeat as her anxiety ratcheted up at meeting all his friends. He had told her a little about them, so she knew they had met in a foster home, except for Jaxon who, of course, was his identical twin. She could not help but glance between the two of them, stunned to find someone whose looks were so like his while being slightly different.

As the group chatted, digging into the food, she was relieved that no one was staring at her as though they could not understand why Jayden would be with her.

"How's the food?" Zander asked.

She realized that his question may have been for all of them, but he was looking at her. Swallowing her delicious bite, she said, "It's really good. The wings are perfectly seasoned without being too hot."

"All right!" Zeke exuded, his fist pumping the air. "They're my specialty."

She met his easy enthusiasm with a smile that felt less forced and looked back at Zander. "I've never been in here before. You have a really nice place."

He grinned and leaned back in his chair, his arm resting across Rosalie's shoulders. "Thank you, that means a lot. This place was a real dump when I first bought it, but these guys helped me bring it to life."

Rafe nodded and said, "You wouldn't believe what this place looked like. The bones of the building were good, but it was literally falling apart on the inside."

Cael jumped in and agreed. "It took a lot of rebuilding, but I always liked how Zander kept the concept simple."

"Hell, at first all I wanted was just a bar. A place where a few locals could come in and drink and no one would get in their business."

Zander smiled at Rosalie, and Ruby noticed the sweet looks they gave each other. She felt something on her shoulder and jumped, realizing that Jayden had also put his arm on the back of her chair. With a quick glance around the table, she observed it was a position all the men had with their women. Claiming or affection, she was not sure, but she had to admit it felt nice.

Zander continued, saying, "I can't remember which one of you convinced me to get a jukebox, but at first, I thought it was a waste of money. Then we moved a few tables around so that people could dance if they wanted to. Again, I thought it was a waste of space. But," he shrugged, "the neighborhood began a revitalization program and lots of new businesses came in. With that, my clientele changed from just the people who lived around here to a lot of workers who stopped in before heading home. Grimm's even became a meeting place, and we get bachelor and bachelorette parties in here, although quite frankly, I can do without those."

"Hey," Morgan complained, "I met Jaxon here when I came with a bachelorette party."

Jaxon leaned over and kissed Morgan on the cheek and said, "Best thing that ever happened to me—besides Miss Ethel—was you bumping into my chair."

"What do you do, Ruby?" Rosalie asked.

Immediately self-conscious, she hesitated, her fingers twisting in her lap. "Um…I have several houses that I…um…clean during the days, and…well…um… until last night, I was a server at Carter's Truck Stop and Diner."

"Ugh…Carter's. Heard about that place. Rough crowd," Zander said. "You're better off not working there."

Before she had a chance to respond that any job was better than starving, the other men nodded their heads in agreement with Zander.

"See, I knew it was right for you to leave there," Jayden said.

Eleanor, her voice soft, asked, "Are you planning on taking on more houses?"

Shrugging, she replied, "I'm afraid I haven't thought about it very much. I only left Carter's last night. I'd like to get another serving job because the tips can be really good if it's the right job."

After a moment, everyone began chatting as they finished the food and drinks. Jayden's arm was still resting on the back of her chair, his fingertips playing absentmindedly with her shoulder. His attention was on his brothers as they conversed, and she remained quiet, listening to some of the conversations. Within a few minutes, she had discovered that Rosalie was a high school English teacher, Eleanor was a nurse, and she, along with Rafe, ran a home for burned veterans. Morgan now taught swimming at the clinic Eleanor ran, and Regina worked on restoring old movies at the University. She was never ashamed of working hard to make ends meet, but these women all seem so self-assured.

She wondered what they thought of her, a simple young woman who cleaned houses and served beer and food to a rough group of men.

The room suddenly felt very small, and the need to escape was overwhelming. Pushing her chair back quickly, she mumbled, "Excuse me. I need to go to the ladies' room." She was grateful when Jayden scooted his chair over to give her a quick way to escape, and she made the correct assumption that the hall at the end of the bar led to the bathrooms. Barely able to breathe as she reached the door, she threw it open and stumbled inside.

14

Going directly to the sink, she wet a paper towel and held it to her face before soaking it again and holding it to the back of her neck. She sucked in a deep breath of air and let it out slowly, lifting her head to stare into the mirror. Small in stature, she knew what it was like to feel lost in a crowd, sometimes wondering what it must be like to be a tall, long-legged woman, turning heads as they walked through a room. Her face was heart-shaped, and she was proud of her clear complexion, but makeup was an expense that she gave up several years ago. Moisturizer, mascara, and a cheap lipstick that she could swipe over her cheeks as well as her lips to give her face a tiny bit of color was all that she used. Her hair was long but with both of her jobs, she had pulled it back tightly, rarely letting it down.

Her curves were slim, and she always felt like her elbows were too bony and her wrists too thin. Dropping her chin, she grimaced. *Stop...just stop, Ruby. Stop putting yourself down.* Sucking in another deep breath, she closed her eyes, the other women moving through her mind.

Jayden's friends were all gorgeous and appeared so self-assured. She did not resent the other women's college educations or their careers because Granny had always taught her that there was nothing wrong with an honest day's work. But sitting there with him, she had wished she could have dazzled them with her story. *Oh, I'm a surgeon...I work in a law office...I own my own business...*

Before she had time for her thoughts to go further, she startled when the door opened and Morgan walked in, smiling brightly at her before moving into a stall. After a moment, Morgan came out and washed her hands at the sink next to Ruby.

"I was hoping you were still going to be in here," Morgan said, her smile warm. "I know meeting everybody can be kind of intimidating. That's how I felt when I first met the gang. But I wanted to have a private moment to let you know how glad I am that you're with Jayden."

Blushing, she babbled, "Oh, I'm not with him, not like that. We're just...um...I guess we're just friends."

Morgan shook her head, a soft laugh escaping and smiled as she gently laid her hand on Ruby's arm. "Of the two twins, Jaxon's the louder, goofier one. But Jayden? He has a big heart, the desire to care, but I always knew that I'd be able to tell when he found that someone special. Believe me, Ruby, it's you. And I couldn't be happier. Heck, all of us are."

Rubbing her palms on her jeans, she admitted, "Everyone is so nice, but you're right...it's a little...um...intimidating."

"Don't worry, Ruby. I can tell you'll fit in just fine."

Scrunching her nose, she pondered Morgan's assurance but blurted her confession. "I'm not like the rest of you. You all have careers and I...clean houses. I'm not ashamed, but—"

"Good grief, don't let that bother you, Ruby. None of the guys went to college. They all joined the military and then found jobs that they wanted to do and love. Believe me, you really do fit in just fine with our group. No one judges you other than how you make Jayden feel."

Not knowing what to say, her shy smile was her reply. Letting out a relieved breath, she felt some of the tension leave her body. It appeared his friends were happy for Jayden. Morgan wrapped her arm around Ruby and led her back out to the table.

Jayden jumped up, his eyes searching hers, a worried expression on his face. As she started to sit, he leaned close and whispered, "Are you okay?"

She simply nodded but placed her hand on his thigh and gave a little squeeze. She was thrilled when he responded by wrapping her hand in his and squeezing back.

One of Zander's servers walked over and delivered new drinks. She looked down at Ruby and smiled widely. "Hey, it's nice to see Jayden here with someone. I'm Lynn."

"It's nice to meet you," she said, noting Lynn's smile

was relaxed and not forced the way her smile had always been at Carter's.

"How's the family, Lynn?" Jayden asked.

Rolling her eyes, she replied, "The kids are growing like weeds. It's good thing bossman pays me so well so I can keep my son in shoes since he outgrows them every time I turn around."

The others laughed, and Jayden explained, "Lynn's got two kids. She has the kids during the day, and her husband has them at night when she works here."

"How's it going, Lynn? Zander asked.

Lynn turned around and cocked her hip. "Since Janelle left the other day for maternity leave, we're dying here, boss. You've got to hire someone soon."

Rosalie looked over at her husband and agreed. "Zander, stop stalling and hire someone. You need another server!"

He began to grumble, saying it was hard to find someone reliable. He lifted his gaze to Ruby and asked, "I don't want to put you on the spot, but are you serious about wanting to find another serving job?"

A spark of hope deep in her chest began to flare, and she nodded. "Yes, I am. I'm available some afternoons and any evening." Her shoulders slumped, as she admitted, "But I didn't leave Carter's under the best of circumstances. There's no way he'll give me a reference."

Zander barked out a laugh and said, "I wouldn't take a recommendation from that asshole anyway!"

A giggle slipped out, watching Rosalie playfully slap

her husband's arm, and she slid her gaze up to Jayden, who was squeezing her shoulder.

Zander had a piece of paper he was scribbling on. Uncertain what he was doing, she was surprised when he shoved it across the table toward her.

"The top figure is what your hourly salary would be, and the second figure is the average tips that my servers make per week. I've also jotted down the basic benefits that I offer my employees as well. I know it's only temporary until Janelle comes back or you find something else. You can look that over, and if you're still interested, let me know."

She stared at the figures on the paper and was unable to hold the gasp back. *That's way more than I was making at Carter's,* and she jerked her gaze back to Zander. "I don't have to think about it. I'll take it."

Jayden heaved a sigh of relief upon hearing Ruby's acceptance of Zander's offer. Grimm's would offer her a safe work environment. Not only did Zander have a reputation for keeping an orderly bar, but he did not have his servers dressed provocatively, and he hired several bouncers to deal with anyone who got out of hand. Zander had met Rosalie when she was injured just outside his bar, and he was not about to let that happen to another woman.

With his arm around Ruby's shoulder, Jayden squeezed her tightly, pulling her closer. Her smile was bright, and as she turned to beam up at him, he leaned forward, unable to keep from kissing her. It was a light kiss, the barest meeting of lips, but it seemed to surprise them both. He blinked as she startled, not having meant for their first kiss to be so public. But the feel of her soft lips on his was imprinted onto his brain.

He dropped his gaze from her wide eyes down to her mouth, still slightly open, but battled the desire to have that touch again. Her attention was distracted from the congratulatory cheers from the others at the table, but he could see the blush rising over her face and feel the heat pouring from her body.

While it had not been much of a kiss, he leaned back, grinning widely, anxiously awaiting the next time he could take her lips, giving them the time and attention they deserved.

A few minutes later, the group began to disperse. Zander and Rosalie wanted to get home to their little girl, but he made arrangements with Ruby to come in and fill out the employee paperwork the next day. Eleanor said that she and Rafe had an early morning at their clinic the next day, and they were ready to call it a night. Cael and Regina were working on restoring an old house, and they decided to head home. Asher had already said his goodbyes and quietly slipped away, and Zeke and Cas headed into the kitchen.

The gathering had dwindled to just he, Ruby, Jaxon, and Morgan. While she had appeared to enjoy meeting his other friends, having the group now just be the four of them, he felt the tension in her body relax. He had been worried when she left the table to go to the ladies' room, stress evident on her face, but when she and Morgan reappeared, she seemed happier.

"I have to confess that I've got a nosy question for you two...did you ever switch identities, just for fun?" Ruby asked, shifting her gaze from Jaxon to Jayden.

"We tried it the very first time we met Miss Ethel, but even though she'd only just been introduced to us, she already knew which of us was which," Jayden said, shaking his head, still not able to understand how she had been able to do that.

"Yes, but most of our teachers were never that astute," Jaxon said with a wide grin and a wink.

"You were in the same classes?" she asked.

Before Jayden had a chance to answer, Jaxon jumped in. "Nah, but that didn't stop us. Every once in a while, when we got bored, we'd go into each other's class. Our teachers never noticed." Shrugging, he threw out, "It helped."

Morgan's brow lowered, and she asked, "Helped?"

Jayden's chin dropped to his chest, eyes closed, and sighed, knowing what his brother was going to say. He felt Ruby shift in her chair and felt her attention riveted on him.

Jaxon barked out a laugh and replied, "Jayden was better in English, and I was a little better in math. We didn't do it often, but occasionally, if he had a math test, I'd spend the day pretending to be him and take that test. He'd do the same for me when there was an English test."

Both women gasped at the same time, and Jayden's head jerked up, pinning Jaxon with a glare. "You make us sound like a couple of cheats." He looked down at Ruby and added, "We only did that a few times."

"Yeah, but it came in handy," Jaxon continued. "We even switched up on a few dates."

Morgan rolled her eyes, but Ruby lifted her eyebrows. "Seriously?"

"It wasn't my fault," Jayden protested. "Jaxon would ask out more than one girl for the same weekend, forgetting that he'd already asked somebody. Then he'd get me to go out with one of them, pretending to be him."

Morgan and Ruby burst into laughter, both shaking their heads. Ruby said, "For some reason, when I asked the question if you two had ever switched identities, I sort of expected you to say no."

"I have a feeling Miss Ethel has more stories to tell about the two of them," Morgan said, winking at Ruby.

As the four of them continued to chat, he noticed that Ruby had barely touched her beer, preferring the water instead. When Lynn came around one more time, he ordered water as well. When Jaxon and Morgan's attention was diverted, he reached over and slid her untouched beer to the end of the table. She shot a grateful look his way, and he winked.

Thirty minutes later, the four walked outside. Jayden stood to the side as Ruby accepted a hug from Morgan. Her face registered surprise and then she appeared to relax, a smile sliding over her face as she hugged her in return.

Jayden loved seeing the genuine smile on her face, having seen it when she talked to Granny. It was so simple, as though she did not expect anyone to be nice. Sliding his arm around her as he steered her to his truck, he was determined to do everything in his power to keep a smile on her face.

Driving her home, he listened as she chatted about his friends. He wondered if she did not get out very much, considering that she was always working. He and his brothers had always gotten together no matter how hectic life became, Miss Ethel's lessons about the importance of family having been drilled into them.

As they pulled into her driveway, he realized that she had grown quieter. Turning off the engine to his truck, he shifted around in his seat so that he could see her pensive face.

She glanced over at him and then back down to her hands clasped in her lap. He liked how she was quiet, even shy, but wanted her to feel at ease with him. Just as he was getting ready to ask what she was thinking, she spoke.

"I really liked meeting your friends," she said.

He smiled, relieved, and reached across the console to take her hand. Rubbing his fingers over her knuckles, he replied, "I'm glad."

"I was nervous," she confessed. "It was kind of over-whelming to meet them all at once."

"I could tell," he said. "I didn't want you to feel nervous. I didn't mean to spring them on you all at once, but, well...I didn't really think about it making you anxious. We get together a lot, so it just seemed natural to me. I'm sorry that you were nervous."

"I don't get together with groups. I don't really have a lot of friends," she added, stealing glances at him between staring at her hands.

"Why is that? You're so pretty and so sweet."

She grimaced, and he wondered what her reply was going to be, hating that he put that expression on her face. She was silent for a moment, and he was not sure she was going to answer.

"I was always just someone who kept to themselves. Then it seemed like I was always working or taking care of Mom. Kevin never liked me being close to anyone, and at the time, it didn't seem too bad, since I'm shy." She shrugged her shoulders and continued, "I guess that seems strange coming from someone who worked at Carter's. Of course, that's probably why my tips were not as good as some of the other flirty waitresses."

"I can't tell you how glad I am that you're not going to be working for him anymore. Even if you're still mad at me, I just couldn't stand to see you there."

She nodded slowly, saying, "I was angry last night. I had no idea how I was going to be able to pay my bills." He opened his mouth to speak, but she rushed to add, "I know you said you'd take care of things, but I can't have you do that."

Once she began to speak, she opened up more and said, "I've just been really busy for the last several years. It's hard to make friends when my days were spent alone cleaning houses, and my evenings were spent at Carter's trying to avoid people other than those I had to serve." She looked down at his hand covering hers, and her fingers flexed before giving a little squeeze. "I do envy the close relationship you have with your friends. I know that things were terrible for you when you were younger, but when I see the relationship you have with those other men, it seems as though Miss Ethel was able to work miracles."

He smiled his agreement, and they sat for a few more minutes in comfortable silence, their hands still linked together.

She finally looked up toward the house and said, "I'd better go in. Granny is getting better and stronger every day, but I still like to check in on her."

He hated to end their connection but nodded, giving her fingers one last squeeze in a silent plea for her to stay until he opened her door. Pleased that she seemed to understand it was important to him, he rounded the truck and assisted her down. Walking to the front door, he wrapped his arm around her shoulder, tucking her closely into his side. As they stood on the porch, he towered over her, and she leaned back looking up. He noticed a blush cross her face and tilted his head, asking, "What's going through that pretty head of yours?"

Her lips curved into a smile, and she said, "I was

thinking that I seem way too short. But…I feel very safe when I'm with you."

Her words warmed his heart and gave him hope. He slid his hands from her shoulders up to cup her jaw, his thumbs sliding over her cheeks.

She continued to stare, her eyes focusing on his lips. She leaned up on her tiptoes, as though drawn upward by an invisible thread that connected her to him. Not disappointing, he leaned down and gently took her lips.

The kiss was soft and sweet, but she felt her toes curl at the sensations that moved throughout her whole body. With his hands still cupping her cheeks, he tilted her head slightly so that he could take more of her lips.

She sighed, and his tongue slid between her open lips, caressing hers. She was glad he was holding her up or she would have slunk down to the porch, her body a mass of jelly. *How could a man with such strength and power kiss with such gentleness?*

She had only been kissed by one man, and Kevin took more than he gave. The only reason she was sure of that was because of the romance novels she read. She often wondered if romance novels were purely fiction, written by women who wanted to tempt others into thinking that there could be kisses of perfection. But now, as Jayden slid one hand around her back, pressing her tightly to his length, she knew how a real man could kiss. And as much as she was reveling in all of the sensations, the realization slammed into her: *He's ruined me for any other man.*

His tongue slipped deeper into her mouth, gently exploring. Self-conscious at her lack of kissing experience, she nonetheless responded naturally. Her tongue tangled with his before exploring on its own.

She wanted to shove all thoughts of Kevin from her mind, but it was hard not to compare. Kevin had often tasted of stale beer or whiskey and cigarettes. But Jayden tasted of spice and sweet, and something that was uniquely him. Closing her eyes, she allowed her tongue to wander, seeking his essence while memorizing it, knowing it might be the only kiss she ever shared with him.

Suddenly, cool air moved between them, and she dragged her gaze from his lips up to his eyes, questioning the end of the kiss. He had leaned his head back and closed his eyes, the expression on his face one of pure agony.

Oh, God, I was terrible. He must be used to beautiful women knowing exactly how to kiss a man, and here I am fumbling through what, to me, was amazing.

She lowered her heels back to the floor, and her hands, which had been gripping his shirt, now flattened on his chest as she pushed herself backward. The heat of embarrassment flamed through her, and she wished she could disappear.

His chin jerked down, and his eyes landed on her, his brow furrowed as though in pain. "Ruby, I'm sorry."

Desperate for the evening to end, she forced a smile upon her face and shook her head in jerky movements.

"No, no. It's fine...um...I'm the one who's sorry. I'm sure that was...um...terrible."

She tried to step further away from him, but his arm banded tighter around her back. Cocking his head to the side, he asked, "Terrible? You thought it was terrible?"

Blinking, she chastised herself for insulting him. She rushed, "No. No, not for me. But...um... I'm not very good...um...experienced. So...um..." By now, the desire to cry was overwhelming, and she tried to push further away from him, desperate to go inside the house. *Anywhere to get me away from his penetrating stare.*

"Ruby," he said, his voice soft. When she refused to look up at him, he squeezed her gently. "Ruby, please look at me."

A tear escaped, and with his thumb, he wiped it from her cheek. "That was anything but terrible," he said.

Uncertain of his meaning, she sucked in her lips, continuing to blink in an effort to hold the tears at bay.

"Oh, babe, that kiss was amazing," he admitted, holding her gaze.

She swallowed deeply and whispered, "But you stopped. And you looked like you were in pain...like it was awful."

She watched as a smile curved his lips but was no longer able to read his emotions. "Please don't toy with me," she begged. "I don't know how to play this game."

He moved her body closer to his, erasing all space between them, and lowered his head so that he was right in front of her. "Ruby, this is no game, and I'm not playing with you. The look on my face was one of pain, but it was not pain from the kiss, but knowing that the kiss was going to have to come to an end, and I didn't want it to."

Her eyes widened, and she gasped, "You didn't?"

"Why would I want to end the best kiss I've ever had in my life?"

Her mouth opened but no words came out as she continued to stare, seeing only honesty in his eyes. Stammering, she finally said, "I thought you didn't like it."

He shook his head slowly and smiled, his thumb still stroking her cheek while his other arm still held her tightly.

Her breath caught in her throat as she felt the evidence of his arousal pressing against her stomach. She knew from Kevin that when a man was aroused, he wanted sex. Still whispering, she said, "We can't...you know. My grandmother's inside."

His smile dropped immediately from his face, and his brows lowered. "What are you talking about?"

"I can tell. You're...um...ready. I don't want you to be mad at me, but we—"

"Ruby, I'm not mad. Not at you. Sometime soon, though, I need you to talk to me about what that asshole did to you because I need to know how to undo every-thing negative that he did. But for right now, all you need to know is that just standing here with you on this porch tonight, with you in my arms, after sharing the best kiss I've ever had, I'm a happy man."

Her tears started anew as she looked into his strong, handsome face. *Me. He had his best kiss with me.* Her heart beat so loudly she was sure he could hear it, but all he did was lean down and gently touched his lips to hers one more time before stepping back.

Nodding toward the door, he said, "Go on in, and let me hear the lock. I'll talk to you tomorrow."

A smile still on her face, she did as he asked before moving to the window. Standing at the front window as she had the other night, she watched him drive away. Once his tail lights were gone from sight, she grinned widely. Twirling about the room, she did a happy dance with her arms waving in the air. *He had his best kiss with me!*

Ruby stood in the employee workroom which was little more than the supply room with a few lockers and an old couch in the corner, and checked herself in the mirror. Dressed for work, she was wearing blue jeans, sneakers, and a soft, dark green Grimm's Bar T-shirt. She could not help but smile at the comfort she felt.

She had worked two afternoons at Grimm's but was so experienced already that Zander put her on evenings. The door opened, and she saw Lynn hurrying into the room.

"Oh, I'm so glad you're here," Lynn said, throwing her purse into a locker before moving next to Ruby at the mirror. Her hands went to her head as she finger-combed her hair into a ponytail, securing it with a holder.

"Are you okay?" she asked, seeing Lynn huffing in frustration.

Chuckling, Lynn said, "Yes, just the regular madhouse at home. I'm trying to get out the door, and the baby is crying, and the preschooler was trying to flush her shoe down the toilet. I just looked at my husband and told him to take care of everything, I had to get to work!"

A giggle slipped out, and Ruby said, "I'm sorry. I don't mean to laugh."

Lynn replied, "Honey, if I didn't laugh myself, I'd end up in the loony bin!" She looked Ruby up and down and said, "You look like you're ready."

"I confess, I'm nervous. I don't really know why, other than I don't want to let Zander down."

Lynn threw her arm around Ruby and said, "You'll be fine. Zander is easy to work with, and I promise he won't let anyone bother you. And we servers all keep an eye out for each other. If you have anyone that bothers you…hell, anyone that even makes you feel weird, you let us know!"

Shaking her head, she admitted, "This is so different from Carter's. I know he wanted to make money, but he didn't care what happened to us in the process."

"Well, Zander is not like that!" Lynn grinned and said, "And I don't think Jayden would've pushed for you to have this job if Zander didn't run a tight ship."

She looked at Lynn in confusion, but before she was able to ask for clarification, one of the other servers threw open the door and said, "Hey, ladies. Looks like we've got a large group coming in."

Lynn dropped her arm from Ruby shoulders and replied, "We're on our way!"

Ruby followed Lynn out, and within a few minutes,

she was quickly immersed in her new job. She moved between her tables, taking orders, running drinks between the bar and the clients, and making sure the food was delivered. She ran up tabs on those who wanted them and took the payments from those who paid as they went.

The servers were each assigned a group of tables, but she loved the camaraderie. Any server could jump in and help another if it was needed. She got into the swing of things, smiling as Zeke winked when she picked up an order from the kitchen, laughing at the antics of the bartenders, and reveling in the fact that the two bouncers kept an eye on anyone who might be tempted to get rowdy.

As the evening wore on, she watched her tips increase and mentally added up how quickly she could pay off Granny's last bills from rehab if this was a typical night.

Coming off her break, she looked over in surprise, observing Jayden sitting at one of her tables.

Her feet practically skipped toward him, and she was unable to keep the smile from spreading across her face. "Hey," she greeted.

He stood as she approached, and placing his hand on her waist, bent to offer a kiss on her cheek. "I wanted to come by and see how you were doing. It looks like a lively evening. How's it going?"

She nodded, looking around at the busy bar. "It's good. I've already made more in tips than I did in my usual night at Carter's." She watched as he settled back into his seat, his hand now holding hers. Remembering

Lynn's comment, she asked, "Did you get me this job with Zander?"

She watched him blink, but before giving him a chance to speak, she added, "I mean, I can't be mad about that, but I just need to know the truth."

He squeezed her fingers and admitted, "I let Zander know that you had left Carter's. He was glad because he knew that place's reputation. And yes, I knew that he had a server who went on maternity leave, and he hadn't hired anyone."

She nodded, biting her lip, her eyes drifting down to their clasped hands.

He squeezed them again, gaining her attention, and asked, "Why does it matter?"

Sighing heavily, she said, "Our scales are so unbalanced, Jayden. I keep needing, and you keep giving. I can't deny my need, but I'm beginning to feel overwhelmed. You're like a fairy godfather, and I can't figure out what I'll ever be able to do to pay you back."

Chuckling, he said, "Fairy godfather?"

"You know what I mean," she huffed, tugging her fingers but finding them clasped firmly in his.

"Sometimes, Ruby, things just feel right. They seem to click. That's what I feel with you."

As always around him, her heart beat faster, and as she stared into his eyes, she whispered, "I feel that with you, too."

With another squeeze of her fingers, he smiled and said, "You need to get back to work, because if you don't, I'm going to want to drag you out of here and kiss you senseless."

She laughed and replied, "Well, I don't want to get fired on my first evening shift, so I'll get back to work."

"I'm going to hang at the bar and chat with Zeke and Zander. I know I can't be here every night you're working, but I really wanted to be here on your first."

Her heart lighter, she watched him walk toward the bar, and she rushed around her section to make sure her customers had everything they needed. The room became more crowded, and she often lost sight of Jayden as he sat at one end of the bar, but whenever their eyes did meet, he always greeted her with a wink.

At one point, she stood to the side and glanced over the room, just checking to see if there were any tables that she needed to take care of. Her eyes landed on a man, but before she could blink, he disappeared into the crowd. *Kevin? That looked like Kevin.* She squinted, but without glasses, she could not be sure who she had seen. *It must've been my imagination. He wouldn't even know where I'm working.* Forcing air into her lungs, she breathed deeply for a moment.

"Hey, you okay?"

She jumped, jerking her head to the side, seeing Lynn. "Oh, yeah. Uh…yeah."

"Do you need a break?" Lynn continued, placing her hand on Ruby's shoulder.

Shaking her head rapidly, she replied, "No, no. Not at all. I was just lost in thought for a moment." Feeling her cheeks heated with blush, she said, "I guess that's not a very good trait for a server, is it?"

"Shoot, honey, we all need to take a breather every

once in a while. Sometimes this room can get so crowded and noisy, I think I'm losing my mind."

Just then, Zander walked over. "Everything okay, ladies?"

"Sure thing, boss," Lynn replied easily, moving on to her next table.

"You're doing a great job, Ruby," Zander said. "Keep up the good work, and let me know if anyone gives you any problems."

She smiled her thanks and followed Lynn through the tables, her eyes still darting around, but she saw no other sign of Kevin. Heaving a sigh of relief, she hated that even the thought of him had interfered with her first night at her new job. Forcing him out of her mind, she brightened her smile, served the customers, and at the end of the night, reveled in her tips. *Life is finally turning around.*

Jayden sat on the top step of Granny's porch, waiting for Ruby to arrive. Zander had already sent him a text saying that he had personally walked her to her car. The lights were dim on the inside of her house, and he knew that her grandmother was already in bed asleep. Leaning his head back against the post, he smiled, anxious for her to get home. The neighborhood was quiet, most of the residents tucked in their homes. He wanted that for Ruby also…to have a job where she did not have to return to her home after midnight most nights.

"If wishes were fishes, we'd all casts nets." Startled at the quote that popped into his mind, he remembered Frank Herbert using the line in The Dunes Storybook. At the time he read the book, Miss Ethel had him research the line and he discovered it actually came from an old Scottish proverb. *Well, if wishes were fishes, I'd cast a net for Ruby, that's for sure.*

As if conjured by his desire, he looked up as headlights came down the street. Standing as she pulled into the driveway, her look of surprise made him smile wider, and she bounded up the front walk toward him. Recognizing that she had no plans of stopping, he spread his arms as she leapt, catching her in his arms as she wrapped her legs around his waist.

He was so much larger than she, it was easy for him to counterbalance her as she threw her arms up into the air and leaned back, a joyful smile on her face. "I had the most amazing night at Grimm's! Everyone was wonderful. None of the other servers are catty. The crowd was good but nice." She flung her body forward, her arms wrapping around his neck, and gleefully added, "And my tips were phenomenal!"

"Glad to hear it, babe," he said, chuckling, his heart light at her obvious joy.

Her hands slid from behind his head to his square jaw, her thumbs rubbing over the stubble. He held her gaze for a few seconds, and then she caught him by surprise again when she leaned in to kiss him. Getting over his shock, he did not hesitate to take the kiss deeper.

He held her slight weight easily in his arms, the feel

of her pressed against him sending his blood southward. The porch light illuminated her halo of dark, shiny hair and crystal blue eyes. He could feel the hesitancy in her kiss but was thrilled she was taking the initiative.

Angling his head, he slid his tongue inside her mouth, meeting her thrust for thrust. This time she was the one who ended the kiss, pulling back slightly. Her smile lit his heart, and he chuckled at the blush moving across her cheeks.

"Wow, babe," he heaved. "This time you were the one who stopped, which is probably a good thing. I don't think your grandmother would like us making out on her front porch like teenagers."

Giggling, she said, "Granny is so infatuated with you, I don't think she would care where we made out."

As her feet slowly slid back to the walk, his arm still banded tight around her, he held her gaze as she peered up at him. "Good to know. Your Granny's approval is important to me."

Pressing her lips together, she hesitated before asking, "Why?"

"It's important to me that the woman I'm dating has her family's approval."

"Dating?" she croaked, her eyes widening.

His brows snapped down, and he scowled. "Yes, dating. What did you think was happening?"

"I wasn't sure," she admitted. Her fingers clutched his shirt, and she added, "Please don't be mad, Jayden. I guess I really didn't know exactly what was happening. You've been my rescuer and good friend, but…"

Her head turned to the side, as headlights moved down the street. The car passed slowly by but did not stop, and its red tail lights turned the corner and drove out of sight.

He slid one hand up, lifting her chin with his knuckles, making sure he had her absolute focus. "I admit that my feelings for you were initially one of wanting to help. But the more I've gotten to know you, the more I want to be with you. So, if you'll have me, I want to be yours."

The passing car apparently forgotten, her eyes latched onto his, and her lips curved into a beautiful smile. "I want to be yours as well," she replied.

He bent to take her mouth once more, his thumbs gently caressing her cheeks.

"I'm so glad you had a cancellation this morning," Granny said.

Blowing out a breath that puffed her hair away from her face, Ruby groaned, "I don't work, I don't get paid."

"One housecleaning cancellation won't kill us," Granny retorted. "Anyway, this gives you a chance to go out and have some girl time."

"I have girl time with you," she said, standing in the living room, running her hands down her jeans, making sure her blouse was tucked in.

"Ruby, girl, listen to me."

She obediently turned and squatted next to Granny's chair, placing her hand on her grandmother's knee.

"I love the time that I spend with you, but I'm doing a lot better, and it would make me happy to have you go out today with your new friends."

She wanted to protest that they were actually Jayden's friends, but she knew that was not necessarily true. In the past week, Morgan and the others had sent her texts, checking on her and planning a lunch together. When she let Morgan know that her Saturday cleaning client had canceled, the women quickly jumped on the opportunity.

Smiling at Granny, she nodded. "Ever since I met Jayden, I almost feel as though my life is out of control. It's kind of like the rollercoaster I rode with Dad the last summer we went to the amusement park, and I was scared but thrilled at the same time."

Her grandmother tilted her head to the side and patted Ruby's arm. "Does that feel bad?"

"Not really. I guess it's just different, and that makes it seem weird." She saw her grandmother's continued, questioning gaze and tried to figure out how best to explain her tumultuous emotions. "I just depended on myself for so long. Now, suddenly, if my car has a problem, Jayden fixes it. If someone treats me poorly at work, Jayden jumps in. I'm gone for years without any close girlfriends, and suddenly, there's a small tribe wanting to have lunch with me."

Granny continued to pat her arm and nodded. "I think that's the sign of a good relationship. Jayden wants to make your life better. He wants to take some of the burden off you. He sees what he can do for you and jumps in before you even have a chance to worry about it because you're worth it, and you deserve that."

Ruby dropped her gaze, worrying her bottom lip with her teeth as she pondered her grandmother's words. "What you're saying is he's the total opposite of Kevin."

"Yes, darling, that's exactly what I'm saying. Looking

back, I can see how much Kevin dominated you and isolated you. I just didn't realize it at the time, and I hate that."

Her eyes darted back up to Granny's, and she said, "Oh, please, don't blame yourself. If anyone should have put a stop to that relationship earlier, it was me and only me."

"You did. You are so strong, my darling Ruby, and I'm so proud of you."

A car drove into their driveway, and she looked over her shoulder through the window. "That's Morgan."

Granny met those words with a huge smile and said, "Go, Ruby girl. Have a wonderful time, and you can tell me all about it when you get home."

With a nervous smile, she kissed Granny's cheek and headed out the door. Morgan waved to her from inside the car and she jogged over, climbing into the passenger side. She breathed a sigh of relief to see that Morgan was similarly dressed in jeans and a blouse.

"Thank you for picking me up," she began.

Waving her hand in a dismissive gesture, Morgan said, "Oh, don't mention it. You live on the way to the restaurant."

Morgan was easy to talk to, and before she knew it, they were pulling into the parking lot of a trendy new bistro.

"Have you been here before?" Morgan asked.

Not wanting to admit that it had been a long time since she had been out to a nice restaurant, she shook her head.

"None of us have either, that's why Rosalie thought

it would be a good place for us to check out. I know their dinners can be a little pricey, but I looked online and their lunches are super reasonable. I've also heard good things about their soups and salads."

Breathing a sigh of relief, Ruby relaxed. The two women walked inside, immediately spying Rosalie and Eleanor. After hugs and kisses all around, Regina came rushing in, and the greetings ensued once more.

The hostess took them to a large, half-circle booth near the back, and the five women scooted in, with Ruby in the middle. Holding her breath as she perused the menu, she grinned as she discovered the lunch specials were very reasonably priced...and looked delicious.

Finally at ease, she placed her order and leaned back, enjoying the camaraderie of the other women.

"Jayden tells us that you don't live too far away from Miss Ethel," Rosalie began, grabbing a piece of garlic bread from the center of the table.

"Oh, God, these are amazing," Morgan moaned. "I'm gonna have to swim more laps today to work these off."

"I've still got baby fat to work off," Rosalie added, "but I don't care. As soon as we finish this basket of bread, I'm going to have them bring another!"

The others laughed together, and it hit Ruby that they had body issues as well. She had always been self-conscious about being so small, appearing more like a young teenager than a woman. *Jesus, do all women focus on their bodies too much?*

Pushing that thought to the side, she was nibbling

on the buttery goodness when Eleanor prodded, "You live near Miss Ethel?"

Chewing quickly and swallowing, she nodded. "Well, my Granny does. I moved in with her when my mother passed away several years ago. I didn't need the family home, and it gives me a chance to help her."

"I'm so sorry about your mother," Rosalie said, her eyes holding a specter of sadness. "My parents are both deceased, as well."

Before she had a chance to express sympathy, Eleanor nodded. "Me too."

"Same," Regina said. "Well, almost the same. My dad is the one who raised my brother and me, but he passed away. My mom, who walked out on us years ago, is still around somewhere with, I think, husband number three. She's not in my life, so it's pretty much the same as having both parents gone."

"I'm sorry for you all," Ruby said, laying her breadstick back on her plate. "I haven't really had a lot of friends to chat with, so I began to wonder if I was the only person my age whose parents were gone."

Morgan, sitting next to her, patted her hand. "You're not alone anymore. And I have to tell you that I'm the oddball in this group. Both of my parents are still living. I'm closer to them now than I once was."

"I remember reading that your dad was your coach," Ruby said, then immediately wanted to kick herself for bringing up something that might have been painful. "I'm sorry, I shouldn't have—"

"Don't worry about that," Morgan said brightly, waving her arm that showed thin, white surgery scars from her car accident. "You'll find that between all of us, we have few secrets." Grabbing another breadstick, she added, "My dad was my coach, and that sometimes made our relationship difficult. But now, he helps out at Eleanor's center along with me. I think our relationship is much better now that the pressure of trying to make the Olympics is over with."

She turned her smile to Morgan, saying, "That sounds really nice."

"How is living with your grandmother?" Regina asked. "I heard Jayden tell Cael that he met her, and she reminds him so much of Miss Ethel."

Her face melted into a smile, and she took another bite of her soft, garlicky breadstick. "Granny is wonderful. When my father died, she and my mother and I sort of clung together. We didn't live too far from her, and it was easy for me to visit often. My mom was her daughter-in-law, but they got along beautifully. When my mom developed cancer, Granny was the one that helped us so much. When my mother died, I sold the small family home and moved in with Granny. I loved my parents dearly, but with all that went on, Granny has been the one consistent person in my life."

Rosalie blinked, and Ruby noticed that the others seem to be battling tears also.

"I think that's so beautiful," Rosalie said.

Before anyone else had a chance to speak, the server arrived with their soups, sandwiches, and salads.

After a few minutes of only yummy sounds being heard while the gathering dug into their food, Morgan looked over, a twinkle in her eye, and said, "So, tell us about you and Jayden."

Caught off guard, she almost choked as she took a large gulp of her iced tea. "Uh…I…uh…"

Laughing, Morgan said, "Don't worry. We're not trying to dig out all the details—"

"Yes, we are," said Regina. Catching Ruby's eyes, she said, "We just like hearing a good love story."

Shaking her head back and forth quickly, she said, "Oh, no. That's not us. We're just starting. I mean, he said he wants to be…uh…I guess I'm not very good at this." As she glanced around the table, she saw the mixture of confused and concerned expressions on the other women's faces.

Eleanor laid her fork down and smiled at Ruby. "How about you start at the beginning, and just tell us your story with Jayden."

Never having had a group of friends to unburden herself with, the request almost seemed too personal. But as she stared at their faces, she felt a longing deep inside that she truly wanted to share with these women.

"I recently had a boyfriend. Only one, and that was enough. I'd known him for years, having met him in high school. He was sort of a loner, like me, and I guess we gravitated toward each other. We weren't dating then, just friends. He always seemed to have big ideas and grand goals, and after having watched him be bullied by his dad, I really wanted his big plans to work out. My mom got cancer when I was in high school, and her treatments took most of our money, so college was never an option for me. Looking back, I was either in school or working, and my only friend was Kevin. We stayed friends, even when he went off to college, but he never finished. I think college was too slow of a way for him to make it big. We stayed friendly for years, and then just slid into being a couple."

"I hear a *but* coming," Eleanor said.

Nodding, she said, "I think I tried to convince myself that I was in love with him, but I was really just lonely. And the big plans that he used to talk about as a teenager were no longer very exciting as an adult when none of them came to fruition. He was always after a get-rich-quick scheme and got very angry when they didn't work out."

Her palms begin to sweat as she thought back to the gradual changes that she could now see so clearly in Kevin. Swiping them on her jeans, she was determined to follow through with her story with her new friends. Sucking in a deep breath, she let it out slowly, choosing her words carefully. "He started drinking, stopped working, and became angrier and angrier with each passing day. Thank God I never moved in with him, knowing that Granny needed me."

Rosalie whispered, "Was he abusive?"

She felt Morgan's fingers wrapped around her wrist, giving a gentle squeeze for support. Shaking her head, she said, "Not terribly. Not every day." Seeing the alarm on the other women's faces, she hastened to say, "He never hit me, not really…but would grab me and jerk me around sometimes. And of course, nothing I did was ever good enough."

Rosalie gasped, "Ruby, I'm so sorry!"

Shrugging, she rushed to say, "It's my own fault for staying with him so long." Her brow furrowed as she looked down at her almost-empty plate for a moment. Lifting her head, she amended, "To be honest, I don't know why I stayed with him as long as I did. Maybe I believed what he was saying about me."

"What was that?" Eleanor asked.

"That I was lucky to have him because no one else would want me." As soon as the words came out of her mouth, she wanted to pull them back, embarrassed at having exposed so much of her thoughts. But she was quickly assaulted with the other women all chattering at once, exclaiming how she was wrong.

"What a dickhead!" Rosalie bit out.

Regina chimed in, "Don't you believe it, honey. My dad always told me that a real man would never put down a woman. Your ex-boyfriend was just a jerk!"

Hearing their exclamations, she could not help but smile, her nerves easing.

"Oh, Lordy, you better hope that Jayden never comes across that guy," Morgan said.

She stared at Morgan's wide-eyed, lifted brow expression, and blurted, "He did." Gasps were heard from the others, and she explained about the day they first met.

After she finished her tale of how Jayden stopped to help her but she begged him to leave, she finished her story by admitting, "I stood by the side of my house, watching him ride away, and realized I had just met a real man. In bed that night, as Kevin lay passed out drunk, I just felt something in here," and she rubbed her chest right over her heart. Tears stung her eyes, as she said, "I figured I would never see that man again, but I just knew Kevin was not what I deserved."

"And Jayden is everything you deserve," Morgan pronounced as the others nodded in emphatic agreement.

"And Kevin?" Regina asked.

"I broke up with him right after that."

Morgan, her hand still on her wrist, asked, "How'd he take that?"

Shrugging, she admitted, "Not well. At first, he begged me not to break up with him. But then it was mostly bluster...telling me that I wasn't worth his time, and he was the best thing that I could ever have."

"Oh, no!" the women all groaned in unison, causing a smile to curve Ruby's lips.

The rest of the lunch was spent with Ruby listening as they told their own stories of how they met their men. She stared in rapt attention as Rosalie described being beaten unconscious and how Zander stayed with her in the hospital, brought her back to his house for her to recuperate, and helped her learn her identity.

Eleanor described her injuries suffered while in the military and how she lived in seclusion until Rafe met her and encouraged her to live life to the fullest again.

Her eyes widened when Regina shrugged and said, "Cael and I met one night and agreed to no-strings sex only. His niece had cancer, and then I had a recurrence of cancer. For a while, it just seemed like we had too much on our plates, but he swooped in and took care of me during my recovery. He and all of the guys became stem cell donors."

Morgan nodded and said, "My story with Jaxon is more public since the media got hold of me after my accident took away my Olympic hopes. Jaxon made sure I was taken care of, and I even moved into his place for a while."

Shaking her head, Ruby blurted, "I kept thinking that Jayden was doing too much for me, but it seems to be in their blood."

Rosalie winked and said, "Jayden is a good guy and would want to help anyone. But believe me, what he's doing for you, he's doing it because he really, really likes you."

Grinning, Regina added, "If you want our advice? There's nothing better than one of Miss Ethel's boys falling in love with you."

18

As Morgan drove her home, Ruby's heart was much lighter than on the trip to the restaurant. She discovered that she had gained four new friends, each with their own interesting personalities, but the one thing that bound them all together was their love for one of Miss Ethel's boys.

Interrupting her musings, Morgan looked over and said, "I hope you forgive me for putting you on the spot earlier, asking about you and Jayden. I just knew the others were as interested as I was about your relationship. And I suppose that since I'm involved with his twin, I'm even more nosy."

Laughing, she assured, "Because I haven't been used to having girlfriends, it did feel a little strange at first. But all of you are so sweet, it was really nice to have someone to talk to."

Morgan pulled into her driveway and put her car in park, shifting in her seat so that she faced Ruby. "After spending time with you, I can see why Jayden is so taken with you." She reached across the console and grabbed Ruby's hand, giving it a squeeze. "Keep in mind that there's a huge difference between a man who wants to help you because he genuinely cares and a man who just wanted to take over your life because he didn't want you to have a life of your own."

Allowing Morgan's words to seep deeply into the cold places that Kevin had created, she nodded. "I'll do my best," she promised.

"Well, you've got my number, so don't hesitate to call anytime you need me," Morgan said, her smile bright.

Feeling giddy, she said goodbye and bounded up her porch steps, waving to her new friend as she drove away. Opening the door, she called out, "Granny, I'm home, and I had the most amazing time!"

She stopped short as her gaze landed on a visitor in Granny's living room. The woman was tall and thin, dressed in a buttery yellow shirtdress, cinched at the waist with a light blue belt. Her white hair was pulled back into a neat bun at the back of her head, and her grey eyes peered at Ruby from behind wire-rimmed glasses.

Startling, she said, "Oh, my goodness. I'm so sorry to have yelled when I came into the house. I had no idea that Granny had company."

The woman's face creased as her smile widened, and she stood, moving toward Ruby with her hand outstretched. "Please don't apologize, I'm so pleased you had a good time. I'm Ethel Wiseman."

"Miss Ethel," she whispered reverently, taking the older woman's outstretched hand. She had no idea how she knew the identity of the woman, but she was exactly as she imagined in her mind.

Laughing, Miss Ethel nodded. "Yes, and I'm so glad to make your acquaintance. My Jayden speaks highly of you."

Blushing, she glanced between the two women, sure her confusion was evident on her face.

Granny beamed and said, "Would you believe that Ethel and I know each other?"

Mouth falling open, she asked, "You do?"

Ethel explained, "We were both volunteers at the local library many years ago, and I'm so ashamed to say that over time, since we were no longer meeting there, we lost touch. But when Jayden told me about you, I realized that I knew your grandmother. I confess that I had been wanting to visit, but when the girls told me that they were taking you to lunch, I thought it was the perfect opportunity to renew my friendship with Jewel."

Miss Ethel walked over to where Granny was sitting and bent to offer her a hug as Ruby was still processing the strange coincidence. The two older women embraced, and with promises to come back again, Miss Ethel moved toward the front door.

"May I offer you a ride home?" Ruby asked, glancing out toward the street and not seeing a car.

Miss Ethel grinned widely and said, "Only if it would be convenient."

"Absolutely," she replied, pulling her keys out of her purse. Looking over her shoulder, she assured, "Granny, I'll be right back."

Granny waved and said, "Take your time."

She walked to her car and made sure Miss Ethel was settled and buckled in safely. Rubbing her palms on her jeans, she breathed easier as Miss Ethel's smile put her instantly at ease.

Following the directions that Miss Ethel indicated, she weaved out of her neighborhood and into another one close by. She felt the older woman's gaze on her and glanced nervously to the side.

"Don't worry, my dear," Miss Ethel said. "I'm sure you've spent your lunchtime talking to the girls about your relationship with Jayden. I'm content to just know that he has found someone worthy of him."

"Worthy?"

"My Jayden always considered himself to be nothing more than a simple, hard-working man. But he has a protective streak." Shrugging slightly, she said, "Actually, all my boys have that same protectiveness. I knew that Jayden would fall for someone that he could care for, but that the woman would be strong on her own. You, my dear, are a kind and giving woman. I think you're very worthy."

Sucking in her lips, she blushed hearing Miss Ethel's praise. She confessed, "I once had someone in my life who made me feel less. Granny says I took that to heart."

"Oh, the words of others can be so cruel," Miss Ethel said. "I once read a beautiful memoir by Yvonne Pierre, who said, *'The enemy uses those things you're insecure about. Free yourself and take your power back by being secure in who you are - flaws and all.'*"

Nodding, she reveled in the older woman's hug and watched as she safely walked up to her house.

Driving the short distance back to Granny's house, her mind raced. Her parents had always told her that she was a good person, but Kevin's belittling over the last several years had taken its toll.

As she walked back into the house, she headed down the short hall to the kitchen, seeing Granny standing at the counter with her walker. Glad to see her grandmother able to move around more independently, she immediately enveloped her into a hug.

Granny turned, smiling, and said, "Oh, my, Ruby. You look like your day went well."

Holding her grandmother tight, she replied, "I'm ready to let go of the past and see what the future holds."

Granny leaned back and held her gaze. "And does the future hold Jayden?"

Her smile lighting her face, she said, "I don't know, but I'm willing to find out!"

"Praise the Lord!" Granny cried, hugging her back tightly.

Jayden lowered the car down from the lift and gave the signal to Cas that he was finished. Hearing his name, he looked over and saw Jaxon waving from his office. Cleaning his hands, he passed by the other bays and walked up the couple of steps, entering his office.

"Hey, bro," he greeted, shaking Jaxon's hand, noting

his brother's Cheshire cat smile. "What's got you so happy?"

"Just talked to Morgan," Jaxon replied. "Seems like the girls took Ruby out to lunch today."

"Okay," he said slowly. "I wanted Ruby to spend some time with them. That asshole ex-boyfriend of hers kept her isolated so she really hasn't had a chance to have any friends. But you smilin' like that is making me nervous."

"Oh, I think it went fine. But according to Morgan, they all started quizzing her on her relationship with you."

With his hands on his hips, he tilted his head back and looked toward the heavens. "Fuckin' hell, Jaxon. Knowing she's skittish, I'm trying to ease her into the idea of a relationship, and now you're telling me that the women all ganged up on her? Damn, now I'm gonna have to go undo everything that they just did!"

Throwing his hands up in front of him, Jaxon said, "Hang on, Jayden. You know good 'n' well the women had her best interest at heart."

He dropped his chin and pinned his brother with a stare. "Their intentions may have been good, but I'm the one who'll be left calming Ruby's anxiety. I know she already felt kind of intimidated by them."

"I don't think you gotta worry, bro. According to Morgan, they had a fabulous time and Ruby seemed to be thrilled to have some other women to talk to."

He eyed Jaxon carefully, afraid to hope.

"I'm telling you the honest truth, straight from Morgan's mouth," Jaxon assured. "She said Ruby seemed nervous at first, but they all started talking, explaining how they met each of us and told her that they thought she was great with you."

"You think she believes them?" he asked, hearing his own anxiety in his voice.

"Jayden, I've got no idea what women talk about or how they think. But I do know that if Morgan tells me that Ruby had a good time and seemed happy by the time the lunch was over, I don't think you've got anything to worry about."

Nodding, he reached out and clapped Jaxon on the shoulder. "She's working tonight at Grimm's, so I was going to go and see her. I'm glad you stopped by and told me. Give Morgan a hug for me."

The twins shook hands, and he watched as Jaxon jogged back out to his truck. Jayden sucked in a deep breath through his nose and let it out slowly, his mind firmly on Ruby. He had so wanted her to go out with the women who would make good friends but had not considered that they would be talking about him. *Fuck, that was stupid.* He loved those women like sisters and knew that they wanted him to find someone special, too. *I should've known that they would do everything they could to push Ruby to me.*

He scrubbed his hand down his face, running Jaxon's words back through his mind. His lips curved into a smile as he thought that perhaps the lunch may have been the best thing that could have happened to them. *Hell, if they sang my praises, that can only be good!*

Anxious to see her that evening, he headed back into the garage, ready to tackle the next vehicle. He had only taken a step toward the garage when his phone rang. Pulling it from his pocket, he spied Miss Ethel in the caller ID. She rarely called him during the workday, and he quickly answered. "Miss Ethel? Are you okay?"

"Oh, my, yes," she assured. "I'm so sorry to bother you at work. This is why I almost never call, because I hate to interrupt what you're doing."

"You can call me anytime," he said, breathing easier.

"I just wanted you to hear it from me, but I met Ruby today."

His chin dropped to his chest as he stared at his boots. "This seems to be the day for her to meet everyone," he said.

She laughed and said, "Yes, I understand that the girls took her to lunch. I can assure you that she had a lovely time. While she was out, I went by to see Jewel, her grandmother. It was nice to spend time with an old friend and have a chance to catch up."

Lifting his head, he smiled. Cas caught his eye, motioning toward the vehicle being driven into one of the bays, and he nodded toward him, lifting up his finger to let his mechanic know he would be right there. "And Ruby?"

"I was there when she got home from the luncheon, and she was kind enough to give me a ride back home. We just had a lovely chat, and I had no reason to call other than I wanted you to hear it from me."

"I'm glad, Miss Ethel. I'll be heading to Grimm's after work today to see her, but how about if I come over for a visit with you tomorrow?"

"You're always welcome," Miss Ethel said before disconnecting.

He slid his phone back into his pocket, both thrilled that Ruby had had a good day and knowing that she must have felt overwhelmed. He glanced at the old clock over one of the workbenches and sighed. *Three more hours to go 'til I can see her again.*

19

Jayden walked into Grimm's, offering a chin lift greeting to the bartenders as he headed to the last stool. He had just called out his beer order and his ass had barely made it into the seat when Zander clapped him on the back.

"You gonna be a new fixture at Grimm's now?" Zander asked.

"I usually make it in here a couple times a week," Jayden retorted, his eyes scanning the crowded bar.

Laughing, Zander said, "She'll be out in just a minute. I had Lynn showing her the stock room, but they're due on the floor now that the crowd has gotten bigger."

"How's she working out?"

Zander stood with his back against the wall, facing Jayden and the rest of the bar, his habit of always keeping an eye on the place. "She's good. No problems. I guess that asshole Carter must've given her plenty of experience because she can handle a crowd, keep the orders straight, and seems to be able to keep the customers happy. My regulars know that I don't put up with any moves made on my servers, and if someone is new in here, they learn that real quick."

Nodding, Jayden said, "Good to hear." He watched a smile spread across Zander's face, but before he could interpret it, he felt a light touch of hands on his back. Grinning, he twirled around on the bar stool, seeing Ruby next to him. "Hey, babe," he greeted. Deciding to stake his claim at Grimm's in spite of Zander's statement that the regular crowd knew how to act, he enveloped her in a hug and took her lips in a possessive kiss.

He felt her body stiffen, and just as he was about to end the kiss, she relaxed into him. He lifted his head in time to see her lust-filled gaze as her eyes opened. Kissing the tip of her nose, he leaned back, continuing to hold her hand.

She blinked for a few seconds, staring at him, a smile plastered to her face." Wow," she whispered. "That was quite a greeting."

"I hear you had a busy day," he said, studying her face for signs of nervousness, but instead, her smile spoke volumes.

"It was amazing!" she gushed. "I had such a good time at lunch with the girls."

"Good. I'm really glad." Sighing, he added, "I can't stay too long tonight so I thought I'd go all caveman on you and let anyone in here know that you're mine."

"I wondered when you'd realize you can't spend

every night at the bar just because I'm here," she laughed.

"Yeah, well, I would, but I've got payroll taxes to work on tonight," he said, a grimace on his face at the idea of spending the evening doing paperwork.

"Is there anything I can do to help? I've been doing Granny's taxes for years, and when I started cleaning houses, I had to learn how to do them for myself."

She was staring up at him so earnestly, he slid his hand up to cup her face. "You've got enough on your plate," he said. "I'm a big boy and can handle my own mess. Cas keeps telling me that if I would stay organized all year long, it wouldn't be so hard."

"Smart man," she quipped.

The hand on her waist gave a little squeeze, and he grumped, "Hmph."

She shook her head, a smile dancing on her face and her blue eyes bright. At that moment, she appeared so lighthearted and happy his heart pounded. He kissed her again, this time light and quick, knowing she needed to get to work. "It looks good on you, you know."

She tilted her head to the side and asked, "What does?"

"Happiness."

Her smile widened even further, and his breath caught in his throat at her beauty. She laughed before lifting on her toes to give him another kiss. "I've got to get to work, and you've got to go back to the shop."

He stood and looked down, holding her gaze with his. "Before I go, I wanted to ask you for a date tomorrow night. I know you only have two houses to clean tomorrow, and you're not working at Grimm's."

She nodded, her smile now beaming, and said, "I'd love to."

With one last kiss, he watched her grab a tray off the end of the bar and began moving through the tables before he headed outside to his truck.

Five hours later, at the end of her shift, one of the bouncers walked Ruby and Lynn to their cars. Once she was in and had the engine running, he waved and ambled back into Grimm's. Per usual on a busy evening, the parking lot was still full. As she pulled out of her space, she noticed a man standing in the distance, partially hidden in the shadows. Squinting again, she could ascertain his hair was shaggy underneath a ball cap, and he had a full beard, all which served to make his appearance difficult to distinguish. A sliver of unease moved through her, giving her the same feeling she had had the other evening when she thought she saw Kevin in the bar. She pulled out onto the street, but when she looked in her rearview mirror, the man was gone.

Giving herself a mental shake, she forced thoughts of Kevin out of her mind. *He's gone out of my life, and I won't allow him to haunt me.* She thought of Miss Ethel's quote as she drove home. *I will free myself and take my power back.*

Jayden watched as Ruby fiddled nervously with her dress, her hands rubbing over the skirt. He reached across the console and placed his hand over hers, forcing them to still.

"You're beautiful," he said.

She glanced sideways and smiled. "Can I tell you something? And you promise not to think I'm weird?"

"Of course. You can always tell me anything you want."

She sucked in a deep breath, and then said in a rush, "This is the first date I've ever been on."

His hand flexed over hers, squeezing her fingers as he looked sharply to the side. He knew she had been with her ex-boyfriend for a while, so he did not understand her statement.

"Not a real date, I mean," she explained. "When Kevin and I were first together, it was just as friends. We would meet somewhere, or he'd drop by to see me, but he never asked me out to dinner. And then, when he became my boyfriend, we just sort of slid into that relationship. But we didn't really date...not like...um...go out anywhere."

He watched as her brow furrowed, as though she were pondering her former situation, analyzing it for the first time. He gave her a minute, letting silence offer her a chance to think, while he reined in his fury. *Asshat Kevin probably just got physical without giving anything back to her.* The idea of Kevin using her just for sex shot through him.

"I guess that's why I'm kind of nervous, even though you and I know each other. You're the first man who's asked me to dinner."

Tamping down his anger, he grinned widely, squeezing her fingers again, only this time on purpose. "I'm glad, babe," he said as they pulled into the parking lot of a local steakhouse. He glanced up at the restaurant known for excellent steaks before shifting his gaze back to hers. "I confess that I was just looking for good place for us to go eat. But now, I wish that I had chosen a fancier place to take you for your first real date."

"Oh, no! This is wonderful," she said, her eyes sparkling. "I'd be too nervous if we went someplace fancy."

He gave a gentle pull on her hands, and as she moved forward, he kissed her lightly. Wanting to take the kiss deeper, he pulled back, determined to be a gentleman. Hopping out of the driver's side, he walked around and opened her door. With his hands on her tiny waist, he assisted her down. When she wore her sneakers, she barely came to his shoulder, but with heeled sandals on, she tucked just under his chin.

Her dress was deep, royal blue, fitted at the bodice and full in the skirt. Her dark, wavy hair was down about her shoulders. *She looks fuckin' amazing.* With his arm wrapped around her shoulders, they entered the restaurant and followed the hostess to a private table near the back. They sat next to a window overlooking a small pond.

He could not take his eyes off her, watching as the light moved across her face while she took in the restaurant and then focused her gaze to the pond outside.

"I haven't been to a place this nice since my dad died," she said, "He used to take me, Mom, and Granny somewhere special on our birthdays."

Quickly calculating, he realized it had been over ten years since she had been to a steakhouse. "Then let's enjoy every minute of being here," he said. "You're definitely overdue."

He ordered a beer, and she asked for iced tea with lemon. Looking at her drink, he asked, "Do you mind if I have a beer? I noticed you don't drink alcohol, and I don't want to offend you."

Giving a quick shake of her head, she exclaimed, "Oh, no, not all. My parents didn't drink, and the only alcohol I've ever been around was with Kevin. His behavior was such that it wasn't something I wanted to try. I don't have anything against someone drinking alcohol...um...in moderation."

He accepted her explanation quietly, and as they waited on their food, she filled him in on the luncheon she had with Rosalie, Morgan, Eleanor, and Regina. He listened as her eyes were bright and her hands waved with excitement as she talked about her conversations with her new friends. Then she described meeting Miss Ethel.

"My Granny was always the person who gave me such good advice after my parents passed away. And now that I've met Miss Ethel, I'm so glad that you had someone in your life like that." Finishing her salad, she said, "And you won't believe what she did just before we said goodbye. She quoted a line from a book to me that fit me exactly! It reminded me of when you quoted Winnie the Pooh."

He chuckled and nodded. "Growing up, books were always a huge part of our life in Miss Ethel's house."

Reflecting for a moment, he looked up as she prodded, "Tell me more. Please."

Plunging right in, determined to let her know the worst of his story, he said, "My mother was a drug addict. I have no idea who my father is or if she even knew." He forced himself to hold her gaze, wondering what he would see in her eyes. But her face was filled with sympathy and concern.

Blowing out a breath, he continued, "Jaxon and I don't remember our mom, because she died when we were very little. An overdose. Our grandmother got custody, but she also died when we were very young. We ended up with Mom's sister, a really nice woman, but she was overwhelmed with toddler twins. On top of that, she was dating a man who had no desire to have a ready-made family when they got married. So," he shrugged, "we ended up in the system. But as you already know, we landed in the best place possible, with Miss Ethel. Zander had been her first foster child, and she taught him how to read because he'd been on his own for years and had not been in school."

She gasped at that news, and smiling, he added, "Once Zander learned how to read, there was no stopping him."

She reached across the table and wrapped her fingers around his hand, squeezing for support. He loved the feel of her gentle touch on him, as though all the wrongs in the world could be righted...just like he felt with Miss Ethel.

"Every night, Zander would read from a huge, abridged version of classics, including fairytales. We also had tons of books in our room, and I confess that often I preferred the fairytale storybooks better than the real ones." Chuckling, he said, "The real fairytales scared me."

"It's been a while since I've read those, but I remember that you're right. They weren't written for children, were they?"

Shaking his head, he said, "No. We would always discuss the stories that we read, and Miss Ethel taught us that they were written to give moral guidance. Anyway, as we grew older, literature was a huge part of what she wanted us to learn. She always said that we needed to memorize passages that meant something to us, because literature, not just fairytales, taught us about life."

Blushing, she said, "I had no idea who she was quoting, but when I got inside, I looked it up on the Internet. I can't believe how it fit what I was feeling."

Turning his hand over so that they could link fingers, he said, "It's one of Miss Ethel's many gifts. I know I'm not the only one who's learned from her. I think anyone who's ever come in contact with her has walked away a better person."

The server brought their meal, and for several minutes they focused on the delicious food. His eyes continually drifted toward her, watching as she devoured her meal with relish, smiling when she met his gaze.

"Can I ask you a question?"

"Babe, you can ask me anything you want," he replied easily.

"Tell me more about you...I know you were in the Army—"

"Marines."

Eyes wide, she mouthed, "Oh," before admitting, "I guess I don't know very much about the different military...uh...services."

He grinned widely and shrugged, "Zander, Rafe, and Cael all went into the Army. Jaxon and I thought about it, but we talked to a Marine recruiter in high school. We liked what he had to say, so we both joined. We did boot camp together but then went to different MOS schools. Jaxon ran ambulances, and I became a mechanic. It was the first time in our lives that we were apart."

"That must have been hard," she said, barely glancing up as the server brought dessert.

Nodding, he agreed. "It was weird. We were both sent to Afghanistan but rarely saw each other there. When we got out at the same time, we headed back here to live. Zander had bought Grimm's, Rafe had a modeling career that took him to California, and Cael had a sister in this area."

"Was it bad over there? I know that sounds so stupid, of course it was bad," she added, shaking her head.

"Honestly? Not as bad as I thought it would be. I worked on gasoline and diesel engines, trucks of all sizes. I was mostly at the base, being sent out some to recover vehicles that had become disabled." He thought for a moment and then said, "I know some guys who came back changed from what they had seen or done over there. But for me? I was lucky. I was proud to work on the vehicles, making sure they were in peak condition…well, as peak as they could be over there with the harsh conditions. But I didn't see heavy combat…don't have war stories that keep me up at night. For me, it was on-the-job-training in tough conditions and makes what I'm doing now seem like fun."

"Fun?" she asked, incredulity in her voice.

He chuckled. "When I have to work on a vehicle and it's the middle of July and the temperature is in the high 90's, I remember that I used to work in that heat, including dust storms that could choke us, and there was no relief in sight. At the end of the day, I would still be in that heat and dust. At least now, I can go home, shower, and get cool. Same with the winter now, as well."

She sighed softly and said, "You're amazing."

"No more amazing than you are, Ruby." He watched her open her mouth, sure to protest, and he said, "You've suffered loss, but you get up every day ready to tackle whatever you have to do to make your and Granny's life better. You were strong enough to get rid of a negative person in your life. And brave enough to do what you had to do to make it all work. That, sweet Ruby, is amazing."

She blushed, her smile curving her lips as she took another bite of chocolate mousse. A small dab was left on her lips, and he longed to lean over and kiss it off. Instead, he settled for reaching over and caressing her lips with his thumb. Heat flared in her eyes, and he had no doubt it was in his, as well.

When the meal was finished, they walked hand-in-hand behind the restaurant toward the pond. The evening was still early, but the sun had dropped beyond the tree line, and the path was illuminated with Christmas lights draped in the trees.

With a slight tug on his hand, she stopped him, and he turned to look down at her. Her beauty in the night shadows and the twinkling lights glistening off her hair and sparkling in her eyes halted his breath. At that moment, she appeared as a fairy sprite, rising from another world to cast her spell on him.

"I've never seen anyone more beautiful than you," he breathed, watching as her blue eyes widened at his words.

She peered up at him and said, "I never thought I had a chance with a man like you, but here you are."

"I watched my brothers fall for women, ones they seemed to know immediately were right for them. I believed it for them, but never believed it would happen to me. But here you are with me."

He bent and kissed her, feeling her immediately melt into him. Her confidence rang out as she owned the kiss as much as he did. Noses bumping, tongues tangling, both taking and giving at the same time. His cock swelled painfully within the confines of his pants, and he knew she must have felt the evidence of his desire.

Their lips separated, but their eyes stayed glued to

each other, both panting as they fought to draw oxygen into their lungs.

"When do you need to get back to Granny?"

Shaking her head so that her dark waves bounced about her shoulders, she replied, "Not for a while. She's doing much better and insisted that I not come home early."

A slow grin moved across his face, and he said, "My place isn't too far. Would you do me the honor of coming back to—"

"Yes!" she rushed.

His grin widened as he said, "Then your chariot awaits." Grabbing her hand, they hurried back to the parking lot, where he tried not to break the speed limits on the way back to his place.

20

On the drive to his apartment, Jayden and Ruby remained silent, but the sound of their breaths echoed in the cab of his truck. Their fingers linked, and the electricity zapped throughout her body.

Part of her wanted to call a stop to their destination, fear of not being pretty enough or good enough almost overwhelming. She had only ever had sex with one man, and Kevin had filled her head with his belittling. The more he drank, the less he was able to perform, but his words had sliced through her as he laid the blame on her shoulders.

Opening her mouth, she snapped it closed quickly, once more remembering Miss Ethel's words. *I will not let Kevin take this moment away from me.* Sparing a glance toward Jayden, she was once more awed that this man wanted to be with her. From the moment he had picked her up for their date, she had continually taken the measure of him, from his thick, long, wavy hair, to the slight scruff over his square jaw. Out of his usual T-shirt, the blue dress shirt with the sleeves rolled partly up his forearms still managed to showcase his muscular body. Khakis instead of jeans encased his legs, and she had to fight to keep her eyes from the bulge she had felt behind his zipper.

Before she knew it, he parked, and her eyes jerked toward the windshield, viewing an older, three-story apartment building. "I wondered where you live," she said.

"It's not much, but it's home for now. The rent is low, so that allows me to save for when I want to buy a house someday."

Excited to see his apartment, her leg bounced with impatience as he rounded the front of the truck, then assisted her down. She met his smile, and they linked fingers once more, walking toward the building.

"I live on the top floor, which gives me decent views of the park in the back. From the living room, you can even see the river in the distance."

As soon as he unlocked the door, she was surprised. Having expected more of a bachelor pad, she walked into the living room, spying the comfortable sofa, matching coffee table and end tables, a widescreen TV on the exposed brick wall, and huge windows.

Staring out the window, she leaned into him as his arms wrapped around her from behind. They stood in silence for a moment, until the tangible wanting became too much for them to ignore. Turning in his arms, she placed her hands on his shoulders and peered up into his face.

"Do you want something to drink?" he asked, his eyes boring into hers.

Gathering her courage, she shook her head and replied, "No. I only want you."

———

"Oh, thank fuck!" he growled, his hands finding her cheeks, angling her head slightly as he took her lips in a searing kiss.

His tongue thrusted between her parted lips, tasting the chocolate from her dessert while smelling the light floral scent of her shampoo. The delightful combination was singularly hers, and he was determined to memorize it.

He felt her fingers grasping at his shoulders, clinging as though hanging on for dear life. His arms banded around her middle, and he lifted her. His erection was painful, but he forced the thoughts of sex with her to the back of his mind, knowing they would only go as far as she was comfortable.

Her hands slid from his shoulders to the front of his chest, and she began to unbutton his shirt. Her lips slid from his, over his stubbled jaw, down to his neck where she continued to place kisses.

"Fuck, babe… I—"

"Please, Jayden. Please."

Still holding her in his arms, he groaned, "Please what, Ruby? You gotta speak plainly because I don't want to do anything to hurt you."

She leaned back and held his gaze, her eyes bright

and her lips kiss-swollen. "I want you, Jayden. I want us."

He continued to stare, trying to discern her exact meaning, and she grasped his cheeks, pulling him close, and said, "I want you to make love to me."

Relief warred with excitement as he turned quickly with her still in his arms and stalked down the short hall to his bedroom. Somehow, he managed the feat while their kiss did not break. Once he reached his bed, he bent and laid her gently on the mattress, following with his body so that he lay next to her.

Not wanting to rush a single moment, he propped his head up on his left hand with his elbow bent next to her head and his right hand stroking her cheek. He kept the kisses light, wanting to savor the taste and feel of her.

As his tongue gently explored her mouth, he slid his hand over her shoulder to her waist, his fingers almost spanning her entire stomach. She moved slightly toward him, her hand gliding up his arm, her fingers clutching his shoulder. Her body was liquid fire under his kiss, and he fought to keep from moving too quickly.

His hand moved up her tummy, resting just underneath her breast. With a sweep of his thumb, he felt the hard bud of her nipple, and she moaned into his mouth. His hand inched upward until he was cupping her breast. She was petite, but her breast filled the palm of his hand, and he desired to have her lying next to him with no clothes as a barrier. He tried to remember how her dress was fastened.

Gliding his hand around her back, he discovered the

zipper and slowly lowered it from her neck to the bottom of her waist. As he began to pull the strap over her shoulder, he was distracted by the feel of her tongue now exploring his mouth, the sensation zinging straight to his cock which was already impossibly painful as it pressed against his pants.

It slowly dawned on his lust-filled mind that with them both lying down it was almost impossible to get undressed while still kissing. *How long has it been since I slept with someone? It's been a while, but Jesus, I should be smoother!*

Regretfully, he lifted his head and watched as her eyes fluttered open, the brilliant blue holding him captive. "I hate to tell you this," he began. He observed as a dark blush moved from her chest over her face, and she immediately struggled to pull her strap back over her shoulder.

"I'm sorry," she gushed.

Holding her shoulders, he said, "Hang on. What just happened here?"

Her eyes looked everywhere but at his as she said, "You were about to stop what we were doing. I get it..."

He lifted her chin with his knuckles and said, "Get what, Ruby? I wasn't about to stop anything. I don't know what you're talking about."

"Oh," she murmured, looking confused.

Considering the asshole she had been with before him, he was fairly sure he knew what she was thinking, and it was not going to make him happy, but he asked anyway. "What are you thinking?"

Her voice barely above a whisper, she replied, "Sex. I'm not very good at it."

Scrubbing his hand over his face, he counted to ten in an effort to quell his anger. Sucking in a deep breath, he let it out slowly. He slid his hand from under her chin, around her cheek, his thumb sweeping over the soft skin. "Ruby, I need you to listen to me, sweetheart. Really listen to me." He observed as she kept her eyes on his, nodding her acquiescence.

"I don't know what that asshole told you, I just know he treated you in ways that a man should never treat a woman. My guess is that he was inadequate and lay the blame on you. But he's not here. He's not in this room, baby. It's just you and me."

She stared at him, her eyes wide, seeming to absorb every word, so he continued.

"This is the beginning of you and me. We're gonna learn about each other, and that includes our bodies. I already know that you're beautiful, inside and out. I already know that whatever we do together is going to be beautiful."

"You and me," she whispered. "You're right. I'm working to get him out of my head, and I don't want him in here with us."

"Yeah, just you and me," he said, nuzzling her nose.

Her brows lowered in concern, and she added, "But you were stopping..."

He chuckled and said, "I wasn't stopping, babe. I just needed us to shift around some because I had us lay down before I realized you were in a dress and there was no way I was going to be able to get it off of you without us both getting all tangled up."

"Oh," she mumbled. Just then, her dress strap slid off her shoulder, and she giggled. "It probably would've been easier for us to have gotten undressed before we got in bed." She lifted her gaze to his and said, "I'm sorry. Have I ruined it for us? Tonight, I mean?"

He crawled over her and climbed from the bed, taking her hands in his and gently pulling her up with him. "No, babe, nothing's ruined. I guess I just wasn't as smooth trying to get you undressed as some guy in a movie or a book."

Sucking in her lips, quelling the smile that was slipping across her face, she said, "If you had been perfectly smooth, then I would've felt completely inadequate." Her hands moved to his buttons, and she began to flip them open one at a time, starting from the top and finishing as she pulled his shirt out from the waist of his pants.

The lower her hands went, the more he felt his arousal swell. Now that her body had easier access, he slid both straps over her shoulders and down her arms. She let go of his shirt long enough for her arms to be free of her dress, allowing it to the pool at her feet.

She stood before him in her white, lacy bra and panties.

"Jesus, you're beautiful."

She held onto his arms as she slid her heels off her feet. She now had to lean her head way back to hold his gaze, and she stood on her tiptoes to push his shirt off his shoulders.

"You're so big," she said. "I know I'm short, but being around you makes me feel absolutely tiny."

"I promise I'll never do anything to make you fear my size," he vowed.

She blinked and looked up at him, a crinkle between her brows. "Jayden, I've never been afraid of you. I always think of you as my protector."

His heart warmed at her words, and he bent to take her lips again, cupping her cheeks with his hands. Slowly, he became aware of the tugging on his shoulders, and he grinned as he stood to his full height. She was struggling to get his shirt over his muscular biceps, and he assisted, dropping the offending material to the floor.

Eyes wide, with a smile playing about her lips, she slid her hands over his chest, tracing the line of muscles down his abs. Her fingers struggled with his belt buckle, but it soon came undone, and as she unzipped his pants, he groaned at the relief of his cock being released from its confines.

He took over, kicking off his pants after toeing off his shoes and divesting himself of his socks. Snagging his billfold from his pants, he pulled out a condom, tossing it to the bed.

They stood, a foot apart, dressed only in their underwear, their eyes devouring each other. "This is more like it," he said, his hands moving to the front clasp of her bra. With a quick flip, he drew the material off her shoulders, exposing her small but perfect breasts. The dusty rose nipples, hardened to a peak, beckoned him.

Wrapping his arms around her again, he lifted her, and this time as he gently laid her on the bed he hooked his fingers into her panties and dragged them down her legs. Now, she lay before him, completely naked, completely beautiful.

And he intended by night's end to make her believe that she was as perfect as she was in his eyes.

Ruby lay on her back, her eyes filled with the sight of Jayden standing in front of her. Barely aware of her own nudity, she was mesmerized by the play of muscles that rippled in his arms and chest with every movement. His hair, long and wavy, hung down around his shoulders, and she could swear her fingers itched at the desire to tangle in his tresses.

His eyes had not left her, but she watched as they dragged over her body, heat flaring in them. Her gaze dropped to his tapered waist, and she held her breath as he hooked his thumbs at the top of his boxers and pulled them down his legs.

Holy moly. He had said that he did not want Kevin to be in her mind, but there was no way to not make a comparison at the sight of Jayden's perfect cock. Having no experience with men before Kevin, she made the assumption that all men were basically equal in that department. But staring at Jayden's long, thick cock, her breath rushed out of her lungs. *I don't know if we'll fit.*

He chuckled and said, "Don't worry, sweetheart. I'll make sure you're ready, and I promise that we'll fit."

Embarrassment flooded her as she realized she had spoken her thoughts out loud, but he gave her no time to stay inside her head. He dropped to his knees on the floor, lifting each of her legs over his shoulders. She rose on her elbows, her eyes wide at the sight of his hands at the apex of her thighs, and gasped. "I've never...I don't think...it's—"

Her words halted as his face disappeared between her legs, sweet kisses as soft as butterfly wings on her inner thighs, moving toward her core. Once more, her breath halted in her lungs as she was assaulted with sensations she had never felt before.

He settled his mouth over her folds, licking gently before moving up to her clit and giving it a nip. Lifting his head just enough to speak, he ordered, "Breathe."

She gasped once more before flopping back onto the mattress and closing her eyes. Giving herself over to the tingling deep inside, her fingers clutched the bedspread. He licked, sucked, pressed his tongue to her, and just when she thought she could not take any more, he gently thrust his finger inside her sex.

A coil in her womb tightened, and she wondered if it would snap. Her hips began to undulate, seeking movement and friction in an attempt to alleviate the overpowering need. Barely aware that his hand had slid up over her tummy, her eyes jerked open as he lightly pinched her nipple. Suddenly, her inner muscles spasmed, and she squirmed as she felt herself squeeze his finger.

Oh, God, so this is what an orgasm feels like!

He continued to tweak and suck until her legs flopped off his shoulders, leaving her completely exposed to his perusal. Weightless and boneless, she no longer cared about anything other than the feeling of ecstasy coursing through her body.

The mattress pressed down around her, and opening her eyes, she watched as he crawled over her body until his face was right above hers, his long hair casting his features into shadow.

"You've never had an orgasm before?"

Realizing she had spoken her thoughts aloud again, heat rushed over her, this time from blush instead of sexual satisfaction. Holding his gaze, she did not speak but shook her head slowly from side to side.

"I swore I didn't want him in this room," Jayden growled. "But are you telling me that he never got you there?"

She felt the angry vibe radiating off of him but understood that he was not angry with her. She lifted her hand, her fingers threading through his coarse hair, pushing it back so that she could clearly see his eyes. And so that he could see her tears. "Honey, everything I never felt before just means that it's something I can feel with you."

The anger that had been burning in his gaze slid away, his smile easing through her.

"Oh, baby, how did I ever get so lucky?" he breathed.

She whispered, "I've been wondering the same thing."

His elbows bent, and he lowered himself so that his

223

chest was barely brushing her breasts, kissing her deeply. Whereas before he had tasted of dark wine and chocolate, now was the heady taste of herself on his tongue.

He leaned up and rested his ass on his heels as he rolled on the condom. Settling back on top, he lined his hips between her thighs, maneuvering his cock to her entrance. Sliding the tip through her slick folds, he entered her slowly.

She clung to his shoulders, feeling her sex stretch, fearful of the oncoming pain which she had always felt before. But Jayden pushed in slowly, then pulled back out before moving in again, shallow thrusts allowing her body to gradually adjust.

Her fingers squeezed his muscles, and she closed her eyes as a smile crossed her lips. *It doesn't hurt!* She heard him growl, and her eyes jerked open. "Shit, I said that aloud, didn't I?"

He did not answer her but continued to thrust slowly until he was completely seated deep inside her sex. He held her gaze, and she smiled encouragingly.

"Please, Jayden. I need...I need..."

This time he answered with a grin and said, "I know what you need, baby." With that, he began thrusting, deeper and harder, creating the friction that she desired.

The coil that she had felt tighten earlier was back in full force, only this time she knew the bliss that awaited when it snapped. Her hands wrapped around his neck and moved up and down his back, feeling the play of muscles with every motion that he made.

It did not take long before her nails dug into his shoulders, and she cried out his name as her body tightened around his cock.

Jayden watched her body shudder as her orgasm washed over her, stunned at the heavy emotion he felt at bringing her pleasure with the joining of their bodies. He was humbled that she had given him such a treasure, and his chest puffed with pride at the idea that he was the first man who had given her an orgasm. He hated that her ex-boyfriend had treated her so shabbily but refused to give any more thought to that asshole, determined to spend the rest of his life proving to her that he was the right man for her.

It had been a few years since he had had a girlfriend, preferring to keep things simple, but watching her face as she gave way to ecstasy, he could not remember the face of any woman he had before her.

Reacting to the feel of her body squeezing around him, he began to thrust faster as her juices lubricated her channel even more. It only took another moment before he felt his balls tighten, and with his fingers fisting the covers by her head, he roared out his orgasm, pumping until the last drop was gone.

He barely caught himself from falling onto her chest, managing to shift to the side. Not ready to lose their connection, he wrapped his arms around her and rolled, allowing her slight weight to rest on top of his.

With her head on his chest, he knew she must have

felt the pounding of his heart as he fought to catch his breath. He lost track of time as they lay together, recuperating.

She was so still, other than her breathing, he was not sure she was awake. "And the marvelous rose became crimson, like the rose of the eastern sky. Crimson was the girdle of petals, and crimson as a ruby was the heart."

She lifted her head from his chest and whispered, "What is that from?"

"After I met you, I remembered a passage that talked about a Crimson Ruby. Unlike Miss Ethel, I couldn't remember the exact quote, so I did some searching. It's by Oscar Wilde." He remained quiet for a moment, before adding, "It's from his short story The Nightingale and the Rose. When I first read it, I thought it was horribly depressing. A boy, in love with a girl who only wanted a red rose, searched but could not find one. A beautiful nightingale discovered that if she pierced herself with the rose thorn her blood would turn a white rose red. So that's what the nightingale did, but in the end, she dies, and the girl rejected the boy's red rose anyway."

Ruby's brows lowered in confusion and said, "That *is* a horrible story."

Jayden lifted his hands and pushed her hair back from her face, cupping her cheeks and holding her gaze. "I thought so, too, until Miss Ethel explained the meaning. Scholars may spend time analyzing the boy and the girl, but the true moral of the story comes with the love that the nightingale had for the boy and its willingness to die to give him anything he needed. For a skeptic, they would see it as the futility of love. But truly, it tells of the power of love."

Her breathing deepened, and she blinked several times, but a tear slid down her cheek, to be captured by his thumb. "That's so beautiful, Jayden," she whispered.

Slowly, he slid his hand down to palm her perfect ass, the other hand moving up to cup her head, his fingers trailing through her long tresses. "No more beautiful than you are."

She shifted her body, looking down at him, and smiled.

"Are you okay, babe?" he asked, his eyes searching hers. "I wasn't too rough, was I?"

"I've never felt like that before," she admitted. "It was as though I could feel every nerve in my body tingling."

He smiled, his heart soaring at her words, pride that he had given that to her.

"Is it always like that?" she asked.

He shook his head slowly and said, "I don't know. It's never been like that for me before." He watched her eyes widen, and he hastened to say, "I'm being honest. That was different than anything I've ever felt. I've had sex... but I've never truly made love."

He watched as her smile brightened, her face so beautiful it was almost hard to breathe. A light pink blush rose from her chest over her cheeks, and he lifted his head just enough to give her a soft kiss.

She bit her lip, then asked, "I've never made love either. And I'm so glad that the first time I did, it was with you."

"Same here, sweet Ruby," he said.

They kissed, long and slow, as their bodies cooled. She finally separated slightly and sighed. "As much as I would love to keep laying here with you, I need to go home."

"I know you do," he said, reluctantly letting her go so that he could take care of the condom.

She followed him out of the bed, and they got dressed, then walked hand-in-hand out to his truck. They sat in her driveway for a few minutes, the desire to continue to kiss too overwhelming to ignore.

"Granny is getting stronger," Ruby said. "When I feel like she's completely safe, then I'd love to spend the night with you."

He kissed the end of her nose and said, "I can't wait to hold you all night and wake up with you the next morning. But I get it. For now, you're needed here, and I'll just be satisfied with every moment that I can have of you."

They made their way to the front porch, where they continued to kiss for several long minutes, before he finally forced himself to separate from her, listening for the click of the lock as she was safely inside.

Driving away, his smile was wide and his heart was light as he began planning their next date. As he drove out of her neighborhood, he missed seeing the car that was parked down the street from her house, the lone figure sitting inside.

2 2

Ruby practically danced her way through the large house, making sure everything was perfect. Her mind was filled with the last weeks and the tight band of anxiety that had become second nature to her finally loosening.

Granny was becoming more independent every day, moving about the house easily, even forgoing the walker for a sturdy cane.

She and Jayden had been spending every moment together that they could, including the evenings she did not work at Grimm's, and daytimes on Saturdays and Sundays. Sex with Jayden, amazing the first time, only got better as she was finally able to let go of past insecurities.

Taking a final look at the kitchen she had just finished cleaning, she picked up the check the owner had left on the table, seeing a note paperclipped to the back. Carefully placing the check into her purse, she read the note. The owner thanked her for her diligence, but since they were taking an extended vacation, they would not need her services until further notice.

Sighing, her steps now heavy, she walked toward the front door. Cleaning houses was never a job she aspired to, but it brought in much-needed money, and she knew she was good at it. The problem was never having a steady source of income with her houses changing and always needing to find a new client. Of course, being a server was also not her dream job, but working at Grimm's was fun, and she enjoyed getting to know Zander, Zeke, Rosalie, Lynn, and the others who worked there.

Securely locking the door behind her, she walked to her car, forcing her thoughts to how her life had changed so much in the past month. Thinking of Jayden always made her feel better. *I'll focus on finding another house to clean tomorrow.*

Her phone vibrated a message, and her grin widened. In the last several weeks, she often heard from Morgan or one of the other women. Miss Ethel did not text but occasionally called, and she relished the older woman's presence in her life, almost as much as Granny's.

Once in her car, she dug out her phone and looked down at the ID. It only listed a number, not a name, but her stomach clenched as she saw that it was from Kevin.

Just wanted to say I'm sorry. Hope you are well. Would love to talk to you sometime, just to catch up and apologize in person. Kevin

She sat, not moving, staring at the message on her phone, wondering what to do. She had worked hard, with Jayden's help, to close the door on that part of her life and was not eager to open it again.

On the other hand, she had always been taught to accept someone's apology when it was offered. Her finger hovered over her phone but found that she could not hit delete. Instead, she simply shoved her phone back into her purse and drove away. The house she had just cleaned was the last one for the day, and she had an evening off from Grimm's.

Deciding that she really wanted to see Jayden, even if only for a moment, she drove to his shop. Parking in the lot, she walked toward the office but did not see anyone there. Just as she was ready to turn away, Cas called out.

"Hey, Ruby. You lookin' for Jayden, or somethin' going on with your car?"

She smiled her greeting and shook her head. "I was just stopping by to say hello to him. Is he around?"

Shaking his head, Cas said, "He ran to an auto parts dealer to get some things that we needed." Laughing, he continued, "He forgot some things on our last order."

Shaking her head, she said, "I'm not surprised, the way that office looks!"

"Well, if you can find a chair in there, go ahead and wait. He should be back soon."

Taking him up on his offer, she climbed the two steps from the garage into the office and looked around in dismay. *It's even messier than the last time I saw it!*

She sat in the plain, utilitarian metal chair for a moment, then curiosity took over, and she moved to his desk. While she did not understand all of the automobile lingo that was on the order forms, invoices, and the plethora of other papers scattered around, she found that she could not sit idle.

She began going through the papers on his desk and organizing them into piles. One for invoices which she stacked according to their date. One for order forms, again which she stacked according to the date at the top.

Anything to do with payroll went into another stack. Same for the paperwork that pertained to taxes. Spying a filing cabinet in the corner, she opened the top drawer and glanced inside. Torn between the desire to help and fear that she was interfering, she shut the drawer quickly.

Hearing a noise outside, she turned to see Jayden walking back into the garage, a large box in his arms. He was handing it to Cas before looking up toward the office. She waved at him, and he grinned widely. A moment later, he stepped inside, immediately moving to her.

His arms banded around her, and she lifted on her toes to meet his kiss. He swept the inside of her mouth with his tongue, nipping at her bottom lip.

"What a nice surprise, babe," he said.

Before she had a chance to say anything, his eyes dropped to his desk. "Holy shit, did you do this?"

Following his gaze toward the neat stacks on his desk, she jerked her head back around toward his. "I'm sorry, I know I shouldn't have touched anything."

"No, no, Ruby," he assured, his eyes back on her. "I don't have a problem with you being in the shop or the office. I just don't want you to feel like you have to straighten things here. I keep thinking that I need to hire someone to take over the office management. But I kinda know where everything is, at least enough to get things to the accountant when I need to. Other than that, though, I prefer my time to be spent in the garage working on the cars."

She shrugged her thin shoulders and said, "I like organizing. Cleaning houses isn't my favorite job, but my clients say that I do it really well. I guess I just like things to be in their place."

He dipped his head so that their faces were closer and asked, "What would you like to do as a job?"

Shaking her head, she said, "It's been so long since I really thought about it, I don't know."

"I don't believe that," he said gently, giving her a little squeeze.

She shot a glare up toward him, but before she had a chance to retort he continued.

"Honey, I know you've had to work since you were a teenager. And you've got no idea how much I admire you for that. Shit, you put me to shame. Miss Ethel always told us that our job in high school was to work hard in our classes. We certainly had chores that we had to do around the house, and most of us did get part-time jobs in high school. But that was just for spending money, not necessities." Continuing to hold her gaze, his eyes penetrating, he re-asked, "What would you like to do?"

Biting her lip, she thought for a moment and then replied, "As much as I enjoy working for Zander at Grimm's and am so thankful that he gave me the opportunity, I know it's only until his other server comes back. And that's fine because while the tips are good, I hate never knowing what my actual pay will be. Cleaning houses is something that I'm good at because I like to keep things organized, and it's kind of cool to work for myself. But not having health insurance is terrifying. And," she sighed, "I just had one of my clients cancel on me so now I have to find a new one to take her place. It's a pain never knowing from one week to the next what I'll have."

"So far, you've told me what you don't want to do," he observed out loud.

Shooting him a playful glare, she said, "Hey, I'm getting around to that." She thought for another moment and then said, "I'm not really all that picky. I like the idea of business. I was good at math in high school and like working with numbers. I like organizing things, and I'm good with computers. Throw in that I'd like to be working full-time so that I know what my paycheck will be, and benefits." Looking back up at him, she shrugged again and said, "Now that Granny is getting better, I might start looking to see what jobs are out there for someone with only a high school diploma."

Tilting his head to the side, he asked, "Do you want to take college classes?"

Shaking her head, she said, "I don't think that's in the cards for me. At least not for a long time. With most of Granny's medical bills almost paid off, I'm not about to go into debt again."

Just then, Cas stepped into the office and said,

"Sorry to interrupt, Jayden, but when you get a chance, I need you to take a look at this exhaust system."

Startling, Ruby said, "Oh, my goodness. I never meant to take up this much of your time."

"Babe, I've always got time for you."

Smiling as he swooped in for another kiss, she said, "See you tonight?"

"Absolutely."

Watching Jayden jog over to Cas, she walked back to her car, her mind filled with the idea of her perfect job. *Working for Jayden in his office.* Sighing, she drove away, tucking that thought away, along with so many other unrealized dreams.

Jayden and Cas stood underneath the car Cas had been working on. As they worked together, Cas commented, "Ruby's a real nice girl. I'm happy for you, Jayden."

Shooting him a grin, he replied, "Thanks. I think she is, also."

"You ever think about hiring her to work in your office?"

"Huh?" Jayden questioned, fumbling with the wrench in his hand, halting his progress on the car. Turning to stare at Cas, he asked "Hire Ruby? To work here?"

Nodding, Cas replied, "Sure. You keep saying you need to hire someone to keep the office straight. Every time you have to do taxes you grumble. Hell, even ordering parts drives you crazy. Don't even get me started on bills, invoices, and payroll—"

"Okay, okay, I get it. I know I've been thinking about trying to get somebody, but Ruby?" As soon as those words left his mouth, it dawned on him how right Cas was. "She'd be great, but I don't know that it would be a job she'd want to have."

"You won't know until you ask her."

They continued to work side-by-side for several more minutes, but Jayden's thoughts were no longer on the car. *Man, I don't want to fuck this up.* "I'm gonna let you keep working on this. Now that I'm thinking about what I need to do for my office, I'm afraid I'm going to make a mistake."

Eyebrows lifted, Cas said, "Sorry, Jayden. I didn't mean to mess things up."

Clapping him on the shoulder, Jayden shook his head. "No worries. It's not you. It's just now that you brought it up, I can't seem to keep from thinking about having Ruby working in the office. I'd love to have her here, and I think she'd like to have the full-time work."

"Like I said, boss, you won't know until you ask her."

They lay in bed, a tangle of arms and legs entwined, Ruby's cheek resting on Jayden's heartbeat. The only sound in the room was their ragged breathing as they both recovered languidly from their orgasms.

His fingers traced lazy patterns over her lower back, occasionally moving toward a ticklish spot that made her twitch and giggle. After a few minutes of gathering his courage, he spoke. "There's something I want to talk to you about, Ruby. Well, something I want to ask you. I suppose, though, before I ask you, I need to explain—"

Lifting her head from his chest, she peered searchingly into his eyes. "Goodness, Jayden. Just spit it out. You're making me nervous!"

He shifted up in the bed, tossing some pillows behind him and leaned against the headboard. Easily dragging her up with him, he settled her on top of him, so that they could face each other.

She sucked in her lips, placing her hands on his waist, giving him her full attention but did not say anything.

"When you were in my office earlier today, you saw how messy it was. I told you that I always wanted to work on cars and be a mechanic, doing that as soon as I could get a job and going for that career when I was in the military. When I took over the business, I was thrilled. I knew there was a lot of paperwork to do, but being my own boss and running my own garage was a dream come true. I've done okay with the office management…but I hate it. I could easily hire someone because the shop is doing well enough that I could pay to have a full-time office manager. But," he grimaced, "I've hated the idea of a stranger coming in and going through everything." Shrugging, he added, "So, I just let it go."

He looked to see if she seemed to be getting what he was leading to, but Ruby's face showed concern instead.

"Oh, honey, I'm so sorry you have all that to deal with."

"I'm not telling you this to get your sympathy," he explained. "What I'm really doing is fishing."

She blinked, her face becoming a mask of confusion. "Fishing?"

He chuckled and shook his head. "I'm not doing a very good job of this."

She slid her hands up to his shoulders, and his gaze dropped from her face to her breasts. He realized too late having the conversation while sitting naked facing each other might not have been his best plan. *Eyes back on her face, eyes back on her face.*

Pushing her long hair away from her shoulders so that he could refocus on her beautiful blue eyes peering intently at him, he said, "What I'm trying to do, Ruby, is see if you would be interested in the job."

She blinked again, this time her eyes widening, and her brows reached her forehead. "What? You're offering me the job of working in your office?"

Immediately contrite, he said, "I'm sorry, I shouldn't have done that. I mean, you've got your hands full with everything you're doing and working in a smelly old shop is probably the last thing that you would ever want to do. Just forget I ever said anything."

She grabbed his cheeks and grinned. "Don't you dare take that offer back!"

"You'd be interested?" he asked, incredulous that she would consider his offer. "I thought it made sense in my mind until I just said it. And then I was afraid it might be insulting."

"Insulting?" she huffed. "Why on earth would you think it would be insulting?"

He moved his hand through her tresses, tucking them behind her ears, gathering his thoughts. His gaze was captured by hers when she shifted, placing her face right in his line of vision.

"Tell me," she prodded softly.

"I don't want you to take the job just because you feel sorry for me, thinking that I need the help. I also don't want you to think that I'm insulting the jobs that you already have."

"Jayden, honey, the work I'm doing now, I'm doing because there are bills to pay. But I also know that I'll never have real financial security in those jobs. Granny once asked if I'd like to open my own housecleaning business where I hired other people to work for me. "

Nodding slowly, Jayden said, "You could so do that... own your own business." *Shit, I never thought about that, and here I am offering her to work for me.* "That's something you could do, and I know you'd be successful at it."

Shaking her head, she said, "That's not what I *want* to do. I honestly don't want the hassle of having people work for me. Always having to check up on them, deal with the craziness of running my own business, getting the start-up money. I don't have a problem working for someone else."

He observed as she quieted, thoughts whirling behind her eyes. Her brow furrowed, and he worried where her thoughts had gone. Lifting his hand, he smoothed her brow with his forefinger, sliding it down around to her chin. "What are you thinking now?"

"I'm thinking of the great *what if*. You know, what if we stop seeing each other?"

He had not given that any consideration but knew it was not fair to dismiss her concerns. "Baby, I have no way of knowing what the future holds, but right now I know that I want you in it. If you start working for me and things go wrong, I trust that we'll deal." Leaning forward slightly so that their faces were almost pressed together, he asked, "Can you believe that?"

A smile curved her lips, and she clutched his cheeks, saying, "I totally trust you, Jayden."

Grinning widely, he asked, "So? Do you want the job?"

"What's the dress code?"

Staring at her blankly, his brows drew down as he repeated, "Dress code? Baby, you can wear anything you want."

Laughing, she replied, "Then I absolutely want the job! And I can start tomorrow afternoon!"

23

The next morning, Ruby sent emails to her house-cleaning clients, giving them two weeks' notice. Making sure to not burn bridges, she thanked them for their business and explained that a new, full-time employment opportunity had come along that would give her the benefits she had been lacking.

She quickly finished the one house she had to clean that morning and ran home before showing up at Jayden's garage to start her first day. Barely calling out a greeting to Granny, she ran through the front door and up the stairs to her bedroom.

"Goodness gracious, girl," Granny called out from the living room. "Where's the fire?"

Hanging over the banister, she yelled, "I'm sorry, Granny. I wanted to try to see what I can wear for my first afternoon at Jayden's garage."

She ran to her small closet, throwing open the door. Most of her clothes were bought for practicality. There were the short skirts that were required for Carter's, now shoved to the back. *I need to give those away. I wouldn't even wear those to a nightclub...not that I go to nightclubs!* Then there were the blue jeans that she wore when cleaning houses. Comfortable and serviceable, they did not scream 'I work in an office'.

Her shirts were no better. T-shirts or blouses had always proved to fit most of her needs in clothing. Huffing, she stood, biting her lip, considering her options.

"What are you doing?"

Hearing the words behind her, she whirled around, her eyes as wide as saucers as she stared at Granny. "Oh, my God! Granny, you came up the stairs! You walked by yourself?"

Chuckling, Granny moved to sit on Ruby's bed and replied, "Well I didn't sprout wings and fly up here."

Rushing to her grandmother's side, she knelt in front of her. "Please don't take chances on my account. If you needed something, I would've come to you."

Her grandmother smiled fondly at her and patted her shoulder. "My dear, I've never had any doubt that you would do whatever you needed to do take care of me. But I'm getting stronger, my hip is getting better. I assure you that I have been practicing my walking every day, and I held on very carefully to the railing."

Breathing out a long sigh of relief, she said, "Well, okay. If you're sure. But promise me you won't climb the stairs when I'm not here."

"I promise," Granny said. "But enough about me. What on earth are you fretting about, staring into your closet?"

She blushed and dropped her gaze, saying, "It's nothing, Granny."

Granny reached out and lifted Ruby's chin with her fingers. "Now, Ruby girl, don't fib to me. I always told you that everybody has a right to their own feelings. So, you're obviously feeling something, so tell me what it is."

Eyes bright, she admitted, "Jayden has no idea how much this opportunity means to me. I don't know if anyone does."

"Then tell me, sweetheart."

She stared for a moment into the face that had been with her through thick and thin, through laughter and tears, through good times and hard times, seeing nothing but interest and concern. Unburdening herself to Granny had always been the easiest thing to do, and today was no different.

"When I was working as a teenager in the grocery store, wearing my shirt with the store's logo, I was so proud. But sometimes I would see women coming in wearing skirts or dresses, and heels, knowing that they had just come from whatever business they worked at. And as happy as I was to have the job that I did, there was a tiny bit of hope that one day I would get to dress that way when going to work."

She continued to watch her grandmother, not surprised to see no look of censure but one of understanding. "When I started working at Carter's, I hated the short skirts and tight shirts. I wasn't embarrassed to be a server, but I was embarrassed to wear that uniform, knowing that men had a certain expectation from a woman who dressed that way to work."

Granny's face hardened, her mouth in a tight line. "Oh, Ruby girl, I hated that you worked there. I've never been so glad as when you came in and told me that you'd left that place."

Chuckling, she nodded, having felt the same way. "Cleaning houses, I could dress any way I wanted to, but of course I needed to dress in clothes that could get dirty. Again, I would see women wearing nice clothes and always wondered if there was ever a chance that I could be one of those, too."

Understanding dawned on Granny's features, and she nodded. "And now you have a chance to work in an office and want to dress that way."

Nodding emphatically, she said, "Yes. I know Jayden doesn't expect it, and he'd be fine if I just showed up in jeans and a T-shirt. I also know that it's a small office in a car repair shop, so it's not fancy and not like I'll be around a lot of people." Settling back on her heels, still kneeling in front of Granny, she added, "I know it sounds silly, but regardless of the type of shop, I'm still going to be the office manager. And I want to look the part based on me."

"I see," Granny said, her smile firmly on her face and her eyes twinkling. Looking past Ruby, into the closet, she said, "You do have a few dresses. There are even some sundresses you haven't worn recently."

Scrunching her brow, she said, "I don't think a sundress is the professional look I'm going for."

Granny placed her hand on Ruby's shoulder and

stood. Jumping up to assist her, they walked to Ruby's closet and peered inside together.

"You can certainly buy some new outfits, but until then, I think if you use your imagination, you'll find that you can dress the way you would like to." Granny leaned forward and reached for a hanger, pulling it out. A fitted sundress in pale green was in her hand. Before Ruby could protest, Granny pulled out a lightweight, yellow cardigan "Pair these together, and I think you'll find that you have a very professional look."

A gleam of speculation appeared in her eyes, and she immediately jerked off her T-shirt and slid out of her jeans. Granny laughed at her enthusiasm, and Ruby slipped the sundress on. Breathing a sigh of relief that it still fit, she pulled the lightweight sweater over the sundress and peered into the full-length mirror hanging on the back of her door.

Turning quickly, she dug in the bottom of her closet, coming up with a pair of black pumps. The heels were only about three inches, but they completely trans-formed the look from summer fun to one of business casual.

Twirling around, she threw her arms up in the air as she hopped up and down in joy. "Oh, my God! Thank you, Granny! I know it's not fancy, but this is perfect."

Granny laughed along with her, and the two women hugged warmly. Pulling away, Ruby said, "Let me fix my hair and do my makeup. You sit here with me, and then I'll go down with you to make sure you get back to the first floor okay."

Granny agreed, and twenty minutes later they made

their way downstairs. After a quick lunch of sandwiches, she took a last look into the mirror and headed
out the door. Time for her first afternoon as the new
office manager of J.C. Tire & Auto.

Jayden was glad the shop was full, his four mechanics
busy at work, and he was arms deep in the engine of a
pickup truck. Otherwise, he would have done nothing
but continually stand at the garage doors waiting for
Ruby to pull up.

Cas walked over to speak to him but stared outside
instead. Grinning, Cas said, "Looks like our new office
manager is here, and fuck, man, she's a damn sight pret-
tier than you are, boss."

Jayden turned around, his eyes bugging out of his
head as he watched Ruby stroll toward him, her feet in
heeled pumps instead of sneakers. Her dark hair was
pulled away from her face, the tresses hanging down
her back and curling around her shoulders. Her lips
were slicked with pink, and her blue eyes seemed
impossibly large, highlighted with a little makeup. Her
sweet body was encased in a fitted dress, a demure
sweater over the top, not helping to tamp down the
sexiness of her overall appearance.

Reaching him, she smiled a greeting toward the
other mechanics, all staring at her, their tools unmoving
in their hands. Looking up, she said, "I'm here."

Continuing to stare, mouth open, he finally said,
"Whoa, baby. Hot damn!" He dragged his gaze back up

her body, landing on her face, and said, "You know you don't gotta get all dressed up, right?"

Her face immediately fell, and she dropped her gaze, sweeping her appearance. "Oh," she said, her voice low. "I was going for professional, but is this too much?"

Before he had a chance to answer, Cas intervened, clapping Jayden on the shoulder. "Ruby, I'll go ahead and let you know, you've got my vote for best dressed in the shop. Glad to have you on board," he said, throwing her a wink before he turned and went back to his vehicle.

Glaring narrow-eyed at Cas' back, Jayden felt a delicate touch on his arm and jerked his head around.

"Are you upset?"

He felt like an ass, seeing her worried face. *Shit, she's gone to all this trouble and I'm making her second guess herself.* "No, baby, I'm not upset at all. You look absolutely gorgeous."

He shot a look toward his other mechanics, letting them know they needed to get back to work, and he took her arm and gently led her to the office. Once inside, he turned to her and said, "I just want you to know you don't have to dress like this. Hell, honey, you can come in jeans and a T-shirt."

Her hands fluttered nervously to her sides before she rested them on the skirt of her dress, smoothing it slightly. "I know you said you didn't care. It's just that I've never been able to wear clothes like this to any job I've ever had."

He stepped forward and pulled her into a hug, kissing the top of her head. "It's important to you."

She nodded her head, pressed against his chest, and wrapped her arms around his waist.

"Babe, you can wear whatever you want. Although," he said, leaning away, offering her a stern look, "you'll make it mighty distracting working here looking the way you do." Chuckling, he added, "But then you could wear a paper sack and you'd distract me."

She met his grin with one of her own and stepped back. "Okay, boss, show me what you want me to do today."

He looked around the office and sighed. "I'm not quite sure what to have you start with. Orders and payroll are up-to-date, but maybe you could just start organizing what's here?"

Nodding emphatically, she agreed.

"That'll also give me a chance to get familiar with the forms you use and the lingo of your job."

Knowing he needed to leave her and get back to work, he gave her a quick kiss and headed back into the shop. A few minutes later, he looked toward the office where the blinds were open at the window between their spaces and stared at the beauty that was smiling widely while working. His heart light, he turned his attention back to the truck engine.

The afternoon flew by as Ruby methodically went through one piece of paper at a time. Continuing the process she started the other day, she began by making piles and stacks around the room.

As she read over some of the parts orders, her respect for Jayden rose as high as her confusion. Batteries, brake drums, alternators, gaskets. *Who the hell even knew there were so many types of belts and hoses? It's going to take me forever to learn how to do this!*

Closing her eyes for a moment, she breathed deeply and remembered what Granny had always told her...*One step at a time, girl. One step at a time.*

The next thing she knew, Jayden was walking into the office, and she realized that a couple of the mechanics had closed their bay doors. "The day is over?"

He sat on the edge of the desk and looked around, a smile playing on his lips. Her gaze followed his, and she rushed to say, "It's getting organized. Right now, it's kind of organized chaos."

He chuckled and said, "Come on, babe. Let's go home."

She grabbed her purse and walked out with him as he locked the door behind them. He had said the word *home*, and she knew he was talking about his apartment. She could not help but wonder if one day that word would mean where both of them lived together.

24

Granny and Miss Ethel laughed as Ruby described her first attempts at organizing Jayden's office. Granny had been excited to go somewhere, so upon Miss Ethel's invitation, they had gone to her house for coffee.

Having been to Miss Ethel's house before, she knew that once Granny made it up the front porch steps, she would be fine to settle into the living room. Ruby had looked around the first-floor rooms, curious to see where Jayden had spent his childhood.

Miss Ethel clapped with glee and said, "I'm so glad someone will be able to help him. He truly hates paperwork."

Smiling in return, she explained, "It'll be nice when I can work there full-time. For now, it's only two days a week. I've given my cleaning clients a two-week notice, so I'll have my days free in another week."

"And your work at Grimm's?" Miss Ethel asked, leaning forward to pour more coffee into their cups.

"Zander's server, the one on maternity leave, will

come back in a little over a month. Until then, I can work days for Jayden, two evening shifts during the week for Grimm's, and then Saturday nights there as well."

She observed the pinched lips on both Granny and Miss Ethel and rushed to say, "I know it sounds like a lot. But once my work for Grimm's is over with, then I can just work for Jayden full-time." Shrugging, she added, "It's okay. It's what I want to do."

Miss Ethel leaned back in her chair, her lips curving into a slight smile. "C.S. Lewis once said, *'You are never too old to set another goal or to dream a new dream.'* I think, my dear, that describes you."

Her phone vibrated against her hip, and as Miss Ethel and Granny shared a conversation, she discreetly slid her phone out of her pocket. Seeing it was another message from Kevin, she quickly slipped it back. Glancing up, she spied Miss Ethel watching her. Offering a quick smile, she jumped up and said, "I'll take the cups to the kitchen and rinse them out."

Busying herself in the kitchen, she began to fret. Kevin had texted her every day for a week, his message always the same. He was sorry. He hated that they lost their friendship. He would like to see her.

She finished with the cups and leaned her hip against the counter, her eyes cast downward. Lost in thought, she did not hear Miss Ethel approach, jumping at the sound of her voice.

"We've had such a lovely visit," Miss Ethel said, "but I believe Jewel is ready for an afternoon nap."

She nodded and began folding the dish towel, placing it on the counter.

"I couldn't help but notice that you seem to be quite preoccupied," Miss Ethel observed. "Is anything the matter?"

Shaking her head vigorously, she replied, "Oh, no. Everything's fine." She squirmed under Miss Ethel's scrutiny but was not ready to admit to anyone that Kevin trying to contact her.

With a nod, Miss Ethel patted her arm as they walked down the hall toward the living room. "If you want to keep a secret, you must also hide it from yourself."

Looking to the side, Ruby asked, "I'm sorry?"

"Oh, just something from George Orwell," Miss Ethel said. "I thought about it just now, looking at you. Your face, my dear, speaks volumes."

Before she had a chance to question Miss Ethel further, Granny stepped forward, ready to leave. With goodbye hugs all around, she drove Granny back home. Before spending the afternoon at Jayden's shop, she first drove to a little park.

Walking along the sidewalk, she stopped at a bench under a tree and pulled her phone out. *I should have known that someone as perceptive as Miss Ethel would know I had a secret.*

She scrolled through the messages and pondered what she should do. Sighing, she also wondered what Jayden would think. She knew in her heart that he would not be happy. *If I delete them, will Kevin stop texting? If I delete them and don't respond, is that fair to someone that I knew for years? But I don't want to encourage him.*

Sucking in a deep, fortifying breath, she let it out slowly and hit call. The phone rang several times, and she was about to disconnect when it was answered.

"Ruby?"

Stomach clenching with nerves, she replied, "Yes, Kevin. It's me. I just wanted to call to let you know that you shouldn't—"

"I know, I know," he rushed. "I just hated how things ended with us, and I wanted to let you know that I missed you."

She had nothing to say to that, so chose to remain silent.

As usual, Kevin had no problem filling in the silence. "I didn't mean to make you uncomfortable. I just…well, Ruby, we had a lot of good history."

Silence.

"I wanted to let you know that I got a job. A real job."

Breathing a sigh of relief, she was glad for him. "That's wonderful, Kevin."

"Yeah, it's nothing fancy, but it's a paycheck."

She thought of all the times over the years she had begged him to get a real job, anything that would bring in money instead of all of the scheming he had so often done. "I'm glad for you. Really." Hesitating for just a second, she asked, "I need to ask you something. Have you been following me…or…showing up at places that I am?"

"No," he said in a rush. "Absolutely not, Ruby."

She bit her lip, wondering if he was telling the truth.

The couple of times she thought she saw him he was not there when she tried to discern if it was really him. *Is he being honest, or am I paranoid?*

"How's your grandmother?" he asked, interrupting her musings.

Sighing, she replied, "She's good, thank you for asking. She's getting stronger and getting around better."

"Good, good." Silence filled the air space for another moment, before he added, "It was good to talk to you. Maybe sometime we can have a cup of coffee."

"Kevin, it was nice of you to call and check on me, but I've moved on, and I don't think a cup of coffee would be a good—"

"Just for old time's sake, Ruby," he interrupted. "We were friends for so many years. Just coffee. We can just meet for coffee. Please."

It was the *please*, that got to her, and she said, "Okay. But just this once." Agreeing to the place and the time for the next day, she disconnected, another sigh slipping from her lips. Tossing her phone into her purse, she stood and hurried back to her car. She knew Jayden would not care, but she did not want to be late for work.

Jayden tried to be nonchalant, but he continually checked on Ruby all during the afternoon. They might not have been together for very long, but she wore her emotions on her face. She might have greeted him with a smile, but it did not reach her eyes. She had chattered about the visit between Granny and Miss Ethel, but her enthusiasm appeared forced.

"You okay, Jayden?" Cas asked, coming up behind him.

Swinging around, he nodded. "Yeah, just keeping an eye on the office."

"Ruby's doing fine. She'll learn everything that she needs to."

Realizing that Cas thought he was concerned about Ruby's abilities, he quickly said, "Oh, I know she'll be fabulous. She just seems a little off today."

"Maybe so, but if she notices that you keep watching her, you're going to make it worse." With that, Cas headed back over to his workstation.

Fuck, he's right. Determined to not make her feel self-conscious, he focused on his own work. At the end of the day, he stepped into the office, stunned at how much she had accomplished. "Damn, babe. This looks amazing."

A smile lit her face, this time seeming genuine. "I still don't know what any of the lingo means, but at least I've got a handle on what goes where."

"I know you gotta work tonight at Grimm's, but do you want to grab a bite before then?"

She looked at the clock on the wall and said, "I brought my jeans for tonight's work and was just going to change there. If you want Zeke's wings for dinner, we could go there early."

They closed up the shop together, and he walked her to her car. He gently pressed her back against the driver's door, his body towering over and enveloping hers. Holding her face in his hands, he lowered his mouth, melding it with hers.

The kiss was long and slow and sweet. Pulling back reluctantly, he nuzzled her nose and whispered, "Soon, we can drive to work together."

She sucked in her lips and looked up at him thoughtfully. "Even if I'm still living with Granny?"

"I can swing by and pick you up in the mornings before we come here. Then we can always go back to my place for a little while."

"Oh, really? And just what would we be doing at your place?" she said playfully, her fingers digging into his waist.

Instead of answering, he leaned down and kissed her again, this time allowing the kiss to flame hot. A few minutes later, both breathless, he said, "I know you've got to get to Grimm's, babe. I'll follow you."

An hour later, a platter of wings had been consumed, and Ruby drank water while Jayden had a beer. She disappeared into the workroom, changing into jeans and her Grimm's T-shirt while Jayden and Zander talked.

"I like having Ruby around, but I'm real glad you gave her a job in your office," Zander said. "You needed the help, and I've seen a difference with her here. She seems happier now."

"She's getting the hang of everything, and I think by the time she starts working for me full-time, she'll be ready."

He decided to spend her shift at Grimm's, talking to

his friends while keeping a pulse on her. While she seemed more at ease, he could not get rid of the feeling that something was bothering her. Part of him wanted to force her to confide in him but knew that whatever was on her mind, she would tell him when she was ready.

At the end of her shift, Ruby was in Zander's office, taking off her apron and cashing out the tabs with Rosalie.

She felt Rosalie's eyes on her and was not surprised when her friend asked, "Is everything okay?"

Sucking in her lips, she wondered how to answer. Finally, deciding to take a plunge, she asked, "Do you ever keep secrets from Zander?"

Eyes wide, Rosalie laughed, "I guess it depends on what the secret is. Sometimes I try to sneak broccoli into a casserole, knowing that he hates broccoli, but it's good for him."

Ruby giggled at the thought of taciturn Zander being forced to eat broccoli.

Rosalie sobered and said, "But I get the feeling that what you're talking about is much deeper." Ruby nodded, and Rosalie continued, "All I can tell you is that you're now involved with a man who feels very deeply that he should protect and care for those he loves. And to do so, secrets can undermine all of that. My advice would be that you not keep secrets from him, especially if it's something that concerns you or bothers you. It doesn't mean that he has to jump in and fix everything, but secrets have a way of coming out in the end anyway."

She pondered Rosalie's words for a moment and then nodded again. "You're right. There is something that I need to talk to Jayden about that I've just been holding onto. But I'll talk to him tonight."

"Remember, you can always talk to me or one of the other girls as well. It takes a special person to be with one of Miss Ethel's boys. Believe me, one of us will understand anything you're going through."

The two women embraced, and Ruby headed back to the bar, ready to go with Jayden to his apartment. Only tonight, before they made love, she would tell him about Kevin.

25

"Baby, I can tell that something seemed off with you today, so I've been thinking of how to make it better."

Ruby jerked her head around, staring at Jayden as he continued to drive them to his apartment, not surprised that he was aware that something was bothering her.

"I know I only have a shower and not a big tub for a bubble bath, but maybe I could give you a massage. Something to relax you," he suggested.

"Oh, honey, please don't worry about me." She knew she needed to tell him about Kevin, but the words would not seem to come. *At least not while he's driving. I don't want him angry and behind the wheel. I'll tell him once we get home.* She was sure that he was going to be furious that Kevin had contacted her and terrified that he was going to be upset with her for agreeing to meet with Kevin.

They were almost to Jayden's apartment building, her stomach still clenching with nerves, when she felt her phone vibrate. Looking at the caller ID, she answered it quickly. "Granny, are you okay? Why are you up so late?"

"Oh, Ruby, I'm so sorry to bother you. I'm sure you're spending time with Jayden, but I could have sworn I heard someone on the back porch. The door is locked, but I was afraid to look out the window. Whatever it was, it's gone away. Maybe it was just a raccoon, but it's got me spooked."

"Stay in and stay there," Ruby ordered. "We're on our way!"

"What is it?" Jayden asked, already turning the truck around and heading in the other direction.

"Granny was woken by somebody on the back porch. Or at least she heard something that she thought was somebody on the back porch. She was too afraid to look out."

"She should call 9-1-1."

Ruby replied, "She says whatever was there has gone."

He glanced at the time on the dashboard of his truck and said, "Tell her we'll be there in ten minutes, less if I can push it."

"Granny, stay on the line with me, and we'll be there in less than ten minutes." The time seemed to pass interminably as she and Granny talked. Finally, she said, "We're pulling into the driveway right now." She disconnected the phone, tossed it into her purse, and jumped out of Jayden's truck.

His legs were much longer, and he reached the porch first, with her right behind him as Granny opened the front door. Looking down at the women, he said, "Ruby, go in with her. I'm going around back."

Ruby was halfway through the door when she turned quickly and gasped. "Jayden, please be careful!"

With a nod, he jumped off the porch and headed around the corner of the house. Making sure Granny was inside, Ruby rushed down the hall toward the back door, just off the kitchen. She flipped on all of the back lights, illuminating the yard.

She peeked through the curtain on the door and watched as Jayden walked around, his head down, appearing to search the area. He came up onto the porch, still looking around before he nodded for her to unlock the door.

As he came through, she grabbed his arm with a shaky hand and said, "Did you find anything?"

Shaking his head, he said, "No, but that doesn't mean that someone or something wasn't out there. I don't see anything now."

Granny had come up behind them, clutching her robe around her, her hand resting on the cane. She was getting around so much better and only used it to give her a little stability. She grimaced and said, "I'm so sorry to have interrupted your evening. I must have just dreamed something and then woke up and thought I actually heard a noise. I feel terribly foolish."

Ruby rushed toward her and threw her arms around her, clinging tightly. "Don't you ever feel foolish for giving us a call for *any* reason, real or imagined. If you just had a bad dream and woke up upset, I would want you to call me!"

Jayden walked up behind Ruby, placed his hands on her shoulders, and peered down toward Granny. "Ruby's right. You call her anytime, and if you can't get her, then you call me."

"Well, you two run along and finish your evening. I'm fine, and I'm just going to go back to bed," Granny pronounced.

"Granny, I'm not leaving you."

"Oh, posh, Ruby girl. I'm going back to bed, and now that you two have assured me nothing was out there, I'll be fine."

Ruby shot Jayden a quick glance, and he nodded in understanding. Turning back to Granny, she said, "I was just finished with my shift at Grimm's, and we were on our way home anyway. "

Granny's gaze shifted between the two of them, and she said, "Well, if you're sure." She kissed Ruby's cheek and accepted a hug from Jayden before turning and moving back toward her makeshift bedroom.

Ruby and Jayden walked toward the living room where she quickly whirled around and placed her hands on his arms. Looking up, she whispered, "Did you really find nothing? Did it look like maybe something had been out there and you just didn't want to tell Granny?"

He cupped her cheeks in his hands and leaned forward, kissing her forehead. Offering her assurances, he said, "I didn't see anything, but to be honest I don't know what I might would have found anyway. There are no footprints, but then the grass isn't wet so I wouldn't expect to see footprints on the deck. There were no scratches on the door like someone had been trying to break the lock."

"So, she could have just been dreaming or maybe heard a raccoon trying to get into the garbage can?"

Nodding, he said, "Yeah. Since she's now sleeping downstairs instead of upstairs, she's more likely to hear noises that are directly in the back. And I know when she first came home from rehab, you said that she had some medicine she was taking to help her sleep comfortably."

Eyes wide, she nodded and said "That's right! She's not on that anymore."

"I hate to leave, babe, but I know you want to stay here with Granny."

Ruby leaned forward and rested her cheek on his strong chest. "I'm sorry, honey. I was looking forward to that massage and just having a chance to be with you tonight."

He kissed the top of her head and asked, "Rain check?"

She leaned back, smiling up at him, and nodded. With a final kiss, she walked him to the door, making sure to lock it after he left. Watching from the window as he drove away, she walked to the back and checked on Granny, finding her asleep.

Once upstairs, she quickly got ready for bed, and as she lay there realized that she had not told Jayden about Kevin's call. *Fine...I'll just meet Kevin tomorrow and get it over with. Maybe I won't even need to tell Jayden.* Refusing to give Kevin any more thought, she closed her eyes.

"When does Ruby start working for us full-time?" Tom, one of Jayden's mechanics, asked.

Jayden looked up from the engine he was working on and said, "In another week." Seeing Tom grin, he asked, "Why?"

Tom answered, "Seriously? On the days that she's here, the coffee is a helluva lot better, and she brings in doughnuts."

Cas slapped Jayden on the back as he walked by, chuckling. "Yeah, bro. You gotta admit that your coffee sucked. It's the same old coffee maker so I don't know what she does, but it's a lot better with her."

Shaking his head, Jayden replied, "Just keep in mind that making you guys coffee is not her job. Neither is bringing in doughnuts."

He looked over at Cas and admitted, "But I can't wait until she's here full-time. Right now, she's running herself ragged, doing her last week of house cleanings, working here in the afternoons, and then going in and working evenings a couple nights at Grimm's. I told her to just skip coming in here for another week, but she's only taking this afternoon off."

"I wondered where she was today."

"Yesterday was kind of rough on her, and then last night her grandmother called, afraid that she may have heard something behind her house. I went over and checked but didn't find anything. Once I was sure they were locked up tight I left, but Ruby probably didn't get a lot of sleep."

As the men went back to work on their vehicles, Jayden moved into the office to finish the payroll. As he sat at his desk, his mind was filled with how Ruby would be there, full-time, starting next week. At that thought, he grinned, anxious to get see her that evening.

26

Guilt was eating away at Ruby as she sat in the coffee shop across town. She had not wanted to take a chance that anyone she knew might see her having coffee with Kevin, so she chose a location that was not familiar.

She thought back to the last time that she had been with Kevin, the day she broke up with him. Granny had only been out of rehab for a week, but he could not stand that she was spending all of her time and attention on her grandmother. Finally gaining the courage to break up, they had argued. As usual with Kevin, the argument turned physical before he stormed out, his words cruel.

Blowing out a shaky breath, she wondered why she had ever agreed to this meeting. *What was I thinking? I shouldn't be doing this, and I certainly shouldn't have kept it from Jayden.* With renewed determination, she stood and walked to the door while pulling out her phone to send Kevin a message saying that she was having to cancel.

Before she could hit send, the door opened right in front of her, and there he was. She blinked, staring up at Kevin, stunned at the change in his appearance.

In his younger years, Kevin had been tall and thin, making him an easy target of bullies. As he matured, he bulked out, building muscle, loving the way that women would finally look at him. His appearance was important to him once he discovered the lure of a random hookup. His hair was styled. His clothes clean and somewhat trendy. As he always searched for the next money-making scheme, he wanted to look the part. Ruby could never figure out what part he was trying to look like, but it seemed important to Kevin.

As life did not hand him the breaks he thought he deserved, he began to drink heavily. She never saw him use anything other than alcohol but had her suspicions. Of course, by that time, he had become manipulative, keeping her always on edge.

By the time she finally became brave enough to break up with him, he had gained a beer paunch, his hair was longer and unkempt, and his clothes disheveled.

The Kevin standing in front of her right now did not look like any of the Kevins she had ever known. His body was thinner, but it was difficult to tell underneath the large jacket. His hair was now to his shoulders, but instead of being thick, clean, and sexy like Jayden's, it hung about his shoulders in thin strands. What was most surprising to her was the beard that covered his face and neck as though he had not shaved since the last time she had seen him.

"Kevin?" she said, unable to keep the incredulity out of her voice.

He smiled and gave a quick nod. "Ruby, you look good."

Her mouth opened to politely repeat the line to him but simply stammered instead. "You look…uh…well…uh…different…"

His hand came up to scratch his jaw and he said, "Yeah, thought I'd try growing a beard." He chuckled nervously and glanced behind her at a table. "You have coffee yet?"

Shaking her head, she said, "No. I was just…uh…I don't have much time."

"Well, let's have a cup before you have to go," he said, motioning toward the table to their side.

Not able to think of an excuse, she tried to smile but knew her lips were forming a grimace instead. Turning quickly, she moved to the chair as he ordered two coffees. Sliding into the seat opposite him, she felt his perusal but kept her eyes on her hands resting on the table.

The uncomfortable silence surrounded them, and Ruby searched her mind for something innocuous to talk about but came up blank. Grateful when the server set the cup of coffee in front of them, she busied her hands pouring in the cream and sweetener.

"My Ruby always liked her coffee sweet," Kevin said.

Her gaze jerked up to his, seeing him staring intently at her. Quietly, she replied, "Kevin, I don't want to sound mean, but I'm not your Ruby."

Something flashed through his eyes, but she was

271

unable to identify whatever emotion he was feeling. Unease slid through her, and as she brought her coffee cup to her lip, she noted her hands shook slightly. *This is such a bad idea...such a bad idea!* The coffee scalded her tongue, but she forced down a sip, determined to hurry through as quickly as she could.

She watched as he stirred his coffee, his hands shaking slightly, also. "You said you wanted to see me, Kevin. I really don't have long this morning, so perhaps you could say whatever it is you feel like you need to say."

"You always were a busy girl, Ruby," he said.

She was unable to determine by his tone of voice if that was a compliment or criticism, so she remained silent.

"We were good friends once," he continued. "I always thought we'd just stay together. I could've taken care of you, you know, so you wouldn't have to clean houses anymore or work as a waitress. If you could've just given me enough time, I would've hit it big, and we would've lived large."

Still uncertain what response he expected, she did not reply but busied herself taking another sip of coffee. It did not seem to matter to him if she spoke or not, as he continued.

"I was telling you the truth the other day when I said I wanted to say I was sorry. I know sometimes I could get a little rough, but I would never hurt you. You were just always so busy that I never felt like you were giving me enough attention, I suppose."

Ruby felt anger slowly coursing through her but

tried to tamp it down. *This is not the time or place.* Clearing her throat, she forced her words to steady as she said, "I was busy *working*. I was earning money so that Granny and I could live, Kevin. You know what the bills were like after Mama got sick. I had to be responsible. I had to work jobs that I didn't care for so that food could be on the table. We were not your responsibility, so I never expected you to help out. But I had no choice other than to do what I did. I had no choice but to work as hard and long as I did. And considering that you moved into the house while Granny was in rehab but did not pay any of the bills, it would've been nice to have had your understanding."

With his hair hanging down toward his eyes and his scraggly beard, it was hard for her to discern his facial expression, but she could tell by the way he huffed he did not like what she was saying.

"Yeah, good ol' Ruby was always the one thinking she did everything."

She pushed her cup away and added, "Kevin, this is old business. We had a friendship once and tried to make it more. That was a mistake. I've moved on and I'm happy with what I'm doing and where I am right now. I wish the same for you."

She placed her palms on the table and pushed her chair backward, grabbing her purse and jacket as she stood.

He jumped up as well and said, "Wait, Ruby. I'm sorry. I didn't mean to upset you."

He shoved his hands in his pockets and looked down. For a moment she could see the uncertain, beaten-down teenager that she had befriended many years ago.

Sighing softly, she gentled her voice and asked, "Then what did you want, Kevin?"

He lifted his gaze to her, and once again the specter of something undefinable passed through his eyes.

"I really did just want to say I was sorry for how we ended," he said. "I also wanted to see how Granny was doing...I know she's gettin' up in years, and you never know when something will happen to her. I just don't want you to be all alone. It would be important at that time for you to have a friend who had known you for a long time."

Startling, she blinked, uncertain what he was saying. "Granny is doing just fine and should have many years of good life in her, so you don't need to be concerned about that. And I appreciate your apology. It does make our parting easier."

They had walked out of the coffee shop and were now standing on the sidewalk. He stepped closer and said, "Do you think there's a chance for us again?"

The coffee in her stomach soured, and she shook her head. "Again, I'm not trying to hurt you, but I'm seeing someone." She watched as his body seemed to tighten in response, and she took a step back.

"Yeah, I've seen you with him. Big man on a motor-cycle," he growled.

"Have you been spying on me?" She instinctively took another step back, but his hand snapped out and grabbed her forearm, squeezing to hold her in place.

She jerked on her arm, but all that did was cause pain, considering his hold was tight.

Filled with fury, she warned, "Let me go or I'll start screaming right here on the street."

"I wasn't spying, I promise. I was just driving by one night, that's all." He squeezed her arm again, his eyes wide and filled with something that looked like desperation. "I need some money, Ruby," he groaned, giving her arm a shake. "I owe some people. Please, you gotta help me."

Her struggle stopped as his words hit her. *Of course. This had nothing to do with an apology. Nothing to do with him changing, me leaving, him seeing the error of his ways. He needs money.*

His anger had fled, and standing in front of her was a desperate man who was begging. Stomach still clenching, she sucked in a ragged breath and let it out slowly. Thinking about the tips that were still in her purse, she said, "This is it, Kevin. I can give you a little cash today for old time's sake. But this is it. No more. I don't want you to call me again, or text me again, or try to see me again."

His head nodded in a jerky motion as he agreed. "Yeah, yeah. I promise, Ruby. I'll leave you alone after this."

Her hands still shaking, she reached inside her purse and pulled out a wad of rolled up bills. "There's over three hundred dollars here. That's it. That's all you'll ever get from me again."

He took the money she was holding out to him and said, "Thank you, Ruby. You won't regret this."

He looked as though he was going to say something else, but clamped his mouth shut and headed down the street around the corner. Still shaking, she thought, *I already do regret it.*

A chill ran through her, even though the day was warm. She pulled on her red hoodie, zipping the front up to her neck, reveling in the comfort of her favorite item of clothing. Sighing deeply, she headed home to spend a few hours with Granny before going into Grimm's. Once Zander's other server came back from maternity leave, she could work full-time for Jayden. Deciding to focus on that instead of her disastrous meeting with Kevin, she hurried to her car.

27

Jayden looked up, mesmerized by Ruby's blue eyes holding him captive. He had gotten the message from Zander's bouncer that she was safely in her car and on her way to his place. Standing outside, he met her as soon as she drove up.

Greeting her with a kiss, he had said, "So glad you're almost finished at Grimm's and done with the houses."

She had thrown her arms around his shoulders, staring up at him with a smile on her face. "And then I'm yours."

He knew she was talking about working for him, but the words leaving her lips hit straight to his heart. "Yes. And then you're mine." He hoped she took the full meaning of his words, and they were not just about working at the garage.

They walked into his apartment, and he nudged her toward the shower, knowing she wanted to wash the scent of the bar off her. "Go on, baby. I'll lock up and meet you in bed."

Now, thirty minutes later, with only the moonlight shining through the window, she slipped off her robe, and he worshiped her body.

She was so tiny compared to him, he was always afraid of hurting her, but she accepted him with enthusiasm. He had been sitting in bed when she came out of the bathroom, a dark red robe tied about her waist. Flipping off the lights, she had bathed the room in moonlight before sliding the robe off and crawling on top of him.

She straddled his hips as he reached up and palmed her breasts, tweaking the nipples. Her head fell back, her long hair hanging down to her waist and the delicate line of her pale neck beckoning.

After rolling on a condom, she shifted so that his cock was at her entrance, and slowly settled, sheathing him in her tight body. She leaned forward, her fingers digging into his shoulders, and he watched her exquisite face as her lips curved.

Her beauty undid him, and he held his body still as though to savor the moment just a little longer. Her eyes opened and she smiled as she moved up and down on his shaft. Her body was ready, and the friction created with her movements cast all thoughts from his mind, other than giving her pleasure.

As she began to tire, he moved his hands to her hips and lifted her slightly. Feeling he had the strength of a Titan, he pistoned his hips, continuing the friction they both craved. It did not take long; it never did with his Ruby, for her to tighten her grip, squeeze her eyes closed, and cry out her pleasure.

As she fell forward onto his chest, he barely felt her weight, as slight as it was. Still firmly planted inside her, he rolled, pressing her body down into the mattress. With his weight held off her chest, keeping his forearms planted on the bed next to her shoulders, he clasped her hands into his. He continued to thrust but was determined to savor every feeling. He slowly pressed in and out until she was squirming underneath him.

Her eyes opened once more, and with the moonlight capturing her face, he could see the shadowed blue. Wide and expressive. Without thinking, the words slipped from his lips, "I love you, Ruby."

She sucked in a quick breath, but he could not hold back his feelings and felt no regret in having said the words.

He watched, fascinated, as moisture pooled in her eyes, and as she blinked, two tears slid out, both trailing toward her ears. With his thumbs, he wiped them away before leaning down and kissing each salty trail. "Don't cry, baby."

Her words, starting as a mere croak, then becoming stronger, said, "They're tears of joy. I never thought I'd be lucky enough to have someone like you in my life."

"It wasn't luck. It was destiny. The moment I saw you in your red hoodie, struggling with that lawn-mower, I felt something. I was a pussy for walking away that day, but fate granted me a second chance with you."

Two more tears slid from her eyes as she said, "I love you, too. With everything I have and everything I have to give."

He closed the distance to her lips, his mouth sealing

over hers in a kiss that also sealed their love. He began to thrust once more, this time his tongue matching the actions of his cock. He felt her inner muscles begin to squeeze, and her fingers, still linked with his, tightened.

As though to reach the very heart of her, he plunged deeper, hitting that place that sent her soaring. "Look at me, babe," he bit out, wanting to see into her eyes as they came together.

Biting her lip, she kept her gaze on him, and he watched as her second orgasm moved through her. He followed immediately after, also forcing his eyes to stay on her as his body tensed, every muscle screaming out.

His arms shook as he continued to hold himself off her chest, his orgasm depleting his strength as his heart raced.

Letting go of her fingers, he rolled so that they were facing each other, his now softening cock still in her body, their legs tangled, chests pressed together. They lay for several minutes, not speaking, their hearts pounding, breathing ragged. Slowly they recovered, their eyes still pinned on each other, smiles etched onto their faces.

"Did you mean it?" she whispered.

He knew what she was referring to and wanted to assure her that his vows of love were not wrung from him in a moment of sexual ecstasy. "Oh, yeah, I meant it. I love you with everything my heart, body, and soul can possibly give."

Even in the moonlight, he could see the blush that moved over her face as her smile widened and her eyes lit from deep inside. "I love you, too," she whispered, and their lips sealed once more.

He left the bed only to deal with the condom, then slipped back in, pulling her close. She was exhausted, and as he tucked her back tightly to his front, wrapping his arms around her, he said, "Sleep tight." It appeared she had already fallen into slumber, and he followed soon after.

Moonlight had given way to sunlight, and Jayden woke to the feel of Ruby still in his arms. She usually left after they made love to go back to Granny's house. But last night, she smiled as she said Granny did not want her driving in the middle of the night and that since she was perfectly capable of being in the house by herself now, she wanted Ruby to stay.

As exhausted as she had been, he was thrilled that she was able to sleep a little later. He had already told Cas that he would not be in early today and to go ahead and open up the shop. As far as he was concerned, this morning was for him and Ruby.

So, reveling in the fact that he woke up with Ruby in his arms, Jayden propped his head on his hand with his elbow bent into the pillow and stared at her. She spent very little time in the sun, and so her skin was pale and clear. Her hair glistened in the light coming through the window.

Her thick lashes, light brown in color, lay against her cheeks in crescents. Shifting over slightly so that he could see more of her face as she lay on her side with her hands tucked near her head, his gaze landed on her arm.

Not understanding what he was viewing, he wondered if the sunlight coming through the blinds was casting a shadow. He moved his body more so that he was partially sitting up, gaining a better view.

Her arm was not shadowed but bruised. A large, dark, angry bruise. And the distinct image of finger-prints. No longer worried about waking her, he shifted her to her back so that he could see both arms. Her right arm was not bruised, but the left arm, now completely visible, gave no doubt that someone had grabbed her and held her tightly.

What the hell?

Her eyes immediately jerked open, blue eyes staring up at him, a crinkle between her brows. "Hmmm?" she murmured sleepily.

Realizing he cursed aloud, he continued, "I want to know what the hell happened to you. Where did you get those bruises?"

He watched as she immediately blinked, then her eyes flew open wide as they glanced down to her arm. "What are you not telling me, Ruby? There's no way you could have gotten bruises like that and not know it."

She swallowed deeply, mumbling, "Uh..."

His jaw ticked, his body rigid with anger. He swung his legs around to the side of the bed, reaching for his phone.

She jumped to her knees, her hands reaching out to

his shoulders. "Jayden, what are you doing? Who are you calling?"

"Zander," he bit out.

She continued to crawl across the bed, sliding her body around so that she could look into his face. "Zander? Why would you call him?"

His finger halted over the phone, seeing her look of utter confusion. "That's where you got hurt, isn't it? Last night at Grimm's? Because it sure as hell wasn't there yesterday morning, and I can distinctly see the bruise pattern of fingers on your arm."

"Jayden, please put the phone down. This has nothing to do with Zander."

His body strung tight, her words barely penetrated. "And I'm telling you that if somebody manhandled you at Grimm's last night, then Zander wants to know. And I sure as hell want to know why he, nor the bouncers, took care of you."

Her fingers wrapped around the phone in his hand and she gave a slight tug, pulling it away. He opened his mouth, ready for a warning, when she said, "It wasn't there. This has nothing to do with Grimm's. Nothing to do with Zander, at all. This is all on me."

He watched as she leaned across him to place his phone back on the nightstand before turning back to him. His eyes locked back onto her arm, the bruises standing out in stark relief on her pale skin. Whatever happened, she was terrified, but he had to make sure she was not terrified of him.

Sucking in a raspy breath as though it were hard to draw air into his lungs, he tried counting to ten but only made it to seven. Forcing his voice to be steady, he said, "Baby, I'm trying to hang on here, but you gotta help me. Somebody hurt you. Somebody put their hands on you, and you didn't tell me. You gotta know that is not okay. I'm not happy about you keeping this a secret, but you don't ever have to fear anything from me. But I'm not giving you a choice here, Ruby. I need to know what happened, and I need to know now."

Swallowing deeply, she nodded. She shifted away from him, saying, "Please, let me get dressed. I'd...I'd feel better if I could do this dressed."

He did not want her to move but accepted that this concession was important to her. They both stood from the bed, and he jerked on his boxers and sweatpants, keeping an eye on her as she pulled on her panties, a bra, yoga pants, and her red, zip-up hoodie.

"Can we go into the kitchen?" she asked. He started to protest, but she quickly explained, "My mom used to always say that she and Dad kept anger out of the bedroom."

He thought about those words and how smart and caring her parents were. It sounded like a good plan, so he agreed. They walked into the kitchen, and she turned on the coffee pot. He wanted to rail at her for stalling but forced himself to wait until she felt like she could speak.

She carried their fixed coffee cups to the table and sat down. He followed and sat down close to her.

Her hands clasped together on top of the table near her cup, and she swallowed deeply. Lifting her gaze to his, she said, "Kevin. It was Kevin."

Jumping to his feet, he was surprised he had not knocked the coffee over. He felt as though his head would explode, but she flew out of her chair and placed her hands on his arms, instantly offering a slight balm.

"Jayden, you have to listen to me. You have to let me explain, please?"

Fury coursed through his veins, but as he stared at the woman he loved, her gentle touch on his forearms, her blue eyes pleading, there was nothing he would not do for her. Nodding slowly, he said, "Babe, you don't have to beg me to listen to you. You know I'm already angry, but that's got nothing to do with you. I'm angry at him. So you tell me whatever you need to tell me, and then I'm going to decide what I need to do about it."

Her eyes widened at his last statement, and she opened her mouth to speak, but he jumped in, shaking his head. "No, Ruby. This I will not yield on."

She stood, her fingers clutching his arms, staring up at him for a long moment. Finally, resignation showed on her face, and she nodded. She let go of his arms and turned, sitting back down at the table. Taking a sip of coffee, as though to gather her thoughts, she looked over as he settled back down into his seat.

"He's been texting…not a lot, but some. I've ignored them, until the other day when he said that he wanted to see me to apologize. I started thinking about it, and I thought maybe I should do that."

Jayden wanted to roar at her in frustration but could see the struggle was real for her, so he remained quiet.

"You have to understand, Jayden. Kevin and I have a long history—"

"Yes, one that includes him being abusive," he bit out, immediately hating the expression of pain on her face. Sighing heavily, he said, "I'm sorry. Please, continue."

Lifting her chin slightly, her eyes flashing, she said, "I don't owe you this explanation. If you want to hear my side of the story, then I'll continue, but if you're going to argue at every point, then we can stop right now."

"No, no, baby. I'm sorry. I'm just so upset that he hurt you." He sighed again and said, "I promise I'll listen now. Just listen."

Ruby dreaded telling Jayden about her visit with Kevin, but she knew he was truly concerned about her. She just hoped that she could explain the situation in a way that would make him not want to do anything rash where Kevin was concerned. *I'd just like to forget the whole thing.*

Taking another fortifying sip of coffee, she looked up, seeing his intense gaze staring at her. The tic in his jaw gave evidence that he was barely hanging on. She also could tell that his patience was waning, so she began.

"I've told you that he and I were just friends for many years, from high school on. I knew he was bullied at home, and I always felt sorry for him. He was nice to me for many years." She drew her thin shoulders up in a shrug and added, "There were good times, and I guess I just always made excuses for him. I can see that now. Whatever the reason, it doesn't really matter, because as you know, it all ended in ugliness. I no longer wanted his negativity or abuse. But when I got a message saying that he wanted to see me to apologize, I started thinking about the good times. The times he would listen when Mama was sick and then after she died."

Holding his gaze, she said, "I just thought if he was to the point to where he wanted to apologize, then I should allow him to. I wasn't acting foolishly or impulsively. I truly thought that it was the best thing to do... meet him, allow him to apologize, and then have closure with the whole relationship."

She waited, warily studying Jayden's face. So far, no change. He was not ranting, but then neither did he look pacified. Tucking her hair behind her ear, she said, "I gave him a call, and we chatted for just a moment. He begged me to meet him for coffee to apologize in person, and I agreed. We met yesterday morning at a coffee shop, and I'll admit that by the time he showed up, I was already heading out the door to leave. It no longer felt like the right thing to do, and I hated that I had not told you. I was going to the other night, then all the excitement with Granny happened, and it flew out of my mind."

"That's why you were out of sorts the other day," he said, his voice low.

Nodding, she agreed, "It was bothering me, but I wasn't sure what to do about it. I couldn't deal with it at work or at Grimm's, so I was going to tell you when we came home that night. I decided to just get it over with yesterday morning but hated that I had not had a chance to talk about it with you."

"I appreciate that," he admitted, the tic in his jaw still evident. "I don't want you to feel like there are things you can't talk to me about. If you're upset, or bothered, or just having a bad day, I'd like you to be able to tell me."

Leaning forward, she placed her hand on his arm and said, "I feel the same way, Jayden. I was just waiting for the right time, and then…well, that's why I started to leave before he got to the coffee shop."

His voice still gravelly, he said, "Okay. So, let's get to what happened at the coffee shop and how he went from meeting to apologize to giving you those bruises."

She felt tears prick the back of her eyes, hating that Kevin still had managed to take control over a situation. Blinking, she willed the tears to not fall, knowing it would make Jayden even angrier. "At first it was fine. We chatted, but it was awkward. I finally had to stand and tell him that I needed to leave. It was only as we walked outside that I finally got an apology from him. When he asked if there was a chance again, I told him that I was seeing someone."

Thinking back to what he said, her brow furrowed, and she felt Jayden tense. "He said that he had seen me with you—"

Jayden roared, "What the fuck?"

Rushing to calm him, she said, "I asked him if he had been spying on me, but he said that he had driven past Granny's house one time and seen us. It could have been one of the many times that you and I were standing on her porch."

"Baby—"

"Jayden, stop. This is hard enough without you blowing up every moment." She watched as he almost swallowed a growl, then waited as he brought himself under control again.

"I turned to leave, and that's when he grabbed my arm. He said he needed money." She watched as Jayden opened his mouth, then snapped it shut quickly. The way he was clenching his jaw, she was surprised that his teeth were not cracking under the pressure.

"His grasp was uncomfortable, but I'm the one who probably made myself bruise when I kept trying to jerk my arm away." As soon as those words left her mouth, she shook her head and amended, "That didn't come out right. I don't mean that I'm the one who was responsible for the bruises. It was all on him."

"You were out on the street at this time, and no one came to your aid?" he asked, incredulity resounding in each word.

"It happened so quickly," she replied. She dropped her gaze, unable to hide the shudder that moved through her body.

He jumped up from his seat but this time to scoop her up into his arms. She clung to his neck, as he abandoned the kitchen and moved them into the living room. Sitting on the sofa with her in his lap, he kept his arms wrapped around her.

They sat silent for another moment, this time her mind filled with the difference between Jayden and Kevin. It was true, Jayden could become angry, but it was never directed at her, and she never feared that. Instead, he used his body to shelter hers, enveloping her in a cocoon of warmth and security.

He murmured into her hair, "Is that it, baby?"

She hesitated, considering if she should say more. He appeared calm, and she liked that, wanting to keep that mood. *But this whole situation was made worse because I did not confide in Jayden to begin with.* Knowing what she needed to do, she shook her head. She waited to feel his body tense again, but instead, he kissed her hair.

Murmuring, he encouraged, "Please, baby. Tell me everything."

"I gave in. I gave him some money. All the tip money that I had in my purse. Probably about three hundred dollars."

Jayden heaved a sigh, his warm breath puffing against her forehead. Once more, silence ensued, and she slowly began to relax in his arms, the weight of carrying the secret now released.

Jayden held Ruby for a long time, finally feeling her body relax. Rage still coursed through his veins, but he did not want to do anything to frighten her. Shifting her slightly, he realized that she had fallen asleep cradled in his arms.

Standing, he carried her into the bedroom and tucked her back under the covers. As upset as she had been, he was not surprised that she had fallen back into a deep sleep. *I hate how I woke her up this morning roaring about the bruises.* He also knew that worry and stress had worn her out.

He moved back into the kitchen and grabbed a pad of paper and pen, writing a note that she was not to worry, but that she must understand she was his to take care of and his to protect. He walked quietly back into the bedroom and laid it on his pillow. He grabbed his clothes and moved into the bathroom, gently shutting the door. Once fully dressed, he walked back to the bedroom, stopping to stare at her once more.

The sun was now streaming through the window, illuminating her pale, porcelain complexion, and her hair spilling over his pillow.

Turning, he walked out of the room and carefully shut and locked his front door, determination etched on his face. As he walked to his truck, he pulled out his phone and called Jaxon.

Miss Ethel walked back into the living room, and Ruby jumped up to assist her with the tray, setting it on the coffee table. Pouring two cups of tea, she handed one to Miss Ethel, who had settled into a wingback chair near the fireplace. The material was slightly worn, and it was not hard for Ruby to imagine Miss Ethel sitting in the exact same seat many years ago when Jayden was a young boy.

Taking a sip of the brew, she found that her mind was much calmer in Miss Ethel's presence. Normally when upset, she would have gone to Granny, but in this case, she knew that Miss Ethel was the only one who could help her.

With grey eyes peering at her through wire-rimmed glasses, Miss Ethel set her teacup to the side and picked up her knitting needles. The clicking of the needles filled the background as she said, "Now, child. Tell me what sent you hurrying over here so early this morning."

Ruby had woken to an empty apartment, Jayden's whereabouts unknown other than the note he left for her. While he had told her not to worry, her stomach had clenched at the thought of him going after Kevin. She had no idea where to look for him and did not want to involve any of his friends, so she had hurried into her car and driven to Miss Ethel's.

Taking another sip of the hot tea, she spilled her entire story, starting with her initial friendship with Kevin many years ago, to the first time she met Jayden and begged him to leave, afraid of Kevin's reaction. She continued her story, finishing with the morning's tale of how she had told Jayden of her meeting with Kevin, the bruises on her arm, and the money she had given him. "I don't know where he went, but I'm sure he's gone after Kevin. I'm so scared for Jayden. I don't know what he'll do."

Throughout all of that, Miss Ethel remained quiet, nodding occasionally, her needles continuing to click comfortingly.

Finally, exhausting her story, she sat, perched on the edge of the sofa cushion, wondering what Miss Ethel would say. She did not have to wait long.

"I know that Jayden has told you his story, or I would never presume to tell it for him," Miss Ethel said. A smile curved her lips, and she continued, "I remember introducing Jayden and Jaxon to the other boys the day that they showed up on my doorstep. I had Zander and Rafe at that time, and they were so surprised that Jayden and Jaxon looked alike. I explained to them what twins were, and I believe they were fascinated."

Miss Ethel sighed and said, "Jayden and Jaxon were so used to staying with different people. They really don't remember their mother or grandmother, their aunt being the only person who had taken care of them once they were old enough to have memories. Sometimes their aunt would leave them with friends, and so they were quite uncertain about staying here. I remember the first night, I told Jayden that his name meant *thankful*, and I was so thankful to have them come live with me."

Her heart ached thinking of Jayden as a child, abandoned. *He must've been so scared. Thank God he landed here and had Jaxon with him.* As soon as that thought crossed her mind, she blurted, "Jaxon. That's where he would've gone...or at least who he would've called."

Nodding, Miss Ethel agreed. "I can assure you that wherever he is and whatever he's doing, Jayden is not alone. I have no doubt that Jaxon is with him."

"That does make me feel better," she admitted, "but I still wish he wasn't out looking for Kevin, determined to make him pay for bruising me."

The needles continued to click, and Miss Ethel said, "I had to spend time learning about each of my boys, being very certain to understand that Jaxon and Jayden, while twins, were two individuals. Jaxon, often laughing and joking, was searching. I sometimes wondered if he was not searching for the stability he didn't have during his very early years. Jayden, on the other hand, always seemed to be protecting. I also wondered if perhaps he was not thinking that if someone had been there to protect their mother she might not have ever turned to drugs."

Shrugging, Miss Ethel said, "Obviously there's no way of knowing, but that was just my thought at the time. Point being, Jayden was, and is, a protector."

The room was once more filled with silence other than the clicking of knitting needles. Ruby watched as the yarn turned into a larger piece, held together by the intricacies of the needles' movements. When she had arrived, her mind had been in turmoil, but sitting with Miss Ethel, her body began to relax.

"Do you want to know one of Jayden's favorite stories was when he was young?"

Miss Ethel's question caught her off guard, but eager to learn anything she could about him, she nodded enthusiastically. "Oh, yes, please."

She noticed Miss Ethel's gaze scanned her but did not understand the smile curving the older woman's lips.

"Of all the stories that we read when they were growing up, Jayden loved the Grimm's version of Little Red Riding Hood. He became distraught when Zander would read from an abridged version of the older tales, where the little girl and her grandmother were eaten by the wolf."

Her brow furrowed, Ruby tilted her head, questioning, "The woodsman comes. He chops open the wolf so that they can be rescued."

Chuckling, Miss Ethel said, "Not in the original version. That version came later and was Jayden's favorite." Nodding toward Ruby, she said, "The first thing I noticed when you arrived was the red hoodie jacket that you're wearing right now. I doubt very seriously if he made the connection, but I couldn't help but notice what you're wearing today."

Looking down, a giggle slipped from her lips. "When he rescued me from the side of the road, he said he recognized the red hoodie from the first time he saw me."

The clicking stopped, and Ruby looked up in surprise, observing Miss Ethel folding her knitting carefully into the open bag at her feet before taking her teacup once again. After a few sips, Miss Ethel set it back onto the coffee table and peered at Ruby.

"My dear, do you understand what I've told you about Jayden?"

Blinking, her mind raced through all that Miss Ethel had told her. "Well, you've explained that he's a protector. And I suppose I shouldn't be surprised that he wants to protect me."

"One of my favorite poets was Ella Wheeler Wilcox. You might have heard one of her lines, *'Laugh, and the world laughs with you; weep, and you weep alone.'*?" As Ruby nodded her remembrance, Miss Ethel continued. "There's another quote that I remember of hers that I think defines Jayden very well. *'To sin by silence, when they should protest, makes cowards of men.'* Do you understand?"

Nodding slowly, Ruby carefully considered Miss

Ethel's words. "Jayden should be angry at Kevin. And he should want to protest what happened to me." Tears pricked her eyes as she continued, "But, Miss Ethel, doesn't that make me a coward? After all, I ended up giving Kevin some money instead of protesting what he was doing."

"You are not a coward," Miss Ethel defended. "You are willing to forgive Kevin for his past transgressions. *'Forgiveness is the fragrance that the violet sheds on the heel that has crushed it.'*"

"I know that," Ruby said, her smile wide. "I remember that from high school… It's from Mark Twain."

"Yes, indeed. You are the one who had been crushed, and you are the only one who could offer forgiveness for that, and you were willing to do so. But since that was not accepted, then it is Jayden who will protest on your behalf."

Miss Ethel stood and picked up the tea tray, but Ruby jumped up to assist. The two women carried it back to the kitchen, where Ruby washed out the teacups as Miss Ethel put them away. Leaning her hip against the counter, she said, "All of this makes me feel better. I'm sure now that wherever Jayden is, he has Jaxon with him. And I also understand that whatever he's doing, he needs to do." She glanced down at her hands, biting her lip, before adding, "But I'm scared for him."

"You will always be scared for those you love, but I have no doubt, my dear, that he will return safely to you."

Suddenly filled with the desire to be back at his

apartment so that when he came home she would be there waiting for him, she threw her arms around Miss Ethel. Hugging the woman tightly, she said, "Thank you. For everything."

Miss Ethel returned her hug, kissing her cheek before letting her go. Ruby rushed down the hall, grabbed her purse, and headed out the front door, calling, "I'll let you know how it all turns out."

Following much slower, Miss Ethel walked to the front window and watched as Ruby rushed to her car and drove down the road. Smiling to herself, she turned and allowed her gaze to move about the room, memories flooding her mind. The sights and sounds of many years, with many boys, watching them turn into men.

Never allowing melancholy to take hold, she straightened her spine and walked toward the back door, determined to spend some time in her garden. Stepping onto her back patio, her gardening gloves and shears in her hand, she lifted her face, allowing the sunlight to envelop her. As the warmth soothed her rheumatism, she smiled once again. *Thank you, God, for all the blessings You have bestowed upon me. As always, keep my boys safe in Your arms.*

29

Jayden's anger had not ebbed, but he knew with Jaxon at his side he would be able to maintain control. *The last thing Ruby needs is for me to end up in jail for killing the asshole who put his hands on her.*

He parked the truck in front of an old, brick apartment building that had seen better days. A few sprouts of grass grew tall around the base. The gutters were rusty as well as the metal railings along the stairwells. It was the type of apartment building that had a long, covered sidewalk in front of each of the doors, the apartments opening directly to the outside.

"Jesus, please tell me Ruby never lived here," Jaxon muttered, leaning forward, looking up at the building through the windshield.

Shaking his head, Jayden replied, "No, thank God. She continued to live with her grandmother even when they were dating." He climbed from the truck and began stalking toward the stairs, closely followed by Jaxon.

Hearing the roar of a motorcycle in the distance, he

turned, wondering what new trouble was on its way. At the sight approaching, he shifted his gaze back to his twin. "You thought I couldn't handle it?"

Shaking his head, Jaxon replied, "I called Asher to let him know."

Asher parked next to Jayden's truck and swung his leg over the seat. With his helmet still in his hand, he moved over to the twins. Not speaking, he offered a nod, and Jayden knew that was Asher's way of saying he was with them.

Once on the third level, they made their way to apartment 302, and he lifted his fist, pounding on the door. There was no answer. He pounded again as Jaxon walked to the window, and with his hands cupped around his face, peered inside through the slit in the curtain.

"Don't see any movement inside," Jaxon reported.

The door to apartment 301 opened, and a woman stepped out, wrapping a thin robe around herself. A cigarette hung from her lips, and she glared at them. Snatching the cigarette from her mouth, she blew out the smoke, growling, "What the fuck are you doing here? Making all kinds of noise this early in the morning? Decent folks are still in bed!"

"I need to speak to the occupant of this apartment," he replied.

At his statement, she cackled, then her body was racked with coughing. Finally catching her breath, she said, "Occupant. Fancy word for someone who just crashes here sometimes."

"Ma'am, do you know where he is?" Jayden continued.

The woman took another long drag on her cigarette, and behind her, an equally skinny man walked out. Wearing sweatpants that looked like they could barely hang onto his hipbones and a wife beater T-shirt that had seen better days, he scratched his ruffled hair and said, "What's all the ruckus about?"

Without looking behind her, the woman replied, "These men are looking for Wolfe."

"He ain't there," the man said, now appearing as disgruntled as the woman for having been awoken that morning.

Before Jayden was able to ask any more questions, another man came charging up the stairs. Short, balding, with a beer gut, this man stomped straight over to them and said, "You got a good reason for being here? I'm the manager here, and if you ain't gone in a hot minute, I'm calling the cops!"

Repeating himself, Jayden replied, "I'm looking for Kevin Wolfe. I was told he lives here." Leaning toward the man, he held his gaze, watching as the manager swallowed and took a step back. "I'm not leaving until I've spoken to him."

"I told you he ain't there," the skinny man from apartment 301 repeated.

At that, the office manager swung his head around and stared. "What do you mean he ain't there?"

"Yesterday. He came rushing in, and I heard a bunch of noise next door. Little bit later I was out here having a smoke when I saw him come out. He had two suitcases that were packed so full he could barely carry them. He took them down to his old car, managed to heave them into the trunk, and he took outta here. Never heard him come back."

The manager sputtered and shouted, "He owes me two weeks rent! Are you telling me he left here? Why the hell didn't you tell me?"

The woman tossed her cigarette butt, grinding it on the concrete underneath her slippered foot. She coughed several more times, then rasped, "Ain't our business to keep up with the comings and goings in this place. I was just telling the loud man banging on the door there's decent folks here tryin' to sleep."

Jayden glanced around, seeing several of the people coming out of their apartment doors, obviously checking to see what the commotion was all about. Raising his voice, he shouted, "Anybody see Kevin Wolfe yesterday evening or sometime in the night?" All he received were head shakes.

Jaxon added, "Anybody know anything about him? Where he might be or where he might go?"

The man from apartment 304 chuckled and said, "If he's smart, he'd get out of town."

Jayden pinned him with a hard stare, and the man swallowed heavily, suddenly looking as though he wanted to be anywhere but where he was. "Why is that?"

The man shrugged his beefy shoulders before mumbling, "The man was always talking about big deals. I seen some of the people coming and going from his place and figure the deals he was making wasn't exactly legal, if you get what I mean." Before Jayden had a chance to ask, the man rushed to add, "And don't go asking me about those deals. I keep my nose outta other people's business, and I don't know nothing."

The man gave a curt nod and stepped back into his apartment, firmly shutting his door. A few other people followed suit, leaving Jayden with the manager and the neighbors. Looking down at the manager, he said, "Will you unlock the door, let me take a look around?"

Blustering, the manager worked his mouth as though ready to refuse. Finally, still muttering, he said, "I might as well see what's missing." Pulling a huge ring of keys from his pocket, he unlocked the door, and they moved inside.

Immediately struck by the overwhelming smell of marijuana, Jayden's eyes were still adjusting to the dark when the manager flipped on the lights and began cursing about the state of the apartment.

An ancient sofa sat in the living room, stained and worn. The carpet had cigarette burn holes in it and stains that Jayden did not want to know where they came from. Behind him, both Jaxon and Asher said in unison, "What the hell?"

The manager came from the back, his face red, still cursing. "Goddamn bastard ruined the carpet and the furniture, broke the vanity in the bathroom..." He swung his eyes toward the kitchen, seeing the microwave door hanging at an awkward angle and cursed anew.

Asher had walked into the bedroom and returned,

reporting, "Nothing there. Clothes gone, everything cleaned out."

"Told ya," the skinny man said, he and his wife standing in the doorway.

While the apartment manager stormed out, still red-faced and fuming, Jayden turned to the couple. "What can you tell me about him?"

The man opened his mouth, but the woman whipped her hand up, effectively halting his words. "Seems to me that if we've got any information you might want, it'd be like anything else...you want something, you pay for it."

Jaxon grumbled, but Jayden immediately said, "Will a hundred dollars be acceptable to you?"

At that, both the man and woman's eyes bugged, and she fell into a coughing fit once more. Gaining control over herself, she snickered. "Why, yes sir. I do believe a hundred dollars would be most acceptable to us." This time her hand came up again, only it was palm up, with her fingers twitching.

Pulling the money from his wallet, he put it in her palm and noticed she shoved it into the pocket of her robe instead of giving it to the man.

"Best I can tell from what we heard through the thin walls...not that we ever tried to listen, you understand, but things we just *heard*..."

"Got it. Go on."

Warming to her story, she continued. "Saw a man around here sometimes. Used to be a bookie, probably still is. But I also know he works muscle for someone. Don't know who, don't want to know. That kind of information is too much information. My guess, Wolfe owed somebody money."

The man jumped in, as though tired of being left out of the conversation, and added, "I had the feeling he was dealing. I'd see some bad types hanging around here sometimes, coming and going from this place."

Jayden wondered how *bad* those people would have appeared for the man to have noticed them seeming out of place at this apartment building. "You ever hear anything specific? Anything that might let us know what he's up to?"

The man's face crinkled as he thought but shook his head. The woman's eyes narrowed, and she pulled out another cigarette from her pocket, lit it, and took a long drag. "I heard him say something yesterday morning. Not that I was paying close attention, you understand. I like to keep my nose out of other people's business."

Fighting the urge to roll his eyes, Jayden figured there was very little that went on in the apartment building that this woman did not see or know about. Battling the urge to throttle her to get the information, he growled, "And what did he say?"

"It was yesterday morning. I was getting ready to step out for a smoke when I saw a man coming up the stairwell. I closed my door because I didn't want to have nothing to do with him. But my window was open slightly to allow a breeze to come in."

Jaxon snorted, but with a quick glare from Jayden, covered it.

Her eyes narrowed again, as they jerked between the twins. "Bet your mama couldn't tell you apart when you were babies," she speculated. "It's kinda weird, seeing two men look so much alike."

Pulling her attention back to the matter at hand, Jayden said, "Keep going. What did you hear?"

Huffing, she blew out another puff of smoke and said, "Man went inside, and I heard some yelling. Couldn't hear what they were saying, but as the man left, it just so happened I was standing near the window. The man said that he expected his money, and Wolfe told him not to worry, he was getting it from Ruby. I didn't know what the hell that meant, but I thought maybe he was going steal some jewels."

With a growl, Jayden stomped past them, Jaxon and Asher on his heels.

30

"Drive to Zander's," Jaxon ordered as Jayden climbed behind the wheel of his truck.

Shooting his twin a glare, he did not ask questions but headed in that direction. Fifteen minutes later, he pulled into Zander's driveway. As they approached the front door, it was thrown open, Zander filling the space. With his hands on his hips and a scowl on his face, Jayden assumed Asher had already called him, filling him in.

The four men moved into Zander's living room, and Rosalie appeared, bearing a tray full of steaming coffee mugs. He noticed her eyes were worried, and he assured her, "Ruby is fine. Her arm is bruised, but that's all."

Rosalie offered a quick nod and moved back out of the room toward the kitchen. The men sat down, and Zander quickly asked, "What did you find out?"

In detail, he told Zander everything he knew. As he was speaking, there was a knock on the door, and Zander stalked over, opening it.

"Pete, come on in." Turning to the others, Zander explained, "As soon as Asher called, I sent for Pete."

The men all greeted each other, and Jayden was glad that Zander had the foresight to call their detective friend. Pete Chambers had met Zander when they were both in the Army, and they remained friends when they returned to the States, discovering they were both in the same area.

Once more, Jayden went over all the information he had on Kevin, not surprised when Pete seemed to know who he was talking about.

"Will Ruby come down to the station and fill out a complaint?" Pete asked.

Jayden replied without hesitation, "I'll bring her down today."

Nodding, Pete said, "What I can tell you is that Kevin Wolfe has been known as a small-time bookie for a couple of years. He's never been arrested, but his name has always been associated with just about anything going on. Drugs, numbers games, illegal gambling. I hadn't heard the latest, but based on what you're telling me, he probably owes someone more money than he's got and can't figure out a way to get it. I'm going to do some looking and see if I can figure out what he's up to and if we can bring him in. As soon as Ruby fills out her complaint, then I can send a squad out for him."

With a sigh of relief, Jayden nodded. "I know that's your job, but you've got my gratitude, man." Shaking hands, Pete left, and Rosalie walked back into the room.

She looked up at Jayden and asked, "What can we do for Ruby?"

As the tension slowly left his body, exhaustion was beginning to set in. He glanced at the clock on their television and confirmed that hours had passed since he left her still sleeping. Sighing heavily, he said, "There's nothing right now you need to do. This is all on me. I left her alone in my apartment hours ago, and I need to get back there. She's probably worried sick."

As Zander wrapped his arm around Rosalie, she said, "I hope you don't mind, but I sent her a text when you got here. I figured she'd want to know."

Walking over, Jayden kissed the top of Rosalie's head and said, "Thank you." Turning he looked at the others in the room and repeated, "Thank you all."

As they left Zander's house, Asher said, "I called the garage and let Cas know what was going on. He said not to worry, the shop was fine today."

With man hugs and back slaps, he said goodbye to Asher, then turned to look at Jaxon. The two men climbed silently into his truck, but Jayden made no move to start the engine. Finally, after a long moment, he said, "I love her."

"I know you do, and I'm glad. She's the right woman for you."

He already knew that she filled that place in his life, but hearing his twin offer his confirmation, the thought of her settled warmly in his heart. With a chin lift, he started the truck, dropped Jaxon off at his and Morgan's place, made another quick stop, and then drove home.

Entering his apartment, he barely had time to drop the bags in his hands, before Ruby rushed toward him, leaping at the last second, throwing her body at his.

Her arms and legs wrapped tightly around him, and her face burrowed into his neck. He felt a shiver run through her and he inwardly cursed. *Shit, this is on me. She's scared, and it's because of me.*

"Baby, I'm home. I'm okay…it's all okay."

She leaned back, her blue eyes wide and large, and brought her hands around to clasp his cheeks. "I was scared," she breathed. "I was scared for you, and I was scared about what you might do."

"I'm sorry you were worried," he said, stalking over to the sofa. Sitting down, he settled her so that she was straddling him. "I called Jaxon and had him go with me over to Kevin's apartment."

Shaking her head, she said, "How did you know where he lived?"

"Not much you can't find in a Google search," he said. "By the time I got to Jaxon, he already had an address. I wasn't sure it was still current, but from what the neighbors said, that was where he had lived."

"Had?" she asked as a crinkle formed between her eyebrows.

"It seems that he came in yesterday afternoon and cleared everything out. The apartment manager was pissed when he went inside because the place was trashed. Asher showed up also, and we talked to a couple of neighbors. Since Kevin wasn't there, we ended up going to Zander's place to fill him in on what's going on. Since there's the possibility that Kevin might try to find you again, and you were working at Grimm's, I wanted him to know."

She nodded but did not say anything else, seeming

to just want to assure herself that he was truly there and safe.

Hating to interrupt her quiet introspection, he continued, "Zander's got a friend who's a police detective, and he called him in." Seeing her eyes grow even more impossibly wide, he said, "He wants you to come into the station and file a report. We can also get a restraining order."

Her breath left her lungs in a rush, and she said, "Oh, Jayden, I don't know if that's such a good idea. I mean—"

His fingers resting on her hips gave a squeeze, and he interrupted, "I'm not going to yield on this, Ruby. From what the detective told us, Kevin's been involved in a lot of shit over the last several years. He's never been arrested, but his name has been connected with drugs, illegal gambling, and who knows what else. I'm not going to take a chance on him approaching you again. Ever."

"Oh, my God. I had no idea." Her face fell and she asked, "How could I have not known?"

"He was good at hiding things from you. And the two of you didn't live together, so there was a lot he was able to keep from you."

Shaking her head, she moaned, "I feel so foolish."

"Baby, you weren't foolish...you're a good and trusting person. One that he took advantage of." He leaned forward, kissing her lightly, and added, "That time of your life is over. I love you. And I'll never let anything happen to you."

Ruby slowly nodded, knowing that Jayden was right. She had hoped that Kevin would stay out of her life now, but if everything Jayden said was true, the odds of that were slim. "Okay. You're right. I'll go file a police report." Holding his gaze, she said, "Will you go with me?"

The first grin she had seen from him that day slowly appeared, transforming his face from one of avenging warrior to her gorgeous man.

"Absolutely, babe. We'll go just as soon as we eat."

Blinking, she jumped from his lap, ready to rush into the kitchen. "It'll take me just a minute to fix something."

He snagged the bags off the floor and said, "No need. I stopped by a diner and got breakfast to go."

She had been so concerned earlier when he arrived that she had not noticed the delicious smells coming from the bags. Now, her stomach grumbled in response, and she hurried to grab some plates. Soon they were at the table once more, this time with plates of scrambled eggs, bacon, hash brown potatoes, and big fluffy biscuits.

After focusing on eating, she finally said, "I have to tell you that I went to Miss Ethel's this morning after you left. I was so worried about you but just felt like she was the person to talk to instead of Granny. I hope that doesn't upset you."

Swallowing his bite of food, Jayden shook his head. "Not at all. She's always been the perfect person to go to when any of us needed an ear to listen." He took another sip of coffee, and then asked, "Did she help?"

Nodding, she said, "Yeah. I hope you don't mind, but she told me a little bit more about your very young years." She held her breath, hoping that Jayden would not be upset. When he shook his head, she breathed a sigh of relief.

He said, "I've already told you a lot of what I know, and I've got no problem with Miss Ethel explaining more."

"Anyway, I realized that you would be with Jaxon, wherever you were. I felt better knowing that he was with you if you were going to approach Kevin."

He reached over and took her hand, rubbing her knuckles gently. "I was mad, Ruby. Blood raging, furious mad. But unlike Kevin, I have control over it. I would've never done anything to put what you and I have together at risk."

Finishing the last of her breakfast, she grinned and said, "That's pretty much what Miss Ethel told me."

As soon as breakfast was over, Jayden drove her to the police station, where she gave her statement. Following the incident report, as well as the paperwork for a restraining order, they went back home.

By now it was the afternoon, and she and Jayden went back to bed. Both were exhausted, but falling asleep, wrapped in each other's arms, was just the balm that they needed.

Finally, I'm getting the hang of this! Ruby clicked send on the parts order for the garage and whirled around in her desk chair, throwing her hands into the air in celebration. She heard chuckling coming from the bays and looking through the window into the garage could see Jayden, Cas, and some of the others laughing at her. Tossing them a wave, she poured another cup of coffee and continued to work on invoices.

Life had settled into a peaceful routine, one which she never thought she would have. For the last month, she had been working full-time at Jayden's garage, and she loved the title of Office Manager. She had felt strange with that label at first, considering she had no idea what she was doing. But Jayden insisted, and now the title felt right.

She had gotten her first full-time paycheck, and even after taxes and insurance deductions it was more than what she used to make cleaning houses and being a server at Carter's, and the employment was so much more enjoyable. Plus, she did not mind the deductions, considering that she now had health insurance. *Thank God I hadn't needed medical care when I wasn't insured!*

The first thing Jayden had insisted on was that she go to the eye doctor, and now, with contacts, she could see perfectly.

She looked down at her shoes, skirt, and blouse, loving the way she could dress in the office. Jayden kept telling her that jeans and a T-shirt would be fine, but after wearing those for years, she was determined to dress the way she always dreamed of for work.

Jayden's other employees treated her with respect, thanking her profusely for the coffee and doughnuts. Just as she was considering running out for lunch, her phone vibrated. Seeing it was Granny, she answered it quickly.

"Hello, sweet girl," Granny greeted. "Are you free for lunch today?"

"Absolutely. I was just thinking about lunch. Would you like me to swing by and pick you up?"

Granny replied, "Would you mind coming here? I've got turkey sandwiches already made, and there's something I wanted to ask you about. I thought we could talk over lunch."

Agreeing, she disconnected and moved to the door leading into the garage. Calling out to Jayden, she smiled as he walked over. Telling him about Granny's request, he insisted that she go.

"Take as long as you need," he said. "Whatever Granny wants to talk about must be important, so take your time." He leaned over, careful not to put his grease-covered fingers on her clothes, and offered her a sweet kiss.

She loved that, allowing him to take the lead in their public displays of affection. He never seemed to mind kissing her at work, and she had no complaints.

Twenty minutes later, she stepped into Granny's house, smiling as she heard her grandmother in the kitchen. Moving down the short hall, she observed the table already set with plates of sandwiches, apple slices, and chips. Glasses full of iced tea completed their lunch, and they sat down after hugs of greeting.

"Okay, spill Granny. You've got my curiosity up."

Granny fiddled with her napkin, but in spite of her obvious nervousness, she jumped in. "I'm thinking about selling this house."

Blinking, Ruby dropped the rest of her sandwich back into her plate. Chewing quickly, she swallowed and said, "Selling?"

Nodding, Granny said, "Will you hear me out, please?"

Reaching across the table, she grabbed her grand-mother's hand and offered a squeeze. "Oh, Granny, absolutely. Tell me anything you want, and I promise I'll support whatever you need to do."

With that assurance, Granny seemed relieved and leaned back in her chair. "I've been thinking about the future," she began. "While I certainly get around much better, only need the cane sometimes, and can go up and down the stairs, I still mostly live on the bottom floor of this house. Don't get me wrong…I've loved this house. Your grandfather and I bought it many, many years ago, and it holds good memories. Over the years, I've thought about selling it and moving to a smaller place that has one-floor living. Not another house but maybe a condo for older people."

Surprised, Ruby said, "Granny, you never mentioned this to me."

Shaking her head, her grandmother said, "It never seemed to be the right time. Your mother became ill, and you and she needed me. And then I wanted you to have a place with me as long as you needed it. And I certainly wasn't going to sell while you were still dating Kevin, not trusting him at all." Smiling, she continued. "Now you're with a good man, and I know Jayden and you want to have your own place. You spend most nights at his apartment anyway, and I just don't feel this house is needed any longer."

Taking the information in, she nodded slowly, allowing her grandmother to continue her thoughts.

"I admit that I considered deeding it over to you and Jayden, but you two need to find a place that you can make your own. This house is quite old and rather small for such a large man."

At that description, she smiled and said, "I think that's why his apartment is so open...it gives him more room."

The two women chuckled and continued to hold hands over the top of the table.

"I've already been looking, and I found one that I like a great deal. I wanted to discuss it with you first and wondered if you and Jayden would go there to visit it with me. I would appreciate any suggestions you might have."

They continued to chat as they finished lunch, Granny appearing much more relieved now that her plans were out in the open. Ruby, completely support- ive, was excited to take a look at a new place for Granny to live.

As they rinsed the dishes, Granny filled her in on the activities offered for older people at the new place, and she heard the excitement in her grandmother's voice.

Preparing to leave, she was almost to the front door when her phone vibrated. Checking the caller ID, she grinned widely and heard Granny behind her, say, "Only one man I know gives you that smile."

Laughing, she answered, "Hey, Jayden. I'm just saying goodbye now and should be there soon."

"That's why I was calling, babe. Why don't you take the rest of the afternoon off and enjoy your grandmother?"

"There's no way I'm going to take the afternoon off considering I just started my new job. What on earth would my boss think about that?" He chuckled, and the sound of his mirth vibrated through her.

"Well, considering that I'm your boss, I think we've got this well in hand."

"Granny's got some exciting news that I'll tell you about this—" Hearing a slight gasp behind her, she turned around, her words halting in her throat. Her gaze landed on Granny, with Kevin at her back, a gun in his hand. "Oh, God, Kevin. What are you doing here?"

"Hang up. Now," he growled, waving the gun around randomly.

Heart in her throat, she breathed, "Help," just as her finger hit disconnect.

Jayden stared at the phone in his hand for a few seconds, not moving. "Ruby?" Blinking to focus, he gave his head a quick shake. Turning, he ran through the garage bays on his way to his truck.

Cas called out, "Yo, boss. You okay?"

Shouting over his shoulder, he yelled, "That asshole Kevin showed up at Ruby's grandmother's house. I'm calling 9-1-1 and Jaxon...you call the others."

As he jumped into his truck, he heard Cas cursing but knew he would do what he asked. Jerking his truck onto the road, he dialed 9-1-1 and told them what he knew. Adding, "He's got a restraining order against him, and Detective Pete Chambers knows all about this."

Hanging up before they could tell him to not go to the scene, he dialed Jaxon. Uncertain if Jaxon was on duty or not, his heart leaped when his brother answered. "Get to Ruby's grandmother's house. Kevin showed up there, and I don't know what's happening."

"You got it," Jaxon said, then added, "Bro, hang on to your shit. I'll be right there."

Hanging on was the last thing on Jayden's mind as he floored the accelerator, hurling his truck down the road. Turning onto Granny's street, he slowed down, not wanting to be seen if Kevin was still in the house.

Parking several houses away, he hopped out of his truck just as Jaxon drove up.

Rushing over, Jaxon asked, "What do you know?"

"I don't know what's going on. I was talking to Ruby on the phone and she was here with her grandmother. Then suddenly she stopped in mid-sentence, and I heard her say, 'Oh, God, Kevin. What are you doing here?'. Then I heard his voice in the background tell her to hang the phone up, and just before she did, she said 'help'."

"Shit, man," Jaxon cursed. "Did you get 9-1-1?"

"Yeah, police should be on their way."

"They'll send an ambulance as a precaution," Jaxon said.

Jayden knew his twin thought like an EMT, but the idea that Ruby or Granny could end up needing an ambulance sat in his gut like a stone.

"Have you tried calling her again?"

Nodding, Jayden said, "No one picks up." Not willing to risk waiting for the police, he said, "I'm going around back. I can't just stand here and do nothing."

"Bro, where you go, I'm going, too."

"No, stay here. I called for Pete, and I don't want the police shooting me thinking I'm the intruder."

With a clap on his back from Jaxon, he turned and began running through a neighbor's yard toward the back.

Ruby sat on the sofa holding Granny's hand, heart

pounding as she watched Kevin ranting as he had been doing for the past ten minutes. His eyes were glassy, darting everywhere. He was sweating, his complexion pale. His hair looked as though he had not showered recently, and his clothes had not been washed.

With the gun in his hand and as unpredictable as he was acting, she was terrified, and as she glanced next to her, could see the same emotion in her grandmother's eyes. Now that she knew he probably used drugs, she wondered how she had never noticed it before. *But he was never this bad. Not when we were together.* That recognition gave her very little comfort at the moment as he continued to move about the room, waving the gun, muttering to himself.

"Kevin?" she called out, attempting to keep her voice low and soft.

He whirled around and stared at her, blinking, almost as though he had forgotten she was there. His face contorted, and he groaned, "Don't you see, Ruby? I'm in trouble, deep trouble. The money you gave me is gone, and they're after me."

"Hmph," Granny grunted. "Kevin, you've been playing with fire for a long time, and you know it's gonna do nothing but burn you. And now you break into my house."

"Shut up, Granny!" he growled. "I didn't break in."

Granny and Ruby shifted their eyes toward each other but immediately turned back to him as he dangled a key in his hand. "I took this when I was here…forgot to give it back, so I decided to use it. It's not breaking and entering when you use a key."

Before Ruby had a chance to respond, Granny, her voice shaking with anger, said, "Boy, sneaking into someone's home with a key you were not given and holding us hostage is still a crime!"

His face contorted and he shouted, "Shut up, Granny. I know you gotta have something around here that I can hock." He waved his gun around, emphasizing his impending threat.

Ruby said, "Kevin, you know the police are going to catch up with you. Why don't you turn yourself in, and then you can get their protection?"

Emitting a choking sound, he said, "Are you stupid? How long do you think I'd live in jail? The men I owe have long arms, and they can reach even in there."

"Boy, whatever you want to lug out of this house, you can," Granny said. "I'm an old woman, and you don't scare me. But if you ever cared for Ruby at all, you'll let her walk out of here."

Her fingers flexed against her grandmother's hand as she jerked her head toward her. "Granny, no!"

Kevin interrupted and asked, "What have you got that's worth something?"

Pinning him with her hard stare, Granny said, "There's a box of real silver in the chest that's in the dining room. It's still in there, even after that became my bedroom. I never had much jewelry, but in the upstairs bedroom is a jewelry box with a pearl ring, a diamond ring that belonged to my mother, and some gold earrings that are antique. Other than that, Kevin, you've been here enough to know there's not much else."

He stood, rubbing his hand over his face, his eyes still darting about. Jerking suddenly, he said, "Money. You've got money."

"Only money I keep in this house is just a little cash for necessities. My purse is on the kitchen counter, and it's got about forty dollars in it." Eyes narrowing, Granny added, "You're welcome to it, but I got a feeling those men you owe aren't going to take just forty dollars."

As he paced again, his attention diverted, Granny shared a look with her, and she knew they needed to stall for time. It was going to take a little bit of time for Jayden to notify the police and for them to get to Granny's house. *Oh, Lord, let them get here soon.*

"My purse is right by the door, Kevin," Ruby added. "I don't have as much as I did when I was working for tips, but there's probably about fifty dollars in there."

"No, no! Don't you understand?" he groaned, continuing to pace. "I need a lot more money than that." Suddenly jerking upright, he pinned them with his stare, "The bank! You both have money in the bank!"

Shaking her head, continuing to keep her voice calm, Ruby said, "Kevin, the bank is going to know something's wrong if we try to go in and withdraw a lot of money."

Appearing to not listen, Kevin jerked around, and Ruby feared that he would fire the gun randomly in his agitated state. Uncertain whether to keep talking or to stay silent, she chanced a glance to her grandmother, who appeared equally as uncertain.

His face was showing signs of fatigue, and she wondered about the effects of whatever drugs he had taken. Speaking softly again, she said, "Kevin, why don't you lay the gun down, and let's figure out what to do. You're in trouble, and I'd like to help, but with you waving the gun around, I can't think."

He stared at her for a long moment, then lowered his arm while keeping the gun in his hand. He plopped into the chair across from the sofa, facing them, his gaze settling on the floor. Slowly he raised his head and looked at her, and once more she saw the defeated young man she befriended many years ago. *Maybe I can reach him...maybe there's still a chance.*

"Kevin? Remember when we were teens, and we used to go to the elementary school playground when all the kids had left? My favorite was the swings because for a few moments it almost felt as though I could fly. You used to say that was silly, but then you'd swing next to me and we'd see how fast we could go."

His lips curved ever so slightly, and she was encouraged to continue. "You used to come over to my house, and sometimes we'd come over here to Granny's. We'd sit at the dining room table and do homework."

He nodded slowly, and she could barely hear his response when he said, "It was a lot nicer than my house."

"I knew your grandfather," Granny interjected, immediately drawing his attention over to her. "I also knew your father. They were harsh men, and I always wished better for you."

Ruby did not take her eyes off of him for fear of his volatile state of mind but watched as he blinked away tears.

Jayden had dashed through a neighbor's yard, coming up to the back side of Granny's small lot. Ducking low, he maneuvered his way to the deck, staying out of sight as best he could from anyone watching from the windows. Once there, he could see that the door leading to the kitchen was slightly open and assumed that was how Kevin entered the house.

Straining, he could barely hear voices but could identify both Ruby's and Granny's. *Jesus, thank God!* Not knowing if Kevin had a weapon, he fought the urge to rush inside. Creeping forward, he placed his hand on the door. Able to hear the voices louder now, he could tell they were in the living room. He pushed the door open, ever so slightly, praying it did not make a noise. Providence was with him because the door hinges did not squeak.

Hyper-alert, he squeezed his body through the smallest opening possible, then partially closed the door so that it would be unnoticeable that it had been moved. Glancing down at his heavy work boots, he wished he had taken them off before entering. *Damnit, too late now.*

Tiptoeing a few feet to the right, he moved into the room Granny was using for a bedroom, keeping him out of sight from anyone in the living room. Able to hear more clearly now, he listened as Ruby attempted to calm Kevin, with Granny joining in.

Uncertain what weapon Kevin might be wielding, he continued to move cautiously. A flash of color at the back door caught his attention, and his eyes widened at the sight of an armed policeman nearby. *Jaxon, I hope to hell you let them know I was in here!* The policeman saw him and gave a short nod, forcing a sigh of relief from Jayden. Pete may end up being furious, but if he was able to get Ruby and Granny to safety, he did not care about the consequences.

Suddenly, Kevin's voice rang out loudly, distress evident in his screech, and Jayden's body tightened, ready to rush into the room, fear for the woman he loved the only thing holding him back.

Kevin's gaze moved to the window behind the two women, and he leapt to his feet. "Oh, shit, the police are here!"

She and Granny jerked around instinctively, looking out the window also. From the edge of the yard, she could see a police car parked on the street. Her phone vibrated as it lay on the floor near the front door. It had been vibrating ever since she had disconnected with Jayden, and she assumed it was him calling. *If the police are here, then Jayden can't be far behind!* Scanning outside the window she did not see his truck or motorcycle but knew in her heart that he was there...somewhere. Swinging her head back toward Kevin, her gaze fell upon the gun now being held firmly in his hand once more. Her heart squeezed at the thought of Jayden trying to rescue her, knowing he could be shot.

Her phone vibrated again, and Kevin growled, "Shut it up!"

She let go of Granny's hand and snatched the phone up, hitting connect. "Hello?" she said, her voice barely above a whisper.

"I didn't tell you to answer it!" Kevin screamed.

"Ms. Mantle? This is Detective Pete Chambers."

Staring at Kevin, she said, "It's the police, Kevin." She saw that his eyes were once again wild, and fear threatened to choke her. She listened as Pete said, "Can you put Kevin on the phone, Ms. Mantle?"

Holding the phone out toward him with a shaky hand, she prompted, "They want to talk to you. Please, Kevin. Talk to them. They can help us figure a way out of this."

His head shook back and forth, and he growled again, "They want me dead or in prison."

While he appeared to battle internally over what his next move should be, Ruby noticed a movement down the hall. In her peripheral vision, she caught a glimpse of someone... *Jayden! He came!* Her eyes locked onto his, love and fear tangling in the air between them. Giving an imperceptible shake of her head, she forced her eyes away. As glad as she was that he was nearby, the idea of him possibly getting hurt while trying to rescue her sent chills throughout her body, steeling her resolve.

"Kevin, put the gun down. Let me go with you. We'll go out together, and when the police talk to you, I'll be there."

She watched him waver, barely able to stay on his feet as fatigue pulled at him. Whatever substance he had used, it was either starting to leave his system or had simply worn him out.

Granny stood from the sofa, taking a risk but joining in, her voice warm and loving. "Kevin, let's all go together."

Ruby watched his face crumple as his gun arm slid down to the side of his leg. He drew in a raspy breath and exhaled on a sob. She hesitated, just until he dropped the gun on the chair next to him, and then rushed to him.

Holding him tightly, she moved with him as he slumped onto his knees, continuing to sob. Murmuring softly, she rubbed his back.

Jayden rushed down the hall, pushing Granny behind him as his gaze landed on Ruby and Kevin. Moving quickly, he snatched the gun from away from Kevin's reach. He turned and took Kevin firmly by the upper arms, not trusting that Kevin would not try to use Ruby as a shield. Pete, who had heard the conversation while on the phone, came through the front door as other policemen charged through the back, guns drawn, with Jaxon and Zander right behind.

Ruby's eyes stared up at him over Kevin's shoulder. Tears were streaming down her pale face, and the rage he had been feeling slowly dissipated as he saw that she was unharmed. Softly, he said, "Ruby, honey, let go of him."

She released her hold of Kevin, and Jayden moved back, allowing a policeman to place handcuffs on him. Kevin appeared disoriented, and Ruby whimpered.

Jayden pulled her gently into his arms as her shaking body bucked with sobs. He stood, keeping her firmly in his arms, never wanting to let her go. Now it was his turn to stroke her back and murmur words of comfort.

As Kevin was being led out of the house, he felt her shift around, and she said, "Kevin. I said I would go with him."

Pete stepped closer and said, "Ruby, you did a good job keeping him calm, but he needs help right now."

"Where will he be taken?" Granny asked from the sofa, sitting next to Jaxon, whose arm was around her.

Pete replied, "Because he appears to be under the influence of an unknown substance, we're going to take him to the hospital. They will evaluate him, both physically and mentally, and while he's still under arrest, we'll make sure he's getting the care he needs." He swung his head back around to Ruby and promised, "We'll need to get your statements while he's being taken away. But I promise I'll stay in touch with you, and you can see him when the time is right."

Two hours later, the police had left, but Granny's house was filled to the brim. Zander had called the others, and they all came with their women, including Rosalie picking up Miss Ethel on the way. The living room was small, but everyone crowded in, and no one appeared to mind the intimacy.

Miss Ethel, Granny, and Jayden sat on the sofa, with Ruby tightly held on his lap. Rosalie, Eleanor, Regina, and Morgan filled the chairs in the room, including a few from the kitchen that had been brought in. Zander, Rafe, Cael, Jaxon, Asher, Zeke, and

Cas all managed to settle their large bodies onto the floor.

Ruby and Granny had retold their story several times, but now everyone seemed glad to eat the pizza that had been delivered. Even Miss Ethel, who rarely used paper plates, had brought extra. The mood of the group was neither somber nor elated, but instead, Jayden sensed a calm thankfulness in his extended family as they chatted amongst themselves.

He closed his eyes for a few seconds, the horrendous thought of what could have occurred slamming into him. The touch of a soft, small hand on his face caused his eyes to open. Warmth replaced the cold that was deep inside.

Ruby's wide blue eyes were staring into his. Worried of what was going through her mind, he whispered, "Babe, you did good today."

"You came." Her statement was simple, and he stared, wondering what was going through her mind. She continued, "You came for me."

Lifting his hand to cup her cheek, he rubbed his thumb over her smooth skin, wanting to erase the trail of tears that had dried on her cheeks from earlier. "Don't you know, Ruby? I'll always come for you. I'll always want to protect you."

A smile curved her lips, and she leaned in for a kiss. A soft, gentle kiss, full of all of the emotion he could pour. Pulling back slightly, he whispered, "I love you, my little Ruby."

He watched as exhaustion moved over her, and she

laid her head on his shoulder, allowing his strength to seep in.

TWO MONTHS LATER

"You may kiss the bride."

The large gathering smiled in unison as the groom held his bride closely, bent her over backward, supporting her with his arm, and planted a kiss on her lips that lasted longer than the minister had intended.

As the kiss continued, Jayden leaned forward, catching and holding the eyes of the woman he loved, standing in line with the other bridesmaids. Ruby beamed her smile directly at him and laughed.

Jaxon and Morgan came up from the post-wedding kiss to shouts and claps from the packed church and began their walk down the aisle. Jayden, as best man, stepped to the side, allowing Zander to escort the maid of honor, Rosalie. Cael and Regina came behind, followed by Rafe and Eleanor. Jayden stepped forward, taking the arm of Ruby, his gaze devouring her in the pale pink dress that fit her curves perfectly.

An hour later, they sat down to the delicious reception given by Morgan's parents in the country club near where they lived. After the food had been consumed, Jayden stood, and the bridal party clicked on their glasses to quiet the participants.

Hating public speaking, he reached out to hold his champagne glass and cleared his throat.

"I know these speeches are supposed to be funny—or a roasting of the groom—but that's just not in me today. Instead, I want to honor the man who has always shared my heart. In fact, we shared our mother's womb at the same time which makes him truly the brother of my blood." He looked down at Jaxon sitting next to Morgan and noted the shine in his twin's eyes, but he plunged on.

"Life started out rough for us, bro. But no matter what was thrown at us, where we ended up, we had each other. My life would not be complete without you in it. And we landed easy...our lives changed when we were gifted Miss Ethel." His eyes shot to the table nearby where she sat, her white hair tucked into a bun and her blue gown with its long, chiffon sleeves fitting her thin body. She peered at him through her wire-framed glasses, and he could see tears shining from where he stood.

"She changed our lives, making sure we not only stayed together, but then gave us more brothers to have in our family. And today, your marriage gives me another sister. Another one to love and cherish. So, from just the two of us, bro...we continue to grow." He looked down at Ruby, not surprised to see tears trailing down her cheeks. Holding his glass high, he proclaimed, "To Jaxon and Morgan."

As the cheers rang out, women wiped their eyes, and Jaxon moved to kiss Morgan. Then he stood and embraced Jayden, the two men hanging on to each other for a moment before they back-slapped and separated. Jayden also moved to kiss Morgan on the cheek, then walked back to Ruby. She stood, and as always, fit neatly under his chin, tucked into his chest as he held her tightly.

She leaned back and whispered, "That was beautiful...and perfect, honey."

He kissed her, whisper soft, and relaxed in her arms now that the speech was over.

Five hours later, the crowd had waved goodbye to Jaxon and Morgan as they drove away to spend the night in a nice hotel near the airport, planning on flying to Aruba the next day. The band was still playing, but as the couple left, most of the guests did as well. Zander, Rosalie, Rafe, and Eleanor needed to get home to their babysitters, so Cael and Regina drove Miss Ethel to her house.

Jayden, as best man, his fingers linked with Ruby's, checked with the wedding coordinator to make sure there was nothing left that needed his attention. Looking down, he grinned and gave her a twirl, watching as she threw her head back and laughed. Landing against his chest again, he wrapped her in his arms, and they continued to dance slowly as the DJ played one last slow song before packing up.

He caught her looking at her hand and reached up to grasp her left hand, giving it a squeeze. "Like your engagement ring, baby?"

Her lips curved and she replied, "Love it...but then you know I do."

He was silent for a moment and she reached up to cup his jaw. "What are you thinking?"

Hesitating, he looked around the large reception hall, the workers taking down the tables and cleaning up the bunting that streamed from ceiling to floor. "We haven't talked about what you want. What kind of wedding and reception, I mean."

Shaking her head, she said, "Not this."

He had learned more about weddings in the past few months with Morgan's parents going all out for their daughter than he had ever cared to know. Zander's wedding had been simple, but Rafe and Eleanor had gotten married in her mansion. Regina's brother had wanted to pay for theirs, and so Cael and she married in a church with a lovely reception in a nice restaurant.

"Baby, I want you to have the wedding of your dreams."

She held his gaze, her blue eyes penetrating. "I don't need all this, and I don't want to go into debt to have it. Honestly, this was lovely but not for me. Jayden...just being with you makes all my dreams come true."

He bent, free now to take her lips the way he wanted to. They were soft and pliant, and he plunged his tongue inside her warmth, tasting the champagne and sweet icing, tempting him to find the nearest accommodating place to take her right then. Pulling back reluctantly, he opened his mouth, but she jumped in first.

Breathless, she said, "Take me home...now."

Chuckling, he swooped her into his arms and said, "My thoughts exactly, babe."

The clean-up crew for the country club grinned as the tall, muscular man strode out of the hall, the beautiful woman in his arms.

One Month Later

Jayden stood underneath the large tree in Miss Ethel's back yard. Normally, his mind wandered over the many childhood memories that always seemed to filter through his thoughts, but not now. It was December, but the day was sunny and cool, not cold, therefore those around him were comfortable with jackets or coats. Miss Ethel wore her dark coat and a light blue, knitted scarf around her neck, with gloves on her hands to ward off any possible chill. Granny was there as well, similarly dressed as Miss Ethel, both beaming.

His brothers were all there as well as their women, but he ignored the gathering and focused all his attention on the woman walking toward him.

Ruby, wearing a simple white dress, its hem barely touching her ankles and the lace top delicately covering the bodice. Her long hair was arranged in curls. On her feet, she wore white, heeled pumps, giving her a few inches of the height she craved, but he would not have cared if she wore sneakers. And in her hands, a small bouquet of white and red roses.

What had him staring in stunned reverence was what she wore over the wedding dress for warmth. A red, velvet cape, its hood pinned to her dark curls. It was as though she stepped from the pages of his beloved fairytale story.

She came to him on Cas' arm, having chosen him to walk her down the makeshift aisle in the backyard. They had become close since she now worked at the garage, and with no other male of importance in her life, she asked him.

Jayden glanced at Cas as they approached and could see it in his face that the young man was honored. Reaching him, Cas lifted Ruby's hand and placed it in Jayden's outstretched one. Kissing her cheek, Cas then moved back to sit with the others.

The men had brought folding chairs outside to place in the yard. The dining room was already set with plat-ters of food that Miss Ethel and the women had made and arranged. Granny had gifted flowers for both the table and for Ruby to hold.

The gathering was small, family only. The ceremony was simple...vows said, rings exchanged. Then she lifted her head and smiled as his face descended, capturing her lips in a kiss. He barely heard the claps from the gathering, as his heart soared with his beloved in his arms.

And he knew...fairytales did not have to be for princes...they could come true for a simple man.

Two years later, he knew dreams continued to come true as the nurse placed Opal and Amber into his arms as a tired but smiling Ruby looked up at him. Twin girls and their mama. All a man could want.

Three years later, with Opal and Amber in the waiting room with his brothers, their women, and Miss Ethel, he was blessed once more as Ruby delivered his son, Mica. Now, he had all a man could want. Bending to kiss Ruby, he whispered, "Thank you, baby."

She smiled, her face tired but her eyes bright as she lifted her hand to cup his rough cheek. "You're my dream come true, Jayden."

A few minutes later, he placed Mica in Miss Ethel's waiting arms, swooped a giggling Opal and Amber into his, and accepted the congratulations of his family.

Don't miss the next Heroes at Heart
For all of Miss Ethel's boys:
Heroes at Heart (Military Romance)
Zander
Rafe
Cael
Jaxon
Jayden
Asher
Zeke
Cas

Asher

Zeke

Cas

Lighthouse Security Investigations

Mace

Rank

Walker

Drew

Blake

Tate (August 2020)

Hope City (romantic suspense series co-developed

with Kris Michaels

Hope City Duet (Brock / Sean)

Carter

Brody by Kris Michaels

Kyle

Ryker by Kris Michaels

Saints Protection & Investigations

(an elite group, assigned to the cases no one else wants…or
can solve)

Serial Love

Healing Love

Revealing Love

Seeing Love

Honor Love

Sacrifice Love

Protecting Love

Remember Love

Discover Love

Surviving Love

Celebrating Love

Follow the exciting spin-off series:

Alvarez Security (military romantic suspense)

Gabe

Tony

Vinny

Jobe

SEALs

Thin Ice (Sleeper SEAL)

SEAL Together (Silver SEAL)

Letters From Home (military romance)

Class of Love

Freedom of Love

Bond of Love

The Love's Series (detectives)

Love's Taming

Love's Tempting

Love's Trusting

The Fairfield Series (small town detectives)

Emma's Home

Laurie's Time

Carol's Image

Fireworks Over Fairfield

Please take the time to leave a review of this book. Feel free to contact me, especially if you enjoyed my book. I love to hear from readers!

Facebook

Email

Website

Made in United States
North Haven, CT
02 December 2022

27734288R00212